To Linda

A Note from the Author

I wrote *Sweet Ember* in 1980. It was the third book of a total now of sixty-five and was written for publication in the romance genre. It is therefore quite different from my more recent books in both style and content.

Sweet Ember is a love story from start to finish. It has none of the secondary characters and side plots that my full length novels have. Like many books in the romance genre, its plot hinges on a misunderstanding regarding the "other woman." This misunderstanding keeps my heroine, Stephanie, and her hero, Doug, apart for eight long years. Given that a major change has taken place in Stephie's life during that time, their reunion is . . . hot!

My books are like my children—I love them all dearly for their differences. *Sweet Ember* has a special place in my heart, in that the model I used for PineWinds was the summer camp that I attended for seven years as a child. Those seven summers were the happiest and most carefree of my childhood. Writing *Sweet Ember* took me back there, just as rereading it does now.

Those of you who read *Sweet Ember* when it was first published will know that it was written under the Bonnie Drake pseudonym. That name is gone, as is the original cover of the book. All else remains the same.

Barbara Delinsky
May 1997

Recent Titles by Barbara Delinsky from Severn House

FLIP SIDE OF YESTERDAY
AN IRRESISTIBLE IMPULSE
MOMENT TO MOMENT
A TIME TO LOVE
VARIATION ON A THEME

SWEET EMBER

Barbara Delinsky

This title first published in Great Britain 1999 by
SEVERN HOUSE PUBLISHERS LTD of
9–15 High Street, Sutton, Surrey SM1 1DF.
This first hardcover edition published in the U.S.A. 1999 by
SEVERN HOUSE PUBLISHERS INC of
595 Madison Avenue, New York, N.Y. 10022,
by arrangement with HarperCollins*Publishers,* Inc.
A paperback edition of this book was published in 1981 by
Dell Publishing Co., Inc. in the USA only under the
pseudonym Bonnie Drake and republished in 1997
in paperback format only by HarperPaperbacks
under the same title *Sweet Ember*.

British Library Cataloguing in Publication Data

Delinsky, Barbara, 1945-
Sweet ember
1. Love stories
I. Title
813.5'4 [F]

ISBN 0-7278-5437-2

All situations in this publication are fictitious and
any resemblance to living persons is purely coincidental.

Printed and bound in Great Britain by
MPG Books Ltd, Bodmin, Cornwall.

one

IT ALL CAME BACK WITH THE SWEET SCENT OF the pines. The darkness, the small campfire, the soft bed of leaves. The gentleness of his hands on her skin, exploring her body as no other man had ever done. The rugged feel of his chest against her bare breasts, the smoothness of his hips beneath her questing fingers. The strength of his manhood as, coupled with an exquisite tenderness, he took her, smothering her cry with a soul-fusing kiss, then carried her with him, slowly and inexorably, to the height of desire, the crest of passion, to explode into a thousand shimmering bursts, while the fire before them sent up its own golden sparks, spiraling heavenward, higher and higher, through the bough-edged clearing and into the night sky.

Yes, it all came back, just as she had feared it would, transcending the hurt, the pain, even the beauty of the past eight years, to relive that one night of mindless happiness which had so totally changed the course of her life.

"Mommy . . ." The small voice, its sing-song whine

ample warning of impending complaint, brought her abruptly back to the present and the overall-clad child sitting beside her in the car. "Do I *have* to go? It's not too late to turn back. Please, Mommy?" As her daughter's round gray eyes bore into her with merciless pleading, Stephanie Wright was grateful for the twisting road ahead which, of necessity, demanded her attention.

Momentarily sharing the child's apprehension before catching herself, the auburn-haired young woman sighed. "Sweetheart," she began, rolling her window down farther to let the heady Maine breeze soothe her own warring senses, "we've been over this before. You *know* we're not turning back now. The house in Cambridge is all closed up, Mrs. Hampson is expecting us—counting on me and looking forward to meeting you—and we're both going to have a great summer!"

Where she found the tone of conviction, Stephanie would never know. She had repeated the same words to herself dozens of times over the last few weeks and even then had failed to ease her own qualms.

"But, Mommy," Missy continued, nervously twisting the thick brown length of a pigtail around her forefinger, "I don't want to go!"

"You'll love it!" her mother coaxed gently, playing out the dialogue now by heart.

"But I don't know anybody," the child persisted.

"You will very soon!" Stephanie insisted firmly.

"But I don't want to live with a whole bunch of kids—"

"How can you be against something you've never tried?" Stephanie cajoled, understanding the fear which beset her daughter and trying her best to deal with it. "It'll be such fun for you, Missy. You'll meet a whole new group of friends, do all sorts of different things, and you know that I'll never be very far away! You have the best of both worlds!" *As does your mother,* she admitted silently, knowing that she would never have had the courage to send her daughter off any substantial distance for the summer.

"But I don't want—"

"We can't always have what we want, Missy," Stephanie broke in, her patience finally beginning to fray at the edges under her own seesawing emotions. Unconsciously, she raised a hand beneath her flowing curls to rub the taut muscles of her neck, inflamed both by the length of the drive and by the tension that flared within her at each repetition of this discussion. "There are times when you have to trust me to make the right decision, even if you don't agree with it at first."

The little girl crossed her thin arms over her chest as she scowled ominously. "I'm not going to like it . . . ever!" she vowed stubbornly.

"We'll see . . ." Stephanie's words trailed off as she contemplated them. Had she made the right decision? Would this summer be good for them—for both of them?

In truth, she felt confident that Missy would do just fine. An athletic child, she was a fine little swimmer and a promising tennis player, even at her tender age. Additionally, she had never had trouble making friends, nor been bothered by the lack of them, all of her protestations to the contrary notwithstanding. She was an independent soul, a loner who went her own way whether in the company of friends or not. She was a self-motivator, a hard worker, and a hard player, whose instinct for superiority was threatened only by an underlying distrust of people, a characteristic which her mother recognized and for which she accepted the responsibility.

For it was Stephanie who had erected the protective wall around herself and her daughter during those lonely days of her pregnancy, bolstering it through the bittersweet birth of the child, then cementing it in their mutually sustaining existence. They made their way alone and, particularly after the deaths of Stephanie's parents within a year of each other, they relied on no one but each other. Oh, there were good friends and many acquaintances, but Stephanie always kept that certain distance, that emotional independence which would preclude a repeat of the heartrending anguish that she had once suffered.

Now, for the first time in her life, Melissa Wright would be separated from her mother. And, as much as Stephanie quaked at the thought, she knew how important this would be for her daughter's development. For, counterbalancing any failings she may have had as a mother, Stephanie was a realist. She was the first to admit that she had been overprotective of Missy, her only child, smothering her with the boundless love which, by rights, should have been shared with another. It was inevitable; Stephanie had only to look into her daughter's face to see that of the man whom she had adored, who had possessed her totally, body and soul, so long ago.

The narrow, tree-lined road leveled for a stretch, giving her a chance to cast a sideways glance at Melissa. Yes, it was all there—the thick, brown hair, so different from her own fine auburn curls, the intense gray eyes, alternately veiled then open and ever a far cry from her own jade-spoked ones, the long limbs which, even at her seven years, promised a height in excess of her mother's five foot five.

Sensing her mother's gaze on her, Missy launched a final plea for mercy. "Please, Mommy, if I have to go, why can't I stay with you? I won't be a pest."

Stephanie had to smile at her daughter's proposal. At least, she mused, Missy had accepted the fact of their going. This last, refreshingly novel suggestion would be easy enough to handle. "You're never a pest, sweetie. But there is a bunk waiting for you, with seven other little girls just your age. You know that I'll be nearby, but you're a big girl now. You really don't need me with you all the time. After all"—she glanced sideways through luxurious brown lashes as she injected a kidding note into the conversation—"who wants to have her mother around when she's getting into Lord knows what kind of mischief?" Reaching over, she tickled her daughter in just the place she knew to guarantee a laugh; she was not disappointed.

"Aw, Mom!" Missy exclaimed between giggles.

"And besides," Stephanie continued quickly, eager to make the most of the child's momentary good humor, "I won't be much fun. I'll be working most of the time. Mrs. Hampson has high expectations, you know."

Melissa gave her a knowing grin. "Yeah, I know. My mother, the photographer," she snorted playfully, then turned her small nose to the far window and lent her attention to more pressing matters.

Stephanie smiled at her daughter's words. *My mother, the photographer.* It had been a long haul, but she finally did feel justified in calling herself a photographer. She had begun slowly, during Melissa's preschool years, sticking to free-lancing, planning her schedule around the child's, doing most of her darkroom work in the converted kitchen pantry while Missy was sleeping. It was only when Missy entered school that Stephanie had allowed herself to accept more work, though she still insisted on being home after school and during vacations. As luck would have it, she offered a particular talent at a time when it came into demand. Thus, for the past three years, she had taught photography part-time at each of two exclusive private schools, pioneering in the formation of a photography curriculum for children. She adored both the challenge of the work and the nature of the working conditions, which conformed to Melissa's school schedule, and her curriculum had been widely recognized and applauded.

In fact, it was this very acclaim that had led her on the present northward trek. Two months earlier, she had received a surprise phone call from Sylvie Hampson, the owner and director of the girls' camp in Maine to which Stephanie herself had gone as a youngster, then worked as a junior counselor, and finally as a full counselor that last, fateful summer.

"You've been very busy, I see." Sylvie, gently authoritative in her uniquely gravel-toned voice, had proceeded quickly to matters of business, after the initial enthusiastic pleasantries had been exchanged. "I received the brochure you did for the Damon School for Gifted Children. It was superb, Stephie! And I've seen your curriculum guide . . . very impressive, albeit to my own untrained eye," she had complimented. "It seems you've taken them by storm!"

Stephanie had blushed, even at the other end of the line, her innate modesty forcing her to reply, "You're too generous, Sylvie. Actually, I was in the right place at the right time, as they say. There was a need and I was able to fill it."

"No, no, my dear," the older woman had firmly protested, "you deserve every bit of credit for what you've done. And now I have a further proposal for you. As you well know, at PineWinds we pride ourselves on keeping our activities *au courant,* so to speak, to stimulate our campers anew each year." Funny, stimulation had never been lacking in her own years at the camp, Stephanie had mused wryly as Mrs. Hampson barreled on. "For several years now, Sonny and I have toyed with the idea of offering photography as a regular activity. This summer we would like to act on that idea."

Stephanie had listened intently, subconsciously aware of the dull ache that sparked into life at the mention and memory of PineWinds, not the least of which was the suspicion of what Mrs. Hampson was leading to.

"Since you left, Stephie, the size of the camp has remained very much the same. We have one hundred and twenty girls, ranging in age from seven to fifteen. I want someone who can teach photography at each appropriate level in addition to serving as camp photographer, taking formal pictures and candids." She had paused to catch her breath, or, more likely, to give her listener a chance to catch hers. "Would you be interested, my dear?" Her voice was warm and sincere, a beckoning hand which Stephanie instantly knew she would have great difficulty refusing, if only from the professional standpoint.

"Oh, Sylvie, it sounds exciting!" And it certainly did—far more exciting than any of the other prospects which she'd had for the summer. "But—" she hesitated briefly, doodling absently on a blank piece of paper as she sought to organize her thoughts—"are you sure that I'd fit the bill? I've never applied my curriculum to the camp setting before."

Stephanie smiled in hindsight as she recalled

Sylvie's response, picturing the dismissing wave of the hand she must have made at her end of the line. "Not to worry, my dear. Between what I've read of your program and what I've seen of you—you were with us for ten summers, after all—I think you can handle it. But perhaps you have some questions you'd like to ask me," she had suggested.

Dutifully, Stephanie inquired about facilities and equipment, knowing how efficiently Sylvie Hampson ran her camp, sparing no expense to maximize the experience for campers and counselors alike. Without a doubt, the photographic experience would be incomparable. Yet Stephanie was unsure of how to most tactfully broach the two issues that troubled her. Eventually, she chose to be straightforward regarding the first of the two.

"Sylvie," she began, more timidly than she might have wished, "I have a child, a daughter." Suddenly reminded of her responsibility, she automatically reached to fold the loose pieces of clean laundry—her daughter's T-shirts, jeans, and underthings—which she daily placed on the kitchen chair to make the greatest use of telephone time. Thus, she found she could accomplish this most monotonous custodial chore during times when her hands would be otherwise idle. As a working mother, Stephanie had quickly learned to take precisely such shortcuts.

"How marvelous!" the voice at the other end of the connection had burst out, with an enthusiasm which was typically Sylvie Hampson. "And how old is this daughter of yours?" Again the warmth was genuine, and Stephanie couldn't help but respond.

"Melissa is seven. We're very close. Unfortunately, I don't think I can afford her tuition to PineWinds, and I couldn't possibly leave her home."

Mrs. Hampson had interrupted immediately. "Leave her? Nonsense! You'll bring her!" Then she hesitated, as though searching for the most diplomatic way to proceed. "What about the child's father?" She spoke tentatively, well aware of the generation gap regarding that particular issue, and the fact that Stephanie had continued to use her maiden name.

After more than seven years Stephanie was no longer thrown by the question. "I have no ties other than Melissa," she replied immediately and confidently.

"Then it's settled! Her tuition will be included with your own room and board, all of which, plus a salary, goes with the job. In fact, Melissa will fit in perfectly with the youngest group."

The sheer simplicity of it all, so unusual in her own life's experience, gave Stephanie the courage to face the one remaining barrier. As far-fetched as it sounded, there was always the possibility that he still worked there—and that was the one thing that the mature and self-possessed Stephanie doubted she could handle. This time she chose a circuitous route of gaining the information she wanted.

"Your offer is almost irresistible, Sylvie." She laughed over her nervousness. "Tell me, are any of the same people around? Babs—is she still on the waterfront?"

"Yes, Babs never changes. She's as ornery as ever, but good, very good!" the graveled voice had bubbled.

"How about Suzanna Watts—is she at the Arts Center? Is Larry still at the boathouse?"

Sylvie laughed aloud. "Yes to the first, no to the second. Who else do you remember?"

Quickly Stephanie had gone on. "That tall, dark one, Douglas Weston—is he still a tennis instructor?"

"No—" Sylvie had responded, to be quickly

interrupted by Stephanie's next question, rushed out in hopes of erasing the previous one from Sylvie's mind. Stephanie now had the information she wanted. All that remained was for her to cover her tracks.

"One last one—Jane. Is she still the head counselor?"

"No," the director had responded sadly. "Jane passed away two years ago. She was with the camp for more than thirty years, you know. And she was only sixty-two when she had the stroke. We miss her!" The raspy voice had lowered in emotion; as firm and aggressive as Sylvie was in running her camp, she considered its players to be part of her very own family and, as such, the recipients of all the warmth, compassion, and love that this matriarch could spread around.

"I'm so sorry, Sylvie. I didn't know—"

"Of course you didn't, my dear. Yes, there's been quite a turnover." She purposefully lightened up the discussion. "Some have moved up, some over, some out. But we still have a superb staff!" Stephanie wouldn't have imagined otherwise. "Will you join us, Stephie?" The older woman took the lead.

For the first time in eight years, Stephanie responded with the force of pure instinct, leaving all reasoning for later. "I'd love to, Sylvie!" she had accepted excitedly, lost for the moment in all of the best memories, the fun she'd had at PineWinds, the sense of security she'd felt there, the skills she'd learned, the friends she'd made. All of these things would now be Melissa's—and Stephanie herself would have a profitable summer, rich in teaching experience, wide open in terms of photographic opportunity, and financially rewarding to boot. It all seemed ideal . . . and so much better than a summer of city heat, mildewed shower curtains, and peanut butter and Fluff sandwiches!

During the next month letters flew freely back and forth from Cambridge to Baltimore, where the director lived, with Stephanie listing in detail the equipment she would need and Sylvie sending all of the appropriate forms which would enroll Melissa as a full-fledged camper. Although the reaction of the latter to this new and momentous—from the point of view of a seven-year-old—turn of events was far from enthusiastic, Stephanie remained firm in her conviction that the summer was tailor-made for them both.

It was only as the last few weeks at home approached that Stephanie began to have second thoughts. All of the necessary arrangements had been made, suitable wardrobes had been put together and name-tagged, school and work were, respectively, drawing to an end—and Stephanie's mind turned with increasing frequency to thoughts of PineWinds, past and present. The present she could cope with; it was the past that worried her.

Even in Cambridge, with only her daughter's gray eyes and thick brown mane to remind her of him, his memory was never far from her. She couldn't begin to count the many times she'd lain in bed, her large brass bed, big enough for two, and imagined him beside her, his firm, bronzed body intertwined with her own paler, softer one, giving pleasure and taking it, abandoning reality to the delights of passion, sharing with each other, once again, that very special something that had existed so briefly in what had seemed to be another world.

But now she was headed for that other world. Would she find the anguish greater with each renewed acquaintance? Or would she find, as she had desperately hoped—as had even been at the very hiddenmost recesses of her mind when she had accepted

Sylvie's proposal—that by returning to the scene of such heartbreak, she could superimpose on it more pleasant memories and thereby forever lay to rest the ghost of a relationship that haunted her relentlessly.

"Look, Mommy!" Missy's squeal of delight recalled her mother quickly from her wanderings, jolted as much by the suddenness of her daughter's words as by the spontaneous enthusiasm which had bubbled forth, no doubt to the child's own surprise. But then, Missy had "seen artistically" for years, each time amazing her mother anew, time and again drawing attention to sights which might otherwise have been missed. Now, following the direction of the pointing finger, Stephanie saw a sight so breathtaking that she could not help but gasp. Through the dark forest green of the trees which framed the gently curving roadway, a clearing had broken, a parting of the magnificent pines wide enough to reveal the secret wealth guarded by its evergreen mantle. It was the jeweled surface of a lake, sparkling under the midday sun, crystal clear and mirror smooth, reflecting in all its grandeur the wooded landscape on the far bank, its treed hills rising to a gentle slope extending around the lake in fluted fashion.

"It's beautiful, isn't it!" Stephanie murmured, reveling in the scene, a photographer's dream. "I'll have to come back to photograph it another time." She spoke her thoughts aloud, temporarily forgetful of the hearing ears beside her.

"I'll bet you're going to do the best things on your days off, while I'm stuck at that place," the child whimpered, thrusting her lower lip forward as she suddenly remembered her impending fate.

Stephanie dragged her eyes from the passing scene

and focused back on the road. "Don't be silly! I'm looking forward to my time at camp!"

"Yucch!" the seven-year-old spat out in disgust, causing Stephanie to stifle a chuckle. How typical, she thought, wondering if she had ever given her own parents as much resistance. In actuality the only resistance she could remember, at least as far as camp was concerned, was at the other end, the drawn-out and tearful parting scene at the end of the summer, the misery of saying good-bye to friends whom she would not see for another year, if at all. Stephanie had loved her time at PineWinds, right up until that very last day. . . .

She eased off the accelerator pedal as they approached a small town, quiet and charming in its own rural way, and so typical and unchanged from the local towns as Stephanie remembered them. Houses had sprung up on either side of the road as they had neared, wood frame houses painted in yellows and whites and ivories, many sporting picket fences defining front yards, all boasting the obligatory chairs on the front porch, two or three in a cluster for the evening's entertainment.

The center of the town—if that was what the small gathering of non-residential structures comprised—was here, then gone, a grocery, a drugstore, a general establishment, and several others, flitting quickly and quietly by, one looking as peaceful as the next. As many times as she had passed on this road, it was as though she were seeing it now through different eyes. Again she vowed, though silently this time, to return to photograph this sleepy hollow of a community, if for no other reason than to see if in fact there was someone to pump gas at the lone-standing pump at the far end of the town.

"Are we almost there?" the small voice beside her asked, more meekly than impatiently, and touching off a sensitive chord within Stephanie. Mindful of her daughter's qualms, she reached a reassuring hand over to squeeze the cool one beside her.

"Almost, sweetie. We have only about another half hour to go," she offered gently, smoothing a stray hair from the child's pale face before she put an arm around the slender shoulder and drew her near. "Do you know how much I love you?" she whispered into her daughter's ear as she hugged the child to her. At that moment she knew that she would miss her daughter's constant company, that the separation would indeed be as much of a trial for her as it would be for Melissa.

As though sensing her mother's own emotional need, and once again showing a depth of understanding far beyond her years, Melissa snuggled against her mother's side and wrapped her free arm around her waist. "I love you too, Mommy!" she exclaimed softly, as they both savored the quiet closeness of the moment.

And once more Stephanie knew that regardless of the pain that long-ago love affair had reaped and continued to reap, it had brought her this glorious being, this child who gave meaning to a life which might otherwise have wallowed in self-pity and despair.

"Mommy," Missy began curiously, "tell me what you liked best about camp when you were a little girl."

Stephanie thought for a moment, negotiating a sharp curve in the road as she did so. "The campfires," she offered conclusively, as she straightened the steering wheel. "Way off in the woods, at the end of a long, narrow trail, is the campfire circle. There is a huge clearing, with tiers of benches all around, and a beautiful fire right in the middle. There are songs and stories and . . . well, it's a very meaningful time. At the start of the summer, when you first go there, you still feel a little strange with all of the new people, but somehow the warmth of the setting draws everyone together. By the end of camp, when the final campfire is held, you feel closer to these people than to any others. The songs and the fire make it all that much more beautiful."

Her voice broke as it trailed off, and the child looked up at her, gray eyes as open and warm as they had been in ever so long. "You really loved it, didn't you, Mommy?" she asked softly.

"Uh-huh," her mother agreed, not trusting herself to say more. For her thoughts were no longer on that huge campfire, but rather on another, smaller and more intimate one, in a far-off, more secluded clearing. She had really loved him too. . . .

It had begun and ended during the summer of her nineteenth year. She was a waterfront counselor by day, an overseer of one of the older bunks by night. Soon after her arrival she had become aware of him, as had every female eye old enough to appreciate the opposite sex. He was a tennis counselor, one of three male counselors on the camp staff that summer. And, as a member of the opposite sex, a devastatingly mature specimen at the age of thirty, he was a wonder to behold.

Tall and lean, he had a physique to match that of the most highly treasured model for a life drawing class. His shoulders were broad and well-muscled, as befitted a tennis star, his torso tapering to a narrowness at the waist and hips, with not an ounce of unwanted flesh. His legs, as they tirelessly traversed the courts, were bronzed and sinewy, coordinating with the rest of his body into a harmony of motion whose beauty magnetized the eye.

But while Stephanie shared this appreciation with the many others who cast furtive glances toward the tennis courts as they passed from one activity to the other, what had drawn her even more compellingly had been his face, the darkness of his brown hair, well-trimmed about the neck and ears but falling long and casual across his forehead, the intensity of one-way gray eyes, seeing all, but letting none see within, the confidence in his squared-off jaw, the strength in his firm lips. There had indeed been a quality of mystery about him, the same quality which she would later see so very often in his daughter. But that was a future which she would have least expected during that summer eight years before.

While many of the worshipful entourage made obvious plays for his attention, he parried their moves with good-humored regularity. He seemed a private person, enjoying the more superficial aspects of relationships yet allowing no trespasser into his personal domain. A superb and diligent tennis instructor during the day, he earned a reputation as the rogue of the night, indulging in the passing fling, then moving on.

Stephanie kept a safe distance away. That she was attractive, she did not doubt; neither did she doubt that she lacked the more smashing looks of several of her beguiling fellow counselors. Additionally, she knew that a passing fling was not for her, as attractive as this man might be; there were too many emotional and intellectual needs that cried out for satisfaction, to give in to the pure lust of the night. She was shy in her own innocent way, and far less experienced than many of her companions. Though she was invariably well-liked, she had never been, nor wished to be, the hit of the party, the center of attention to which the others gravitated. She was happier to watch quietly from the sidelines, then go off in her own direction when she felt so moved.

Ironically, it may have been this very reticence, this sense of mystery which so intrigued her in Douglas Weston, that likewise drew him to her. With only three weeks remaining in the camp season, he began, to her great surprise and the unabashed jealousy of many an other, to actively seek her out, walking her to her bunk following meetings, sitting with her at cookouts, inviting her to spend time with him on their mutual days off. At the start she was wary, determined to do nothing to compromise her character, and suspicious of his intentions. Soon to her amazement, however, she found that his reputation in no way approached reality. He never pressured her, enjoying her company as she did his, sensing that she was different from the others and treating her accordingly.

She was, in turn, impressed, charmed, enthralled, fascinated, and, finally, totally captivated by the man—his gentle camaraderie, his subtle wit, his innate intelligence, and, undeniably, his heart-throbbing good looks. It was this last, and her own reaction, for which she had been unprepared. Never before had she trembled in a man's presence, quivered at his touch, thrilled within his embrace. When he kissed her that first time, so deeply yet tenderly, she had responded instinctively, awakened by his very masculine appeal and her own intuitive femininity. For the first time in her life, a spark was lit deep within her, making her yearn for more, much more, than a kiss could give.

As the time for parting approached, she realized she had fallen in love with him. She knew so little of his other life—he had kept that very much to himself—yet she felt she had gained, through the hours of talk and togetherness, an insight into his very nature which was even more meaningful than those other purely biographical facts. It was a combination of pride and fear which kept her from prying—pride in her own strength and that of their relationship yet fear of delving into another life in which she might never belong.

It was perfectly natural for them to go off together that last night. The final banquet had ended, the campers been safely quartered in their bunks to revel away their final hours, the counselors similarly becoming ensconced before the fireplace in the main lodge, beer flowing freely, tongues even more so. It was a scene that had seemed, at that moment, alien to them both, so they had left.

Guided by the light of the moon, he had led her up a narrow trail to their own private campfire. In the center of the small clearing, he built a fire, then drew her down beside him on the cushion of fallen leaves and pine needles to watch the fire take root, then spread, and finally burst about the dry logs into tongues of flame, strewing heat into the cool night air. They talked of the summer, its highs and its lows, each avoiding the turn which the conversation seemed destined to take.

It never did take that turn. At least, not verbally. Rather, their bodies spoke as each reached out for the culminating high of the summer. He was ever gentle, sensing her fears and quieting them. She had responded, then invited, opening herself to his possession. He had undressed her slowly, worshiping her every delightful revelation, chasing away her shyness with each intervening kiss. He had helped her to undress him, thrilling in her unsureness, teaching her the delights of his own manly form. He had caressed and teased, explored and coaxed, drawing her to levels of ecstasy hitherto unknown yet never since forgotten. Their union was one of mutual glory, of shared fulfillment, of breathtaking beauty. When they lay, long afterward, in each other's arms, spent and satisfied, content to let the cool air fan their heated bodies, both knew that they had shared something very special. Stephanie gave little thought as she lay with her head cradled against his strong shoulder and her legs intertwined with his to the moral and physical ramifications of her behavior. She knew but one thing—that she loved him and had needed, for the most compellingly primitive reasons, to give herself to him, irregardless of past or future. It had been, for them both, a passion of the here-and-now, and Stephanie was content to let tomorrow take care of itself.

Unfortunately, when tomorrow came, the bottom fell out of her world. She and Doug had parted shortly before dawn with promises to meet the next day, once the campers had been bundled aboard the appropriate buses to take them each to their own hometowns and a new fall season. Stephanie had neither made assumptions as to a future with Doug, nor did she have demands to make. Rather, she had a single hope—that he would profess the love for her which she felt for him. Specifics were unneeded, details unimportant. The future would be beautiful—if only he loved her.

With that all-encompassing hope in mind, Stephanie headed for Doug's cottage the next afternoon. Bounding eagerly up the steps, she swung open the screen door to stop dead in her tracks at the sight of a young woman, perhaps several years older than herself, and stunning, by all modest estimates, calmly packing Doug's clothes into the open suitcases on the bed.

"Who—who are you?" Stephanie had stammered, warning spasms erupting within her. She knew so little about him . . . so very little. Then the condemning words broke through her rapidly muddling consciousness.

"I'm Diana Weston. Who are you?" the young woman had retorted, her blond hair swinging carelessly about her shoulders as she turned her impeccably garbed form toward the intruder.

It was as though everything, which mere moments before had been full of life and hope, suddenly froze within Stephanie. Wordlessly, she stared at the exquisite face before her, too shocked to speak, too stunned to move. For what seemed an eternity she stood there. His wife—so that was the private life that Douglas Weston had kept hidden from everyone at the camp. And that was what he would have told her today. He was married, and this was his wife, with whom he would certainly have a most joyous reunion on this day.

Stephanie never said a word. Tears blinding her eyes, she stumbled out of the cabin and ran to her own, throwing the last of her things into her trunk, loading up her car, and setting out for home without a glance behind. It was only when she had arrived, late that night, back at the house in Cambridge and had been duly welcomed by her parents, that she escaped to her room and yielded to the deep, soul-rending sorrow which was to be her closest companion in the coming weeks.

Married. . . . He had been married! All the while he had held her, kissed her, and then made love to her, he had been married! He had known that she was a virgin, had paced his lovemaking accordingly, yet all the while he had known that their dalliance could be nothing more than a one-night stand. She had been taken, used, and now was to be discarded. It was almost incomprehensible to her. He had been so tender and considerate and giving, allowing her to make a commitment . . . which he had no intention of matching.

How poorly she had judged his character. It wasn't bad enough that he had deserted his wife for the summer—though Stephanie had known of other such cases in her experience at PineWinds—but to add to that, he had played the bachelor to the hilt. Had anyone else known of his true marital status? If so, why hadn't she been warned?

In vain, she tried to find a whipping boy, a person to bear the blame for the debacle. Yet she could find none. Doug had never lied. He had never promised her anything. It had, indeed, been a total giving of the moment. It had only been Stephanie's naive romantic notion that had given her over to thoughts of love. Neither had ever uttered the word to the other and, for that at least, she was grateful. The treachery was bad enough; if he had declared his love, then spurned her thus, she would have been doubly crushed. As it was, she had no one to blame for her predicament but herself. She had witlessly allowed herself to fall in love with a man whose life had always been a huge question mark. At the time it hadn't mattered . . . or so she thought. If only she had known he was married, she would never have gone out with him in the first place.

As the hours of anguish grew into days, the shock gave way to a dull hurt, which dogged her every step. Her parents were solicitous and she confided in them, though there was little they could say to ease her burden. The anger, the bitterness, the despair all fed on one pervading fact: For the first time in her young life, Stephanie had opened herself up, had given of herself freely, had entrusted another with her love, her very essence—only to find that it had been utterly meaningless to its taker.

At no point could Stephanie say that she hated Doug for what he'd done to her. It was she who had let herself be blinded by love. In her misery, she made a solemn vow that she would never, never put herself in a position to be hurt so again.

Ever mindful of her love for him, there was neither fear nor remorse when she discovered she was pregnant. There was never any thought but that she should give birth to the child and raise it herself. Given her choice, she would not have sought to bring a child into the world without benefit of marriage. But this child had been conceived in love and Stephanie vowed that it would grow and flourish within that very same aura. Strangely enough, it was the very confirmation of her pregnancy that snapped her out of her depression and into a practical semblance of action.

"Is anything wrong, Mommy?" It was Missy, still at her elbow, timidly eyeing the tears that glistened at her mother's eyes. Rescued thus from her reminiscences, Stephanie wiped at her lids with a forefinger.

"No, no, sweetheart, everything is just fine," she assured the child, who, hearing those comforting words, turned to look out the front window. Everything is just fine, Stephanie told herself over and over again as they neared their destination. Everything would be just fine, she vowed, just as things had indeed been fine during the past eight years. And after this summer, she sensed strongly, any lingering ghosts would indeed be laid to rest, clearing the way for a happier future for them both.

One by one, the old familiar landmarks appeared as Stephanie maintained a safe but steady speed on the country road. There was the movie house in which she had spent many an evening, both as an older camper and as a counselor. There was the fish house, where they had bought lobsters to boil on the beach. There was the ancient signpost, a veritable circus of pointing arrows which, when properly deciphered, directed the wanderer to this camp or that. There was the old and stately inn, somewhat more weathered but functional nonetheless, where her parents had stayed, year after year, on visitor's weekend.

"Look, Missy. There's our lake!" she exclaimed, helplessly caught up in the nostalgia of the moment, the excitement increasing with their impending arrival. Melissa got up onto her knees to look out her mother's window for her first glimpse of Blue Willow Lake, its surface gently dappled by the soft breeze which ruffled it. Then it was gone, hidden once more behind the protective barrier of trees. Very gradually the road sloped upward, the lush greenery of the roadside giving way to the amber hues of the wild grasses. They drove past a small farm, or what had once been a farm, though even as a camper Stephanie had seen the dismantled plows and wagon wheels, now given over to rust and the elements, yet still suggestive of the once thriving enterprise that had been reduced to a nearby henhouse and a small herd of dairy cows.

Just as the car reached the top of the climb, Stephanie made a sharp left onto a minimally paved road, part tar, part gravel, as it had always been. Smiling to herself at how little things had changed, she slowly headed the car downward until it was once more surrounded by the richness of the forest growth that held a time-honored claim on the land. How many times Stephanie had passed down this road! How many times she had been thrilled as she was now by the study in contrasts that stretched before her—the rugged grays and browns beneath the tires, the soft and graceful greenery, dark and shaded, of the pines, aspens, spruce, and birch, gathered in on either side to watch the annual parade of humanity, and finally, the light at the end of it all, sunlight beaming a path, beckoning onward to the miniature civilization, carved out of nature's finest, which would be home for the next two months.

As the car rounded the final turn, Stephanie burst into a spontaneous smile as her eyes took in the sight before them. To the left were rows of equipment sheds, freshly painted in the familiar blues and greens of the camp, and the garage which housed the camp transports, rustic blends of bus and truck, open-windowed and emblazoned with the interwoven letters of the camp insignia. Straight ahead were the fields, originating at the end of the small stretch of sand bordering the lake, becoming level and finely mowed where the softball diamond and the volleyball nets stood, then grading as they moved up and away from the gray-blue lake.

Stephanie turned the wheel to the right and slowly accelerated up the main drive toward the dominant structure at the crest of the hill. It was, indeed, the ultimate center of activity, the place of meals, meetings, administration, of rainy-day activities, late-night parties, and leisure-time camaraderie. It was known to the world as the main lodge, to the camp, fondly and intimately, in lazy abbreviation, as the Lodge. A two-storied structure built of unpeeled logs, its first floor was large and open, housing the dining room, the lounge, and several smaller rooms and offices. The second floor extended onto a balcony around the lounge, then closed over the dining room to provide counselor quarters. It was on this balcony that the director's office stood, open and inviting for all to visit at will, a small desk lamp burning almost around the clock, in Stephanie's memory, symbolic of the tireless dedication of Sylvie Hampson.

Following the driveway farther, now curving behind the main lodge to head for the line of systematically placed bunks, Stephanie pulled to a stop before a group of adults, one of whom she immediately recognized. Eagerly she climbed out of the car, stretching her long legs and then straightening her lithe frame at the same instant that the white-haired package of enthusiasm spotted her.

"Stephie!" Even in excitement the voice was as gravel-toned as always—typically Sylvie, part and parcel of her character. "It's wonderful to see you!" Before she knew what had hit her, Stephanie was enveloped in the strong arms of this slim woman, whose head barely reached her chin. Perhaps that too was part of Sylvie Hampson's unique charm—so much insight, compassion, intelligence, and enthusiasm wrapped in such a small bundle, one that showed her every year, but that was, as always, immaculately clad in the white blouse, bermuda shorts, and sneakers she had long since deemed fitting for the director of a highly respected girls' camp.

"Let me look at you," the older woman croaked in command, smiling all the while as she took a step back and surveyed the work of eight years' passing time. Blushing self-consciously under such straight-forward examination, and marginally aware of the approach of the others standing nearby, Stephanie was infinitely grateful that she had changed very little physically since she had last been at this spot. She had chosen to wear chic denim pedal pushers, so practical and comfortable for driving and working, and a pink cotton shirt with rolled cuffs and an opened neck, an outfit which complimented her slim figure even as it offset her coloring to its greatest advantage. If anything, the past years had exaggerated her slimness, while motherhood had lent a gentle shapeliness, a maturity, to heighten her overall attractiveness. Though Stephanie would have soundly denied it, she could hold her own to any beauty.

"You look wonderful." The smile had broadened in approval, and the deep brown eyes, expressive as they had always been, narrowed mischievously. "Now, if you can introduce yourself to that motley crew over there—" Sylvie tossed her head in the direction of the three counselors, who smiled as they moved forward—"I have more important business to attend to." None too subtly drawing Stephanie away from the car and toward the approaching group, Sylvie proceeded to the looks of amused puzzlement to nimbly slide her wiry frame behind the steering wheel of the car, slamming the door behind her as she turned to greet Melissa, who, to Stephanie's heart-stopping notice, bore a look of round-eyed fear almost comical in its intensity. Instinctively, Stephanie trusted Sylvie to know how to handle the child, so she turned determinedly to the three awaiting women and introduced herself. Moments later, with the last of the preliminaries barely completed, all four turned in surprise as Sylvie opened the car door, sliding out as easily as she'd entered, though this time gently drawing Melissa with her. To Stephanie's instant relief and subsequent amazement, the child, who a brief hour before had been begging to return home, now seemed accepting of the situation, only her mother recognizing the veil of caution-tinged resignation which had befallen her expression. Trust Sylvie for her magical powers, Stephanie mused, and, for the first time in weeks, she genuinely felt convinced that, if for Missy's sake alone, she had made the right decision in returning to PineWinds.

The gravel-edged voice broke into her thoughts, now in a conspiratorial tone. "If you all will excuse us, Melissa and I have some exploring to do. Stephie, why don't you drop her trunk off at bunk one, then go unpack yourself. You'll be staying in the Grove, cabin C," she instructed, then turned summarily to lead her young charge off in the opposite direction. Only at that moment did the child falter.

"Mommy—?" she asked, turning quickly back to Stephanie in a final, involuntary moment of insecurity, her gaze momentarily abandoning its protective curtain and softening into a heartrending plea.

Immediately, Stephanie bridged the gap between the two, bending over to give her daughter a firm hug. "I love you, pumpkin. I'll see you a little later," she murmured understandingly into the child's ear.

The small voice was barely audible as Melissa whispered, "I love you too, Mommy." Then the veil dropped over her gray eyes and she permitted herself to be led away to the accompanying chatter of this wondrous child-hearted woman.

Her finely tapered fingers brushed moistness from the corners of her misted eyes as Stephanie watched the two move off down the grassy slope. It was, simultaneously, such a small step, yet a huge one, for mother and child alike. Swallowing away the sentimental lump in her throat, she straightened and, propelled by the force of her own maternal resignation, turned back to the others.

If the three noted the tender moment they had just witnessed, they made no mention of it. Such private partings were common on this day of arrivals, and it was well known that the best remedy for the momentary sadness was a large dose of activity.

"I peeked into your studio," began the redheaded Cheryl, who had earlier introduced herself as the ceramics instructor and, as such, was a next-door neighbor of Stephanie's in the basement of the Arts Center by the waterfront. "It looks super—but there's loads to be done, unpacking supplies and all!" she warned humorously.

Stephanie smiled, slowly beginning to relax as she relinquished the role of mother for the summer and began the transformation into photographer. She hadn't realized how caught up she'd been, during the last few weeks, with the prospect of getting Melissa off to camp. Now it was a *fait accompli,* and, with that most dreaded moment of parting over, she felt her enthusiasm for her work quickly awaken.

Pushing an auburn lock behind her ear, she answered Cheryl warmly. "I can believe it! Perhaps I ought to get moving if I want to get myself settled before I tackle the studio."

The woman named Janet stepped forward, younger by several years than the other two, who seemed to be in their late twenties, and simultaneously more petite, almost elfish. "Do you know where your cabin is?" she asked, a strange note of envy in her light voice.

Stephanie nodded. "I remember all too clearly the good fortune of those assigned to the Grove. This must be a harbinger of good things to come this summer!" She laughed, noting the unanimous agreement of the others.

"You can say that again," chimed in the third, Donna, the drama coach. "Cheryl and I are in the Lodge, which isn't all that bad. Poor Janet, though, has the delight of bunk seven," she cracked, casting a sympathetic grin toward the small one, who, one wondered, might indeed be confused with her wards.

Stephanie laughed with the others, remembering vividly the dubious honor of bunk assignment, particularly with those older girls whose main goal seemed to be stretching the rules. Every bunk had its renegade or two; despite complaints to the contrary, however, they added spice to each summer.

With these fond memories warming her, she made the appropriate apologies, then drove forward to the bunk line, stopping at the very first cabin to drop off Melissa's trunk. Pausing to give a cursory once-over to the immaculate room in which her daughter would live, she noted with satisfaction that the years had done nothing to change the delightful primitiveness of the dormitory-style cabin. Several campers had already arrived, though, so she quickly took her leave before Melissa would return and she would have to go through the good-byes again.

Moments later she found herself in the Grove, actually a large clearing at the end of a short but private road, not far from the bunk line, with three small cabins forming a cul-de-sac beneath the crowding pines. It was a truly heavenly spot, Stephanie reaffirmed as she climbed out of the car—within an easy walk of everything yet far enough removed to escape the sounds with which one would be dealing throughout the day. The air was clean and sweet, an exquisite bouquet of pine needles and natural wood wafting on the light breeze that whispered through the branches overhead. Each cabin was insulated from the heat of the sun by forest parasols hovering above, beside, and beyond their shingled roofs.

Cabin C was the farthest on the right, a large, carved letter so indicating, and Stephanie approached it enthusiastically, bounding up the steps and throwing open the door for the first glimpse of her own home-away-from-home. Although she had never spent much time at the Grove other than to visit a friend, the charm of the cabin far outdistanced even her most ambitious recollections. She had a private cabin, designated for one inhabitant only, with the lone cot against one wall, a large double bureau against the other, and built-in shelves for books, pictures, and other miscellaneous items stretching above each. There was a small back room, with storage space and a closet, and a bathroom just off to the side. As with all the bunks, the showers were separate, in this case in a small shower house behind the middle cabin for the use of all three in the Grove.

Delighted with her accommodations and, in particular, with its location and the privacy it would afford, Stephanie made a mental note to thank Sylvie for the considerate assignment. Although she would never have complained, she feared that it might have been tedious for her to share a cabin with one of the other counselors, considering the most subtle purpose behind this, her return to the scene of so many memories, both heartwarming and potentially devastating. Fortunately, she mused gratefully, he had been living in Blue Cottage that year. . . .

Determined not to let this, her thus far propitious return to PineWinds, be marred so early on by thoughts of that long-ago affair, she gaily swung her auburn head around, set her delicately chiseled chin at an angle of resolve, and returned to her car and opened the trunk to remove her two suitcases and her camera gear. It was on the fourth trip out, as she dug into the farthest reach of the car's trunk, struggling to grasp a duffel bag stuffed with sheets, pillows, blankets, and a quilt, which she knew would be needed on more than one chilly night in the unheated cabin, that she heard the slow drawl of a deep, velvet-smooth voice close behind her.

"It's been a long time since I've seen a pair of legs like those . . ."

Never in her life could Stephanie have forgotten that voice, so cool and confident, humorous yet seductive. At that instant she froze, mind and body benumbed as they hadn't been since that traumatic morning eight years before when she had interrupted the work of a blond-haired woman.

In a kaleidoscopic progression of emotion, the numbness flared into a wave of panic which, tempered by eight years of studied self-control, gradually resolved into a more manageable state of shock. Slowly, very slowly, she sank down against the edge of the open trunk, only then turning to gaze toward the face that she had neither seen for eight years nor been a single day without.

two

IF THERE WAS TO BE RETRIBUTION FOR THIS wildly imagined happening-turned-reality, it was immediate and brief, capsuled in the look of astonishment that struck Douglas Weston's hitherto composed face. As their eyes locked, gray into green, Stephanie knew that he had been unaware of her impending presence and was as disquieted as she with the discovery. Mildly buoyed by this realization, she forced herself into a semblance of composure as she met his puzzled gaze.

"Eight years to be exact." She spoke softly, determined to deny, both to him and to herself, the internal upheaval that had beset her. Her peripheral awareness took in a blue work shirt, sleeves rolled and neck more open than necessary, faded denim cutoffs, and bare arms, legs, and feet, all evenly tanned and infinitely masculine. The face was that of an eight-years-older Douglas Weston, more handsome than ever.

A master of self-possession himself, Doug quickly recovered from the unexpected confrontation. "Then I stand corrected; it's been eight years since I've seen a pair of legs like those." He grinned, his lips parting in a dazzling display of straight, white teeth. Had he been looking at her legs, Stephanie might have been less affected. But his eyes never left hers, their keen grayness piercing her, deeply and painfully. She felt an overwhelming compulsion to run at that very moment, yet doubted whether the well-touted legs would carry her far enough. Experience dictated that she be still, both verbally and physically, letting him take the initiative while she struggled to corral her emotions.

"How are you, Stephie?" he began politely, the steadiness of his tone suggesting, to Stephanie's relief, that this might be an outwardly civilized, even impersonal, conversation.

"Just fine, Doug," she responded in kind, cool and cordial.

Then he did venture to rake her length, head to toe and back, slowly and sensually, in a not so subtle gesture of appreciation, and her sense of relief evaporated. "You've grown even more beautiful than I remember you being," he murmured. Suddenly, she felt a pang of stirrings within her, unbidden and unwelcome. In its wake came a strange anger—anger at his words, despite the compliment they offered, anger at the look in his eyes, so open and insolently appealing, anger at her own reaction, too quick in awakening after a long sleep.

"Memories can be deceiving," she clipped back, of necessity trusting her legs to hold as she rose and turned to grab for the duffel bag once again. It helped, breaking his eye contact, though the respite was short lived.

A roughly haired arm, bronzed and muscular, reached out past her toward the offending bag. "Here, let me give you a hand," his deep voice suggested, as he casually pulled the duffel from the far corner.

After long years of doing for herself, Stephanie somehow found his offer offensive. Mustering her strength, she pulled the bag until it was entirely within her own grasp, only then turning her green eyes defiantly up at him. "I can manage myself, thank you."

The unfathomable look that crept into his suddenly chilled eyes told her that he had perceived her anger and was puzzled by it. But his puzzlement was nothing, compared to the bewilderment that flitted about her own mind. Sylvie Hampson had assured her that Doug would not be here, yet here he stood before her, larger than life, his long frame propped arrogantly against her car, his arms folded purposefully across his chest. It had been a mere hour since she had seen that same gesture in another, so similar. With an imperceptible shiver she wondered fearfully whether there were other such surprises in store for her.

"You're working here this summer, I take it," she stated, attempting to keep the timidity, rampant as he towered over her, out of her voice.

"That's right," he confirmed laconically, reversing the tables now and demanding that she take the lead in conversation. She suspected that he sensed her continuing discomfort and was rather enjoying himself.

"Tennis?"

"Uh-huh." So, Sylvie had misled her. Why?

"Where are you living?" Her hands clutched tightly at the canvas handle of the duffel bag as she awaited his answer. Never one for superstitions, she nonetheless had a premonition, which was instantly fueled by the wicked grin that overspread his lips. Jauntily he cocked his dark head to the side.

"Cabin A."

Stephanie felt her stomach knot, hit by a sudden blow. Why had she sensed what his answer was to be? How could Sylvie have done this to her? What was her great sin, to be thus punished?

To her further dismay, she caught the wry amusement which now molded his features. "You look pale, Stephie," he drawled with distinct mockery. "Are you *that* disappointed we're not sharing Cabin B?"

Convinced that he knew all too well the implication of his words, Stephanie was overwhelmed to the point of fury. Instinctively, she raised a hand and brought it sharply up toward his face, only to have her wrist captured in a viselike grip which burned into her skin even as it thwarted her action.

"It was just a joke, Stephanie," he informed her impatiently, his eyes now steeled, his features taut. As he spoke, he lowered her hand deliberately, releasing it with a thrust, as though he could bear the contact no longer.

Stunned by both his touch and its unceremonious disengagement, she stiffened, flashing jade spokes in her eyes the only outward evidence of anger. "I guess I'm not in the mood for joking," she murmured quietly, struggling for self-control as she dragged her gaze from his to focus on her sole means of rescue, the duffel bag which had yet to be lifted from the trunk. "Now, if you'll excuse me," she began, "I have a lot of unpacking to do."

If she had expected him to graciously back away, she had once again miscalculated. Her punishment was only beginning. Quick, strong fingers took her chin, firmly overcoming her token resistance, and turned her pale face toward his. Everything about him intimidated her at that moment, though she was helpless to move.

"You have grown more beautiful, Stephie," he stated arrogantly, his forefinger lifting to stroke her jawline with a tenderness belied by his fiercely intent expression. "You are also more tense and more angry, if those eyes and this jaw are any indication." His voice had softened dangerously as he concluded, "I wonder what's happened over the last eight years to make you thus . . ." He trailed off, as his hand dropped to his side.

"I've grown up, Doug," Stephanie heard herself say strongly and with conviction. It was the truth, and she suddenly felt a resurgence of strength. "Now, I have to get busy," she reiterated her original intention as she lifted the duffel bag and balanced it against her thigh and climbed the steps. She did not look back, but kept her sights forward as she knew she must if she was to weather this latest storm.

Once within the privacy of the cabin, she became a veritable whirlwind of activity, opening suitcases, piling some clothes in drawers, draping others on hangers, stashing toiletries on the bathroom shelves, and books and technical materials on the shelves in the main room. She quickly made up the bed, stored the duffel bag and suitcases in the rafter compartment, then gave her attention to her photographic equipment, separating what was to go in the studio from that which she'd keep with her.

But all too soon she ran out of diversions. At that moment, as she sank weakly onto the edge of the bed, a shudder shook her tired limbs and her mind turned to the one topic she so desperately wanted to escape. But avoidance, she realized all too painfully, would not eliminate the problem.

What was she to do, her being cried. Douglas Weston was here . . . here at PineWinds! It would not only be the raw memories she would have to battle, but the man, in the flesh. In the tall, dark, and magnificently handsome flesh. She had ventured to return to PineWinds for many reasons, not the least of which was to finally exorcise the haunting past. But, if the earlier encounter was any indication, she seriously doubted her chances for success—particularly with the object of her quandary housed two doors away, where she was destined to see him coming and going each and every day.

She lay back on the bed and threw a shaky arm across her eyes, fighting off a nightmare which threatened to engulf her and draw her into its swirling eddy. And Missy . . . what about Missy? Would Doug know immediately? The resemblance was so strong. Would it be obvious when the two finally came face-to-face? Missy was thoroughly acclimated to a single-parent situation. She must not know yet, not so soon, not until she was old enough to understand.

As she lay there, Stephanie wondered how, after eight years in which she'd directed her life so carefully, she now found herself in this untenable situation. Sylvie had said he wouldn't be here. . . .

Sylvie! She must speak to Sylvie! Perhaps something could be done to ease this situation in which she floundered helplessly. Perhaps she could yet turn around, as Missy had begged, and return home. For, cowardly as that course would be, she questioned her ability to cope with the alternative.

Grasping at this feeble thread of hope, she freshened up, brushing her recalcitrant curls into relative, though temporary, submission, then headed for the door. A cursory sweep of the Grove told her that Doug was no longer there, having gone no doubt in search of more friendly company. Reassured thus, she set out in search of the director, putting the force of determination into the slam of her car's trunk as she strode past it.

As luck would have it, the woman she sought was now in the process of greeting a clamoring busload of girls, the midwestern contingent, which had just arrived from the airport in Boston. Momentarily swept up in the excitement, Stephanie found herself glued to the spot as a memory-laden spectator. She recalled that same bus trip; her parents had always driven her the few miles from Cambridge to the airport, where she would join the newly landed group for the final leg of their trip. She had been one of only a handful of campers from the Boston area, a fact which had appealed to her parents. They were both educators and, as such, placed a high value on their daughter's own learning experiences. To spend the summer with the same people with whom she spent the rest of the year would have defeated one of their primary purposes, and, over the years, Stephanie had come to agree with them. She had first gone off to camp timidly, then had met girls from all over the country, broadening her exposure and vaulting her into friendships which were close, rewarding, and in several cases, long-lasting. Indeed, even now, she kept up a long-distance correspondence with Trudy, her closest friend for six years at camp, who had originally hailed from Cleveland, had subsequently moved to Baltimore, where she had married a doctor, and was now firmly ensconced, with her husband, two children, and a dog, in Arizona. She had seen Trudy periodically over the years, and each time the reunion was a joyous one, the distance between them evaporating instantly, the many months apart forgotten.

Now, as she watched the campers alight, tripping

down the steps one after the other, weighted down by numerous carrying bags and surrogate security blankets, a nostalgic smile curled at her pale pink lips. And there was Sylvie Hampson, hugging each girl in turn, both those whom she knew well from past summers and those whom she remembered only from brief introductions the previous winter. Stephanie recalled how comforting Sylvie had always been in her own moments, both of triumph, as when she had finally passed her senior lifesaving test, and of sorrow, as when she had been struck by the inevitable wave of homesickness that first, momentous year. But now it was Sylvie whom she must confront on a totally different level . . . when she was free and alone. Unfortunately, Sylvie was neither, and, as urgent as Stephanie felt her own business to be, she knew it must take second place to this other, more timely one.

With a sigh she turned away from the scene, only to be checked abruptly by the presence of a tall, dark figure, standing a short distance away in intent observation of her. With a cool stare in his direction, she pivoted sharply and impulsively set out down the grassy slope toward the waterfront. If she had to postpone her talk with Sylvie, she reasoned, she would do something practical. And the farther away from those brooding eyes, the better, she decided. If there was one thing she refused to do, she vowed, it would be to let Douglas Weston know how disconcerting she found his very presence.

Resolutely, she strode across the slope to the pebbled road that bisected the fields and the tennis courts on its lakeward path. When she had first been a camper, there had been only four courts; now there were eight, all clay and in impeccable condition. How much of the credit belonged to Doug, she refused to consider. Rather, she drew her gaze to the approaching waterfront, with its labyrinth of docks virtually unchanged by the years. Just beyond and on the shore stood the Arts Center, with its craft rooms on the main, raised floor and the ceramics and photography areas below, on the dark ground level, where once upon a time Stephanie had hunted for frogs. Now the area had been completely enclosed and finished, providing a perfect setting for her own work.

As she explored this domain, which might or might not be hers, she mused, she felt herself relax, only then realizing the full intensity of her earlier anxiety. She would not let him get to her, she repeated anew, forcefully slamming her fist down on the shiny Formica countertop that skirted the room. Then, having expelled that bit of pent-up anger, she scanned the perimeter of the area to take inventory of the boxes and crates. True to her word, Sylvie had provided everything Stephanie requested—film, chemicals, enlarging equipment, printing paper, and, most importantly, cameras. She carefully examined the cameras and soon found herself locked in an internal battle—the excitement and exhilaration of putting this fine equipment to the best possible use this summer versus the agony of knowing that she would soon be asking Mrs. Hampson to relieve her of the obligation and allow her to take Melissa home. Surprisingly, she found herself disappointed at the thought of all the good things they would both miss if they left. She didn't want to leave, she realized mournfully; despite the painful memories, she didn't want to leave. But the past was not the present . . . why did he have to be here?

Restrained only by the uncertainty of her future, she ached to tear open the cases and delve into the thrilling adventure of setting up the studio. Surely, she mused, there could be no harm in unpacking one camera. Surely Sylvie would understand. . . .

Hesitantly, Stephanie reached for one of the boxes and removed the packing material. Ever so carefully she removed its treasure, turning the camera around in her hand, getting the feel of it, exploring its dials and knobs, savoring the smell which spoke of a newness that would soon be gone. Impulsively, she reached for a roll of film, loaded the camera, mounted it with one of the zoom lenses which had been supplied, and headed back to the main area, intent on capturing the myriad nuances of arrival day.

This time she took the back way to the bunk line, the pine path, as it was called, a broad footpath which led directly through the woods, beneath a continuous canopy of boughs, from waterfront to cabins. Everything was tranquil, everything was silent, save the rhythmic crunch of twigs and dried leaves beneath her own feet.

Several minutes later she arrived at her destination to find that the first bus had left and been replaced by another, this one smaller and carrying the heavily accented, widely adored group of southerners, who had flown directly to Portland and been met there. Again, Sylvie Hampson greeted them warmly and personally as she had done the others.

Lifting the camera to her eye, Stephanie framed the heartwarming scene, cocked then tripped the shutter, repeating the steps over and over again as she moved in and around the action. Satisfied with herself and thoroughly engrossed in her work, she turned and, noting that there were ample frames left, sought to capture the settling-in process, as campers met counselors, unpacked, and had their first introductions to, or reunions, in many cases, with their bunkmates.

Fighting off an urge to look in on Missy, Stephanie quickly moved past to one of the senior bunks and began to photograph, first outside, then inside, until the roll of film was finished. She thoroughly enjoyed herself, meeting people as she worked, having several reunions of her own, as she came across one or two familiar faces. Her only regret, as was often the case, was that she hadn't brought more film with her. But that situation was easily remedied; eagerly she descended the steps and headed back toward the waterfront, only to find herself on a collision course with Douglas Weston.

Involuntarily, she caught her breath, dazzled against her will by his dashing appearance. Dressed in tennis whites and carrying two racquets and a can of balls, his destination was obvious. Similarly obvious to Stephanie was the magnificence of the man, yes, eight years older, but even more compelling than he had been when she had first met him. The years had treated him well, scattering an odd gray hair or two through his lustrous brown mane, etching lines of good humor at the corners of his eyes, giving his skin, with its weathered tan, a rich and rugged cast.

"You're staring, Stephie," he drawled, a faint glimmer of mockery breaking through the otherwise frigid gaze, as he stopped directly before her. It was true, though at the time she could have done nothing else. He was so familiar . . . yet alien. . . .

His eyes narrowed coldly as he offered a further observation. "You looked quite happy a minute ago when you came down those steps." He tossed a quick glance in the direction from which she'd come. "Very much like the Stephanie I used to know. Now you are tense once again." Under his merciless scrutiny, she felt her emotions laid bare, and she fought for some thread of dignity.

Raising fine, arched eyebrows, she calmly protested his claim, feigning a self-confidence which she was far from feeling. "You're quite mistaken, Doug. I'm not tense at all," she stated, even as she felt the muscles in her shoulder tighten beneath the strap of her camera.

"Stephie, Stephie," he chided, his tauntingly condescending tone in odd juxtaposition with the sternness of his expression. "I told you before, it's in your jaw—" He reached out to touch the spot and involuntarily she flinched, taking a step back by way of warning for him to keep his hands in check. His own jaw clenched once, to her satisfaction, before he continued. "And the knuckles around your camera strap are pure white." His voice verged on the angry; then he paused, studying her face intently. Unable to muster an appropriate response, Stephanie stood, tongue-tied, only able to remember the softness and gentleness of that same voice so long ago.

Then, to her surprise, a strange sadness brushed his features, as though he, too, were recalling another time. "Do you hate me that much, Stephie?" he asked finally, cool and composed once more.

Did she hate him? Could she hate him? Had she ever, from that far-reaching day to this, hated him? Without a doubt, Stephanie knew the answer. Hate Douglas Weston? As much as it might simplify things for her, she never could, never would hate him. But then, she had known that all along. What she hadn't known was the effect that seeing him again would have on her.

Suddenly, his face began to blur and, to her utter

chagrin, she knew herself to be on the verge of tears. Soundlessly, she made her escape, passing beside him and heading whence he had just come. She cared neither about last words nor parting pleasantries as she headed singlemindedly toward Sylvie's office. By the time she arrived the tears had dried, leaving behind only the sentiment—raw, painful, and completely baffling to her.

Force of habit took her up the open stairway toward the spot on the second-floor balcony where the director sat, deeply engrossed in some paper work. At another time Stephanie would have delighted in examining the floor-to-ceiling pictures tracing the history of the camp, from the days of middy blouses and bloomers to the present; now she was oblivious to all but the small, white-haired woman seated at the far end of the floor.

"Sylvie," she whispered tentatively, as she approached, her crepe-soled sandals practically soundless on the scrubbed and varnished wood floor and thus failing to alert the other to her presence. Her voice, soft as it was, however, did the trick. The director's head swiveled quickly, a smile instantly illuminating her aged features.

"Stephie!" Reaching a thin, veined hand to draw forward a chair, she gestured for Stephanie to sit. "I'm so glad you stopped by!"

Encouraged by the woman's warmth, Stephanie opened her mouth to get right to the point, when, to her amazement, Sylvie forged on with barely a breath.

"That daughter of yours is a wonder, she is! Such a beautiful child, so polite and well-spoken. You should be very proud of her," she beamed, with a glow that, by rights, befitted a grandmother.

Helpless in the face of this charm, Stephanie smiled.

"I am, very much so, Sylvie!" Again she made to go on, again she was cut off.

"She seemed to take immediately to her counselor, Beth, and I thought I saw her in deep discussion with one of her little bunkmates about a book that the other had. They both were quite excited at one point there!" She laughed, a self-satisfied laugh, justly deserved, upon finding her group assignments so immediately rewarding.

Again Stephanie smiled in appreciation, though her expression was rapidly growing forced as her mind sought a different solace. "I'm relieved to hear that, Sylvie. And thank you for taking her off so tactfully. I was worried—"

"I know you were, my dear." The older woman patted her hand reassuringly. "And you still are, aren't you?"

"Not really—" Stephanie fully intended to pour out the immediate cause of her worry, when she was abruptly interrupted once more.

"You know, there's no need to worry about anything," the gravel-edged voice surged on. "Melissa will adjust beautifully, as will you. Tell me"—her eyes opened wider, as she changed her tack—"is everything in order at the photo shed? Did I order everything you needed? Any mistakes? Omissions?"

Stephanie was aware of the spell which had now begun to work on her. How could she stay tense in this woman's presence? She had the uncanny knack, Stephanie mused admiringly, of recognizing a person's strongest points, then making all other obstacles in life seem insignificant by comparison. In the face of this nearly invincible tactic, Stephanie burst into spontaneous laughter, her eyes lighting up despite herself.

"Yes, Sylvie, everything is wonderful on that score!

The supplies are perfect, the shed ideal, and as you can see I've already begun to make use of the equipment. The subject matter here is inexhaustible! But, Sylvie." She paused for a breath, immediately realizing her error as the white-haired whirlwind struck again.

"What I'd like you to do," she began, her face growing more serious, her brows knitting in emphasis of her expectations, "is to document the entire camp season. Start to finish, high points and low points, everything. We've never attempted anything like this before, but it would be good for us and good for you."

Stephanie grew puzzled, sensing that she was about to hear something new. "You see," Sylvie began in response to the questioning gaze cast her way, "we rarely do any advertising for PineWinds. Word of mouth alone brings us many more applications than we can handle each year. So it's not a matter of attention-getting. No," she murmured, as she looked down at hands intertwined in her lap. Suddenly, Stephanie saw the image of a woman whose life was in large part behind her, with but a few outgoing sparks yet to be fired. Intuitively, Stephanie sensed that she was to play a role, herself, in sending off at least one of those sparks.

Lifting her eyes to meet Stephanie's, Sylvie went on with the sense of conviction which was part of her character. "This camp has been our life's work, Sonny's and mine. With your cooperation, we will have a forum to illustrate the outcome of our work."

"I'm not sure I understand, Sylvie," Stephanie prodded gently, having temporarily shelved her own problems—just as the older woman may indeed have intended.

"This winter Sonny and I will be putting together what we hope to be a definitive book on the camping experience. We have a publisher and a very cooperative editor—"

"That's wonderful!" Stephanie exclaimed enthusiastically, knowing well that such a book would indeed be definitive, considering the wealth of experience shared by this woman and Sonny, whose presence at PineWinds was simultaneously pervasive and invisible. At that moment Stephanie sensed the connection between her own profession and Sylvie's. "And my photographs?" she ventured hesitantly, her jade eyes opening wide in anticipation.

Sylvie took her hand in a touching gesture of supplication. "With your permission, Stephie, we'd like to use them to illustrate the book. Needless to say, you will be given full credit for your work. It could be invaluable to your career." She eyed the younger woman warmly. "What do you say?" she asked, a beckoning tilt of her chin punctuating the question.

Stephanie could only begin to comprehend the full implication of the opportunity. "I'm flattered that you think so highly of my work," she spoke softly, warmed to the core by the other's confidence in her. She knew what her answer had to be. "I'd love to." She smiled, and Sylvie sealed the agreement with a fond squeeze of her hand as she straightened in her chair.

"Then it's all agreed. And you say you've already begun?"

Suddenly a dead weight fell on Stephanie's shoulders as she realized what she'd done, what she'd committed herself to, contrary to her original purpose in seeking Sylvie out. A frown drew her lips into a thin line, and her eyes suddenly clouded with worry. Sylvie immediately picked up on her distress.

"But that wasn't really what you came to talk to me about, was it, my dear?" Mutely, Stephanie shook her head, her auburn curls bobbing around her face, giving her the look of a lost child, which, at that moment, she felt like. "Are you very angry with me?"

Stephanie's brow furrowed. "Angry?" she questioned, totally unprepared for what was to follow.

The elder one held her gaze steadily. "For putting you up there with him?" Whether it was guilt or sympathy on Sylvie Hampson's face, Stephanie was too astonished to notice.

"I . . . ah . . ." As she stammered helplessly, Sylvie's lines softened in keen understanding.

"One of the things on which I pride myself most highly is that I know of everything going on in my camp. You and Doug seemed to be quite taken with each other when you were last here. Unfortunately, you left at the end of the season before I had a chance to talk with you. Oh"—she waved her hand in dismissal of an imagined argument—"some would say that it's none of my business. I disagree." Her eyes flashed in echo of her words. "I make it my business when it concerns my family." Sincerity oozed from her words, concern from her very depths.

"Doug asked about you for quite a while after, wanting to know if I'd heard from you, if you'd be coming back here. Finally, he stopped asking," she confessed, lowering her eyelids. "I felt that there had been something deep there which, for some reason, you chose to deny. Please"—she looked up quickly, leaving Stephanie's rebuttal to die on opened lips—"I'm not blaming you for anything. That is not my place. Neither did I intend to do any matchmaking by putting the two of you up in the Grove; it just worked out that way in terms of practical assignments. Having been a full-time mother for seven years, you hardly needed a roommate, and, for obvious reasons, Doug needed the other single cabin. The middle one was already reserved for our marrieds, Bob and Elaine."

Stephanie had listened with growing trepidation to the monologue, until there was only silence. In a pain-wrought whisper, she asked the question which had nagged at her. "You told me he was no longer here. Why, Sylvie?"

Sensing the anguish before her, Sylvie kept her tone low and gentle. "As I recall, you asked me whether he was still a tennis instructor. I answered in the negative, and correctly so. Doug is the head of the tennis department now, as well as the head counselor. He's taken quite a jump from mere instructor! I was going to tell you, but . . ."

"I cut you off." Stephanie lowered her own eyes as she reluctantly answered her own question. Now she recalled her folly; in her haste to hide that which Sylvie Hampson already knew, she had defeated her own purpose. But, if she felt uncovered, it was nothing to what was about to come.

Slowly, Sylvie leaned forward in her seat, gauging the discomfort already clearly outlined on her young friend's face. "Does he know about Melissa?"

For the second time that day, Stephanie felt as though the breath had been violently knocked from her. She had never before discussed this with anyone but her parents. How could Sylvie have guessed so easily? But then, she caught herself before she had blundered irreparably—perhaps Sylvie had only intended the words at their surface value. Stephanie gambled that this was the case.

"No," she said softly though evenly, "he doesn't know that I have a child." Her green eyes studied the face before her for trace of further suspicion, but, to her relief, she saw none. If Sylvie Hampson had guessed at Melissa's parentage, she had chosen to keep it to herself.

"Are you planning to tell him?" the older woman prodded gently. "He's bound to find out sooner or later, you know. We do have several other Wrights here, but, at some point, there will be a slip."

Stephanie had not given much thought to this particular dilemma, though instinctively she knew that Sylvie was right. Yet she wavered. "No," she finally concluded. "I really see no reason to volunteer that information. It seems somehow . . . inappropriate." Her thoughts flew back to their past relationship and its intimacy. Yes, he would eventually learn that she had a daughter. But for her to actively make a point of telling him smacked of either an accusation or of boastfulness—both unacceptable.

She brightened slightly, remembering her purpose at Sylvie's desk. "I doubt I'll have much discussion with him anyway." He seemed to want it that way, she mused, recalling the ice in his eyes during both of their earlier encounters. "Actually," she went on, raising her face in a gesture of dismissal, "I came to ask you if I couldn't take one of the rooms here." She cast an admiring gaze toward the rooms at the opposite end of the balcony. "As beautiful as is the Grove, well . . ."

The white head bobbed in understanding, as Sylvie filled in the words which seemed to embarrass Stephanie. "You'd rather not be as close to Doug as that?" Stephanie nodded, a faint flush creeping up her cheeks. Why was she so weak, she asked herself. What difference would it really make whether she was housed near him or not? Would this attempted avoidance really help? He would know exactly what she'd done and why. If only she were stronger . . . as it happened, she was neither to return home nor change accommodations.

"Stephie, do you trust me?" Sylvie asked directly, wondering whether the years of inspiring confidence and loyalty in her staff would now stand her in good stead. Stephanie nodded. Taking a deep breath, Sylvie went on. "I want you to stay at the Grove." She paused, then, seeing that no immediate refusal was forthcoming, continued. "Correct me if I'm wrong, my dear. You are a very bright girl. You knew, when you accepted this position, that you'd have to confront some perhaps uncomfortable memories. But you decided to come. Oh, yes, for Melissa's sake, but for your own, as well." As she stopped for a breath, she again looked to see if Stephanie disagreed with her assessment of the situation; Stephanie could only concur.

"You can't run away from him, Stephie. If there's something there, it's there. If it's gone, it's gone. No, I'd like you to stay at the Grove and come to terms with whatever it is that's worrying you."

At that point Stephanie did show signs of distress. Sylvie just couldn't understand the entire situation, she moaned inwardly. It would be torment enough just to see him, let alone to be so near him, even share a shower house with him. Certainly Sylvie would have agreed had she known the full story. Had she known how much Stephanie had adored Doug, how cruelly she had then been used . . .

"Now, now." Sylvie patted her knee. "Don't look so downhearted. You know, Douglas Weston is really quite a man!" *Don't I just know it,* Stephanie mused bitterly. "How much do you know of him?"

"Very little." The auburn curls came up as Stephanie's gaze, unbeknown to her own consciousness, begged for that information.

Sylvie got the message. "He is a brilliant administrator and educator. Tennis is just his hobby, you know," she offered.

"No, I didn't know," Stephanie replied. She had known, that summer, that he worked at a school in Vermont, yet he had never elaborated and she had thus assumed him to be a tennis pro of sorts. "He didn't seem to want to talk about the winter season," she explained unnecessarily.

Sylvie nodded in comprehension. "That's typically Doug. He feels very strongly about his privacy, especially when he's up here each summer. You see, he holds a very demanding position during the year. He likes to make the summer a purely fun time, no responsibility, and so on."

Now it was Stephanie's turn to nod. That did sound like Doug, all right, she thought caustically—love 'em and leave 'em! But she did find herself wondering about what Sylvie had meant by a very demanding position. "What, exactly, does he do?" she asked timidly, curiosity getting the best of her.

Sylvie pursed her lips as she arched one eyebrow. "Now, if I told you that, I'd be violating his confidence, wouldn't I?" As disappointed as Stephanie was, she respected the director all the more for what she had said. Moreover, she felt confident that whatever Sylvie knew or surmised about her relationship with Doug would remain within that remarkably acute mind of hers.

"Suffice it to say," the older woman concluded, "that I had to do quite a bit of arm twisting to get him to serve as head counselor, yet he manages to handle it and the tennis department with equal ease." Her voice lowered slightly then, an odd earnestness in her tone.

"Do try to get to know him this summer, Stephie. He could benefit from someone like you."

"You sound like a matchmaker after all." Stephanie grinned accusingly at Sylvie, her outward calm masking the mélange of confusion and unsureness into which these so innocently uttered words had thrown her. She thought, once, that she had gotten to know him—only to be tragically proved wrong. Oh, yes, he could benefit—using her for the summer to assuage his male needs. But that was certainly not what Sylvie had meant . . . not Sylvie Hampson!

"Speak of the devil, here he comes now, my dear," Sylvie tore into her thoughts. "No, don't panic," she whispered, putting a reassuring hand on Stephanie's arm in response to the aggrieved look which had sprung onto Stephanie's face. "You'll do just fine. But remember what I told you . . . and, you do know, my dear, that my own lips are sealed."

Stephanie had to grin at the words and accompanying impish expression on the director's face. "Thanks, Sylvie," she murmured, "I appreciate that." What she really would have appreciated, as she rose self-consciously from the chair by the director's desk, was a back way out of this place, a laundry chute, fire escape—anything so that she would not have had to face Douglas Weston. But, alas, there was nothing, she mused, as she donned a cloak of composure and headed down the balcony toward the stairs, at the top of which he stood, poised and waiting, his slate eyes following her every step.

If she was grateful for anything, it was for the fact that she did not trip over her own feet, stub her toe, or even worse, collapse under the frightful knocking of her knees. Yet she held his gaze, refusing to be intimidated. When she drew even with him, she thought for an instant that she had it made, with only the stairway to negotiate before she was free of his stare. Her comfort, however, was premature.

As she passed, a well-muscled arm came out and took hers, drawing her to him as he purposely put his towering frame between her form and Sylvie's so far now down the balcony. Stephanie felt the warmth of his body, so close did he stand, and, with only his one hand, albeit made at that moment of steel, to restrain her, she could have fled had she so desired. It may have been Sylvie's words, still fresh in her ears, which kept her. More likely, it was the same magnetism that had always drawn her to him, moth to flame, iron to magnet. He was so attractively masculine as he stood inches from her, the remnants of sweat beading on his forehead and neck from the workout he had just had, the heady scent of man and muscle seeping into her thoughts. But it was his eyes that held her, so cold and gray and threatening.

His stance became more intimate as he leaned forward to speak into her ear. She felt the gentle whisper of his breath against her hair, even as his words devastated her, their tone biting and angry. "I asked you a question before, Stephanie, and I intend to get an answer. You owe me an explanation. But this is neither the time nor the place. We'll talk later," he seethed. With a final frigid scowl he released her, turning his back instantly and heading toward Sylvie's desk. As his physical presence receded, the import of his words loomed before her with the prospect of a confrontation she had neither sought nor would stand by and endure.

Damn him, she swore, totally out of character, but matching her burgeoning anger, as she hastened down the stairs and out into the fresh air. What was he angry about? What explanations did she owe him? What right did he have to threaten her? Well, she, too, could come out swinging, if out of necessity alone. Thanks to Sylvie, she was committed to spending the summer here and to living in close proximity to this man. And she'd be damned if she would let him get the best of her!

Fire flashed turbulently in Stephanie's determined eyes. It was as though she had finally entered an arena which she had carefully avoided for these eight years. Now she would get her explanations, the ones he owed her, before the summer was out! There was no turning back; she accepted that. There would be unpleasantries; she accepted that. She might be tried beyond all previous endurance; she accepted that. What she did not, would not accept was that this man could cow her into submission, could manipulate her as he had once done. No, this time she knew what she was up against, and she would fight tooth and nail to salvage the summer and the future, for both herself and her daughter. She would not be the puppet, dangled witlessly and at the mercy of another. She had been for the last eight years, and would continue to be, her own mistress.

three

WE'LL TALK LATER, DOUG HAD INFORMED HER. As she kept a cautious eye on his whereabouts, Stephanie saw him conversing only with several of the new, younger counselors, fresh, attractive, and appropriately attentive to his charm. To her dismay, this behavior infuriated her more. It was not that she wanted to speak with him herself, but rather that he should be playing the same old game over again, that rankled her. With a scoff she turned away, faintly relieved at having him thus occupied and away from her. Yet it was strange solace. . . .

During the next few days she studiously avoided him, making a point to wait until he had left his cabin in the morning before she did, using the shower only when the counselors' schedule told her that he'd be occupied on the courts. Those she avoided at all cost, using the pine path as a protective screen from his possible view. Eye contact was frequent and inevitable during meals, invariably a two-way frown, scowl, or glower over the heads that separated them. If any were aware of the cold war being waged, there was never mention of it.

Mercifully, her work commanded the bulk of her attention, taking her mind off everything else but the crates of equipment to be unloaded one by one, their contents put in the proper place in the rapidly shaping up photo shed, as it had quickly become known about camp. In the darkroom area she organized and set up enlargers, timers, safelights, trays, chemicals, and printing paper. In the studio she catalogued film, cameras, lenses, tripods, and lights. With her classes not beginning until the following week, she spent any remaining time familiarizing herself with these materials, taking pictures and developing and printing those rolls already exposed.

As she photographed around camp, Stephanie frequently caught sight of Missy through her lens. Repeatedly she had been assured that the child was making a gradual adjustment to her group, its activities, and the absence of her mother as an integral force in her everyday life. Indeed, by the time several days had elapsed, Stephanie had managed to capture on film more than one grin, even a few broad smiles from her unsuspecting daughter. Thus satisfied that the youngster was faring well, she enjoyed her work all the more.

It was, for the most part, when Stephanie was at work that she managed to push the image of a Douglas Weston, cold and angry, out of her mind. Photography had become part of her life after she had known him, thus her photographic memories were free of his touch. Occasionally, and to her professed annoyance, his face intruded into the scope of her lens. At those times she would zoom in or out to obliterate the image, only once catching the derisive glint in his eye before he himself turned away.

By the end of the week she had begun to think that she might have, indeed, come to terms with the ghost of that long-ago lover. True, there was an underlying hostility that stood between the two of them. But his very coldness toward her would hint that the Douglas Weston she had once loved no longer existed. In his place was a man who seemed incapable of showing any warmth or compassion—let alone anything deeper—at least where she was concerned. And, although the ache within her at the loss was as great as ever, she felt that her mind had taken the first step; her body would simply have to follow suit.

Then came the encounter he had promised, or, more accurately, threatened. They had both attended an evening staff meeting. He, as head counselor, directed a number of questions toward her, one more impersonally posed than the next. Actually, Stephanie conceded, he ran his meetings on this consistently businesslike level, behaving no more or less polite to any of the staff. Perhaps it was this equal treatment which put her off her guard. Perhaps she had concluded that he would make no move to seek her out over any of the others, for whatever the reason. She was grossly mistaken.

It was dark that night, the moon only occasionally escaping the heavy clouds that pursued it, such that her walk back to the Grove at the meeting's conclusion was accomplished largely by memory and with not the usual haste that characterized these escapes to her sanctuary. As she neared the clearing, a sudden thunder of footsteps startled her, fast approaching on the earthen road behind her. Turning in fright, she confronted a dark form; its physique and gait were easily discernible, though its face was visible for but an instant as the moon made a short-lived appearance. At this moment of recognition, she whirled to beat a speedy retreat to her cabin, only to be grabbed by the elbow and swung around to face Doug's shaded countenance.

"You seem to have become expert at running away from me," he exploded, not in the least winded from a sprint which would have left other mortals breathless. His fingers dug into her arm with an intensity that frightened her no less than his violent tone—both keeping from her the deeper meaning of his words. How different he had grown over the course of eight years, she thought, before her arm was wrenched again and she winced in pain.

"Let me go!" she ordered meekly, intimidated both by the darkness and his manner. In answer to her plea he merely grabbed the other arm in a similarly confining clamp. If he harbored eight years of anger, she feared it was now to be vented. Even in the pitch black of the night she felt the venom of his gaze, punishing her visually for an as yet unknown crime. When he showed no sign of relenting, she began to panic. "Let—let go!" she screamed, kicking out at his shin to further her demand.

Cursing under his breath, he released one arm. "So you've become a fighter, have you?" he seethed, though his voice was quieter, the grip on her arm less binding. "You never used to fight me." His anger was suddenly laced with a seductive thread which, under the circumstances, incensed her all the more.

"You never used to inspire it," she retorted angrily, tossing her curls back with an arrogant flick of the head. "What do you want, Doug?" Coolly she glared at him, coolly he responded.

"I want to talk with you."

"I believe you had your chance at the meeting.

There is nothing else to say." Trite it was, and wishful thinking. She knew it the moment the words escaped her lips. It was just one of many scenarios she'd played out on her mind's stage over the years. This one she'd dubbed iced indifference. It was not one of her favorites, though its goal, to keep him at a distance, would certainly suit her present purposes.

Undaunted by her denial, he persisted. "I think there is. It's about time we cleared the air. Now will it be my cabin or yours?"

Despite the firmness of his tone, Stephanie was not ready to capitulate. "Neither! I have no intention of discussing anything with you . . . now or ever. You can just stay away from me!"

"Like hell I will," he snarled. Without warning he seized her other arm again and drew her flush against the length of his long, hard body, brutally smashing his lips down upon hers before she could begin to protest. Shock quickly yielded to fury, and then she did fight, struggling at first with the meager bits of strength left in her arms and legs, then twisting her head from side to side in an attempt to escape the violence of his kiss. To her dismay, her efforts only angered him more. With a single, swift movement, he secured both of her wrists behind her within the span of his one large hand, while the other took her neck in its steel grip, immobilizing her face and lending even greater power to the lips which punished hers, bruising them mercilessly against her teeth.

It was a devastating onslaught, knotting her stomach, outraging her senses. Darkness melded with darkness as, gasping for breath, her knees buckled. Only then did he release her, holding her at arm's length as she struggled to catch her breath, glaring at her menacingly as his own breathing steadied. She half expected him to resume his torture; but he was as drained as she, his anger having crested and careened down to a simmering disgust.

"How dare you . . ." she whispered shakily. Her impulse was to either hit him or run from him; neither was possible, however, as the well-corded hands held her shoulders guardedly. After what they had once shared, what he had just done amounted, in her mind, to nothing short of rape. What madness possessed him to attack her so savagely?

Though the darkness shielded his expression from her, an intangible current of tension emanated from his every touchpoint. His voice was low and frigid when he spoke. "Yes, I dare . . . and I'd do it again. Now, which cabin, yours or mine?"

Given the ultimatum, she had no choice. To refuse him further would only spark another attack, and she would avoid that at all cost.

"Mine." No sooner had she spoken than he propelled her in its direction, wordlessly escorting her up the steps and through the door before finally releasing her arm. He flipped on the light, a dim wall lamp above the bed that cast a pale yellow glow in its realm, and leaned back against the door, crossing his arms over his chest as he stood, legs apart, in a stance of mastery which unnerved Stephanie as much as had the darkness. Quickly she moved to the opposite side of the room, turning her back to him as she stared out into the night.

"Why didn't you answer any of my letters, Stephanie?" His words jolted her, the last thing she had expected to hear, a pain tearing at her insides as he waived the preliminaries and shot right to the core of his concern. She trembled as her mind made the dangerous journey back to those first, oppressive months following their affair.

The letters had come for several months. At the time, her nerves were raw and exposed; she was angry, hurt, and desperately struggling to pick up the pieces of her shattered hopes. This was before she even knew that she was pregnant . . . not that it would have altered the situation. She had wanted to wipe her life clean of Douglas Weston, and the best way had been to deny his existence. When she discovered she was carrying his child, she could no longer do that. Yet she refused, even then, to acknowledge him by reading any of the letters that continued to dribble in.

There had been times, over the years, when she had rued this stubbornness, when she would have liked to have known what he had written, if only out of curiosity. But, by then, there were no more letters and she had presumably been forgotten. It was better that way, she had reasoned time and time again.

Now, as her mind flipped into the present and this renewed agony, Stephanie felt driven to revenge, desirous of inflicting pain on its ultimate source. Turning angrily, her eyes narrowed as she lashed out with a venom of her own. "I never read your letters, Doug. Not a one. They were never even opened. I burned each as it arrived." A heavy silence fell between them. Strangely, she felt no satisfaction from the cruelty which she had inflicted. Indeed, she had hit her mark. It was as though he had been struck; visibly he flinched, his lips thinning to a hard line as he drew himself up straighter.

"Why?" His voice was cold and controlled, yet demanding.

As his gaze pierced her very soul, she clutched the windowsill for support. "There was no purpose in dragging on something that had no future. The summer was over. We each had our own lives to lead. You should never have written; there was no point." Much as she believed the oft-repeated words, the sad truth they contained tore at her afresh, diluting her anger with a dose of pure unhappiness.

Slowly and pantherlike, Doug moved away from the door. Instinctively, she stiffened at his approach, knowing that she could no more escape him than its prey the panther. The key was to salvage her dignity, she told herself over and over, as each deliberate step brought him closer. When he was no more than a foot from her, he stopped, his eyes steellike, his jaw taut. His every muscle seemed poised for the kill. Desperately Stephanie fought the trembling that threatened to betray her fear. Anything, she could bear anything, she knew, but a repeat of that earlier violence. It was a sacrilege, that earlier kiss, when compared with the reverence with which he had once treated her. In a fleeting instant of shock, Stephanie realized that her body, traitor and wanton, craved that old, remembered touch, that adoration, that mind-boggling passion which once he had bestowed on her. A blush colored her cheeks, mercifully undetected in the dim light and its shadow, which his tall frame cast over her.

"No point?" His words brought her back to her senses, though now it was their oddly plaintive sound that assailed her. "How can you say that . . . after what we shared."

Suddenly Stephanie came to life, shaking her head as her voice rose in exasperation. "I don't believe you! After eight years do you expect me to come running back to you?" An unsteady arm pointed in the direction of the clearing from which they'd come. "Is that what it was all about out there?" Now she was fighting herself as well as him, and the battle seemed to heat up by the minute.

"Why did you come back here?" he demanded angrily.

"I was offered a very exciting job," she replied, guarding her words, careful to be truthful without revealing her deeper secret. "Had I known you would be here, I would never have accepted." As soon as she uttered the last, she regretted it. Her words had been hateful, yet she did not hate. Why had she spoken thus? What was it which he seemed to bring out in her? It was as though her real self stood helplessly watching while a new, more selfish, infinitely less compassionate human being took command.

Doug's face was hard and strong; even as she regarded it within the aura of anger which enveloped them both, she had to admire its rugged set, its manly cast, the vein throbbing convulsively at his temple, the only sign of any distress she could detect. For a long moment his slate gaze touched her own face, examining each feature in turn, stirring a totally different nerve within her. When he spoke, it was softly and with the same sadness she had noted before, so strange and unexplained yet oddly arousing.

"Just for the record, had I known you would be here, I might have had second thoughts myself." His words stung, poignant and crushing, just retaliation for her own. That he meant them, she had no doubt. In a defensive gesture, she wrapped her arms about her churning stomach, as she continued to regard the hard, dark face above her. He was so near, yet unreachable. So angry, yet so full of sorrow. So forbidding, yet highly magnetic. Lost in a billowing cloud of confusion, she barely heard his sigh.

"We're stuck with it, aren't we, Steph?" he murmured

softly. Then with a final searching probe of gray depths into green, he left.

Standing frozen for long moments afterward, Stephanie realized that he had effectively summed up the situation. They were locked, these two, into a state of affairs which neither would have sought nor could alter. All that remained was to determine how best to cope.

Little by little, warmth crept back into her body, enabling her to go through the motions of preparing for bed. Yet sleep would be a long time coming on this night, as her mind revved up for a marathon session of dos and don'ts, woulds and coulds, whys and why nots.

Of the evening's tumultuous findings, the easiest for her to identify, though by far a challenge to comprehend, was the unexpected violence, the physical attack he had launched, unwarranted and inexcusable, in her opinion. He had never behaved thus toward her in the past. Why had he resorted to such aggression now? As much as his motive puzzled her, she felt that the key to preventing any repeat performance would be to avoid him and, in particular, to avoid giving him any grounds for such extreme reaction. But what grounds had she given him earlier?

Her thoughts progressed to the next puzzlement—the incredible anger, even hatred, that had permeated his mood. As she had asked herself earlier, so now she wondered anew—why was he angry? What had she done to engender such dislike? She was the one who had been wronged, not he. Why, then, did he act as though she owed him an apology?

But, by far the most awesome aspect of the predicament for Stephanie was the undertone of sexuality which had emerged as an omnipresent force, etched indelibly between each and every word. It was to this aspect her thoughts gravitated, about this aspect they congealed, and with this aspect they became obsessed.

Intermixed with his anger had been that recurrent touch of sadness, and the occasional, though assumedly unintentional, thread of seductiveness that even now, in hindsight, triggered a tingling in long-forgotten places. It was an inevitable attraction, which had somehow survived both the passage of time and the tangled web of emotional distaste and distrust, to reappear, unbidden and terrifying.

Yes, Stephanie found herself terrified at the prospect of having to deal with her own primitive instincts, as well as his. Would she be able to maintain the iced indifference she had diligently displayed for his benefit? Would she be able to fight the subtle seductiveness which was the hallmark of his manner, as inevitable as the aristocratic nose on his face?

She would never be his mistress—that she had vowed eight years ago, and to that pledge she would remain steadfast. Strangely, as she looked back on his earlier force, she doubted that his intention had ever been, as she had accused, to pick up where they had last left off. There had been too much anger, too much emotional turbulence in the encounter to attribute it to a purely physical drive. Despite her other opinions of Doug Weston, she wanted desperately to credit him with at least a modicum of integrity, a minimally functioning conscience. Ironically, what disturbed her above all else was that she wanted to respect him.

Darkness had long since cast its heavy shroud about the woods, when finally sleep overtook her. Not long after, she awoke to find a thick fog blanketing the area, tinting the dawn with its gray-white sheen, muting the morning sounds almost to a silence. For Stephanie, on this particular morning, the sudden turn of the weather was a welcome sight and sound—or, more accurately, lack of both. A dull pain throbbed at her temples, a general stiffness at her limbs. She could well have been hung over from the past night's revelries—except that there had been no liquor, no party. Gulping down several aspirins, she caught sight of herself in the bathroom mirror, appalled to see the dark smudges beneath each eye, the pallor of her cheeks, the hardness of her expression. Her only solace was that Doug had fared not much better, judging from the lines of fatigue on his own face, visible to her across the tables at breakfast. He had seen her, too. Of that she was sure. Several times during the meal she looked up to find his gaze darting from her, as though he did not wish to meet her gaze. Avoidance was the operative mode, she had decided; presumably, he had made the same decision.

So it would have appeared over the next few days. There seemed to be an unspoken truce in effect; she went out of her way to avoid confronting him, just as he made no further move to approach her. In fact, there might have never been anything at all between them, if it weren't for the issue of that affair, gray-eyed and pony-tailed, making her increasingly comfortable way through each day.

Photographically, things couldn't have been better. Classes had begun and, much as she had expected, the girls were eager and quick to follow her teachings. For those of them who had already had some experience, she set them to work experimenting with the cameras, all SLRs, which Sylvie had provided. Darkroom work would come for these students after they fully understood the basics of the camera. For the younger campers and those with no prior picture-taking practice, sungrams and photograms were the first order of business, enabling them to understand the positive-negative concept before they confronted a roll of film.

Stephanie herself was having a wonderful time photographing not only the wide range of camp activities, but also the many natural settings and scenic offerings before her. She captured the orange-red of the sunset as it tripped across the rippling lake, she immortalized the flight of the monarch as it flitted among the tall grasses of the field. She documented, as she lay on her back amid the pine needles, the awesome height of the pines, majestic and triumphant in the late afternoon sun.

Stephanie rose very early one morning and hustled into jeans and a heavy sweater to ward off the lingering chill. She made a beeline for the shore, determined to snare the sun as it cast its first pale yellow rays on the hills beyond the lake. Standing on the dock, she was oblivious to a steady motion on the beach until the dull thud of rubber soles on the wooden planks behind drew her around.

To her dismay, it was Doug, clad in sweat shirt and sweat pants, indeed sweating profusely from the exertion which she had evidently disturbed. Camera still in her hands, she would have liked to photograph him thus, though she knew that it would have been a very private picture and one which would betray her own needs. For, this morning, she saw not the immaculately groomed administrator, cool and impersonal, but rather a vibrantly disheveled, sensually grubby jogger. God, she cried, how could he look so good like that? Yet, he did. His brown hair had fallen haphazardly across his forehead, he bore the day's growth of beard which would soon be shaved, perspiration had moistened his skin to a healthy shine, painting dark patterns on the light gray sweat shirt which spoke of raw virility. The rise and fall of his broad chest as his panting gave way to deeper breathing fascinated her. He was, indeed, a spectacle to behold, much as the sun which had barely begun its journey across the sky.

She knew that she was staring again, yet she could do nothing to stop herself. For that matter, he was staring too, and the slowly building physicality which passed between them set her heart to thudding in a slightly too rapid accompaniment for the gently rhythmic lapping of the water against the dock. It was that undercurrent of sexuality which she had wanted to evade. Yet in its face she was mesmerized.

"You're intruding on my terrain." His deep voice finally broke through the silence, his tone velvet, edged with steel. Reflexively, Stephanie opened her mouth to object, closing it again as a glint of amusement filtered through the hard gray of his eyes and betrayed his humorous intent. Trying not to betray her own, she joined the game.

"I'm sorry," she insisted firmly but sweetly, "but this," she tapped a canvas-covered foot on the wood planks, "is *my* terrain. You stay on the shore, I'll stay here, and we'll both do fine."

If indeed she had wanted to appease him, she had played her hand perfectly. His eyes grew openly amused, his face more relaxed than she had yet seen it. With an easy grin and a faintly perceptible nod of his head, he turned, retraced his steps to the sandy strip of beach, and resumed his jog, pacing his steps evenly, moving with the grace of an animal and the ease of a seasoned athlete. Again she admired him, again she fought the urge to photograph him. Yet she indulged herself in following his form as he progressed along the shore, steadily tracing the water's curve as he put distance between them. She insisted that her interest was no greater than it would have been in any other such magnificent a creature, yet she sensed that she was only deluding herself further.

Suddenly infuriated with herself, she twirled and stomped off the dock, heading back to her cabin to deposit her equipment and leave again for the main lodge before Doug would himself return on this, the only path to the Grove. Unfortunately, her timing was off. She had barely made it halfway down from her cabin when he appeared, walking now, head down, apparently deep in thought.

She watched him warily as he neared, then raised his head at the sound of her steps. To her instant relief, though she was later to wonder why, that same glimmer of amusement crept back into his expression.

"Did you get the pictures you wanted?" he inquired smoothly and politely, his eyes falling for an instant to the chest where her camera had so recently rested. It took her every ounce of control to keep from squirming out of his visual clutch; mercifully, the only sign of her discomfort was the blush that bloomed beneath the faint dab of artificial color she had applied moments before.

To her chagrin, she had not gotten the pictures she wanted. To her even greater distress, she had not realized it until this very instant, when he had asked that question. What had gotten into her, she wondered. Where had that ofttimes treacherous mind been?

His gaze returned to hers, demanding an answer. Awkwardly she cleared her throat, as she sought a plausible answer. "Ah . . . no, I . . . didn't. The light . . . changed too quickly. I missed the moment."

If there had been faint amusement in his face before, now there was outright mockery. "I'm sorry." His apology was two-sided, as, she was sure, he had intended. Oh, yes, there was an expression of sympathy that she had missed her moment. But there was that other, more sardonic note, indicating that he fully understood why she had missed her moment, and that he reveled in his victory. After all, she had not particularly disturbed his jogging. . . .

Setting her chin firmly, Stephanie sought to regain some measure of dignity. "It's no problem," she pointed out indifferently. "It wasn't one of the better scenes, anyway." Hoping that she had covered herself sufficiently, she moved on down the road. Well, she rationalized, it could have been a beautiful scene, had not Doug been jogging through it. And, from the looks of his practiced gait, he probably covered the same route regularly. Therefore, she concluded, there would be no cause for her to even consider trying for another morning's sunrise from that spot, for she would not care to risk a repeat of this morning's encounter. It was too dangerous, in a most disturbing sense.

She was brooding on that very danger, curled up in a chair by the huge fireplace in the lounge, a cup of hot coffee removing the last traces of chill from her fingertips. Doug entered the main lodge a while later, having shaved and showered in the interim. He was once more the clean and immaculate Romeo of the camp set, and numerous heads turned to greet him as he passed through the room and headed for the stairs. Though Stephanie kept her eyes glued to the fireplace, she was keenly aware of his gaze as it touched her. Involuntarily she raised her eyes to the point on the balcony where he had stopped and stood, indeed, staring down at her. Their gazes locked momentarily before

Doug moved on; his expression was unfathomable from where Stephanie sat, yet she felt stirred by that same intangible force she was coming to know too well. In a gesture of frustration she downed the last of the coffee, bolted up, and left the Lodge, heading for the photo shed, where she knew she could bury herself quite successfully in her work until her first class arrived.

From the time of that early morning encounter, a very subtle change took place in their relationship, or, more accurately, at that point, their non-relationship. Stephanie saw that subconscious awareness of each other, which time and again caused both of them to look up at the moment of the other's intent regard, as an extension of her torment. For each such episode sparked the throbbing within her which disquieted her above all else. Had it been either anger or indifference, that she could handle. But it was the inevitable attraction, the ever-present sensitivity to the other's presence, that frightened her. Most definitely, she now fought herself as well as him, subtly and wordlessly, with self-reproachment and warning, mindful of the precarious battle being waged and the stakes involved. They were no less than her own sanity, her self-respect, her future. Should she succumb to that most basic drive which, she was convinced, was at the root of this new dimension of their interaction, she would have given up so much of what she had fought for during the past eight years.

It was a mere two days after that early morning meeting that a new and wholly unexpected element entered into the picture, causing Stephanie to temporarily shelve her own, intimate worries, for a very different yet equally as disconcerting one.

She had finished up her work at the photo shed

that particular afternoon and was returning to wash up before supper, when a group of children, easily recognized as seven or eight of the youngest campers, emerged from between the tennis courts to walk along the pebble road ahead of her. The children were engrossed in a game, judging from the laughs and shouts and choruses of their number, such that her own presence was unseen. *His* presence, however, was not; there, in the midst of the peanut-sized girls, walked Doug, his long strides shortened to synchronize with theirs, each hand held by an enthusiastic camper. What froze Stephanie in her tracks, however, was the sight of another of the children, this one looking gallantly down at her friends from the position of honor, the broad, strong shoulders of their adored tennis counselor. It was none other than Missy, sitting so contented, her long pigtails bobbing with his every step. An involuntary shiver coursed through Stephanie's body as she watched; she finally turned her back and crumbled onto a large rock by the side of the road. Coincidence . . . nothing to get alarmed about . . . next time it will be one of the others. Next time . . .

A sense of unease had been born which Stephanie could not shake. Beth had told her how nicely Melissa was adjusting, how much she seemed to be enjoying camp. Stephanie had seen the child frequently, though only for brief moments, and had not pursued the details of her daily activities. It had to have been coincidence, she repeated to herself, pure coincidence.

Coincidence, however, occurred again the very next day. This time, Stephanie was in the lounge of the main lodge, when she heard his laughter, hearty and instantly identifiable amid the giggles of his companions. Against her better judgment, but driven by a nagging curiosity, Stephanie moved to the screen door of the lounge, from whence she could observe the merry group. Her pulse skittered alarmingly as she saw, again, the girls grouped in happy play around Doug, again, Missy at the center, this time on his lap. His arm was wrapped protectively about her waist, and one small hand was clasped tightly around his.

As she watched, Stephanie's eyes filled with tears, touched by the innocence of the father-daughter scene she had never thought she would see, terrified by its implications. For whatever reason, be it destined or accidental, the two seemed to have developed a special relationship. That evening after supper, she sought out Beth in hopes that she would inadvertently shed some light on the situation. She did indeed.

"What activities does she seem to enjoy most?" Stephanie probed indirectly, holding her breath.

Beth responded readily and with a grin. "She's really good in the water and on the courts, so she favors those. But she seems to take to boating also, and ceramics. Must be that inherited artistic bent." She laughed enviously. Stephanie forced a return smile, but her mind was on those other inherited abilities.

"Has—has she made any close friendships? Made any really good friends?" She pursued the issue, trying to remain as subtle as she could.

This time Beth looked more thoughtful. "She's grown very close to several of her bunkmates, particularly little Sara. And"—she paused, throwing Stephanie a mischievous glance—"well, she seems to have remarkable taste in men. She and Doug Weston have quite a thing going there. . . ."

How Stephanie managed to graciously wrap up the discussion, she later couldn't remember. The worst of her worries had been confirmed. What was she to do now? Sooner or later he would know that Missy was her daughter. What then? Indeed, at that moment, Stephanie had no way of knowing that her own overwhelming concern would hasten this very revelation.

Bidden by a morbid obsession which she rationalized as maternal curiosity, Stephanie found herself drawn the following day to the tennis courts at the precise time that Missy's group was in the middle of a lesson. Actually, she had herself come from photographing a diving demonstration and had chosen to return to her cabin by the route which she more commonly bypassed. As she approached, she scanned the courts for Missy, whom she easily spotted on the uppermost of the four pairs of courts; it was toward this one, therefore, that she proceeded, feigning a nonchalance which she was far from feeling. Sure enough, when she had passed the lower courts and come up on the upper one, she immediately saw Doug working with the group of three that included her daughter. He had concentrated his attention on one of the others, working on her backhand grip, and was involved enough to initially miss her arrival. An assistant was with him, and changed places with him as he moved to Missy for similar instruction. Although her camera hung about her neck just waiting to be used, Stephanie was oblivious to it, so riveted was she to the unfolding scene.

Doug had moved behind Missy and was leaning over her to guide her arms and body through first the forehand swing, then the backhand, pointing to her stance and talking steadily and reassuringly by her ear. To her chagrin, Stephanie was affected as she had been the day before, tears springing up involuntarily from her very depths. Yesterday, however, she had been able to escape without being seen. Today she was lost as Doug straightened and then caught her eye. Determinedly, she willed the tears into retreat, a minor victory considering the knotting in her middle, invisible as it was.

If she had hoped he would continue with the children and let her watch in her own misery, she was mistaken. With a word of direction to the girl assisting him, he headed straight for the spot where she stood, just outside the wire fence at mid-court.

"I wondered when you were going to grace us with your presence," he challenged caustically, his slate-gray eyes roaming her body insolently, no doubt appreciating the pull of her batik T-shirt over the fullness of her breasts, the brevity and snugness of her shorts, and the lengths of newly tanned arms and legs. Had the wire mesh of the fence been solid lead, it would not have been dense enough to counter the force of his gaze, alarming, exciting, and thoroughly disconcerting.

"As it happens," he informed her, "you chose an excellent time to appear." Now he was all tennis pro, almost indifferent to her as he turned sideways to see how the group was progressing. "This age is usually more fun than results. These girls are now really capable only of handling the racquet properly. But we do have one little star . . . the one over there with the long pigtails." The description had been unnecessary; Stephanie knew to whom he referred. "She is a natural, look at her." His voice had lowered to a blend of bridled excitement and unbridled admiration; as he paused to watch Missy skillfully return a backhand shot, Stephanie glanced up in shock at the look of pure pride which lit his face. If he only knew . . .

When he went on, his voice silky smooth though entirely nonsensual, there was an added warmth in his tone. "Melissa seems to have an inborn talent for the sport. She has all the right moves, the right instincts." Again he paused to watch, now mercifully, for Stephanie desperately needed a moment to recover from the jolt of hearing the sound of her daughter's name on this man's tongue, spoken so innocently yet so profoundly.

Stephanie stood as Doug instructed her to watch, then rejoined the group on the court and drew Melissa off to the side to volley with her. The initial shock of seeing the two together had begun to abate, enough to allow for the emergence of the maternal pride which welled within. The lessons Missy had taken at home had paid off, though Doug was right; she was a natural, having inherited this superior physical coordination from her father.

When he decided she needed a break, he signaled for Missy to collect and basket the balls and then to rest for a few minutes. He returned to Stephanie, who had not budged throughout the demonstration and asked directly, "What do you think?"

Contrary to her usual reaction to him, Stephanie was suddenly overwhelmed by a desire for mischief. Intuitively, she knew that this particular secret was about to be revealed, and she saw no better time than the present to put him on, though she meant every word she was to say.

Doug seemed taken aback by the broad smile that burst forth into an open expression on Stephanie's usually well guarded face. "You're right!" she exclaimed. "She's great!" Then she thought to carry the mockery one step further, taking control of a situation over which she knew, in the end, she would have very little control. If he were bound to find out, why shouldn't she determine when. "She'll give you a run for your money in another few years, Doug." She paused, then made her move. "Do you mind if I come in to speak to her?" Mildly puzzled by her sudden change of manner, Doug shrugged his shoulders.

"Be my guest. They're taking a breather anyway."

She and Missy had fallen into a subtle pattern of, more or less, paying little heed to each other as they passed during the day. Despite her initial resistance to coming to camp, the child now seemed to want to be just one of the kids, rather than the photographer's daughter. It was a scene which had likewise been played out at school during the year, so Stephanie had been well prepared and was, indeed, grateful. Now, however, as she walked parallel to the fence and entered through the door onto the court, Missy looked up and waved excitedly. She was at a far corner retrieving balls, and Stephanie was able to retrace her steps, this time on the inside of the fence, to reach Doug's side at about the same time that Missy did, her scampering feet responding to Doug's beckoning wave.

"How'd I do?" the flushed face turned up to ask her mother, wisps of dark hair strewn every which way from the activity. Stephanie beamed a combination of pride and happiness that, indeed, her daughter seemed so content. For the instant, Douglas Weston was forgotten.

Stephanie reached out a gentle hand to ease the wayward strands from her daughter's face, smoothing them lovingly over the brown mane. "Just great, Missy! You were super!" she exclaimed. "You've really improved!"

Missy grinned endearingly, and it was all Stephanie could do not to hug her on the spot. "Really?" the child squealed in delight.

"Uh-huh." Stephanie nodded through her own grin. "But," she lowered her voice to a conspiratorial whisper audible to all three, "if you don't get back there now, the others will think you're too big for your britches!" Mother and daughter laughed. Then Missy looked up questioningly at Doug and Stephanie grew aware of him once more. The puzzled look on his face gave way to a rueful smile.

"Yup," he confirmed gently. "Back to work! How about trying the ball-boy?" he asked, knowing full well what the response would be.

"Could I?" Missy shrieked, beside herself in excitement. At his nod of confirmation, she unknowingly took the other, more profound matter, out of Stephanie's hands. "Oh, wow! Now?" Without waiting for an answer, she impulsively threw her arms about her mother's waist; instinctively, Stephanie returned the hug. "I'll see you later, Mommy!" she cried, and then she was gone, leaving in her wake the two adults, one smugly satisfied though laced with growing trepidation, the other clearly and thoroughly baffled.

As Stephanie turned to make her timely escape, Doug spoke. "Mommy?" Incredulity marked both his voice and his face. As she regarded him, Stephanie had to feel the slightest bit guilty for having executed such a dramatic drop shot. Yes, there was a satisfaction at having caught him so unawares, yet it seemed suddenly petty.

"Isn't that what children often call their mothers?" she retorted softly.

"Their mothers? Melissa . . . is your daughter?" Stephanie could have been a totally different person from the one who had moments before walked down the court from the way in which he stared at her.

Under the circumstances, she saw no point in

waffling. "Yes, Doug. Melissa is my daughter." There was defiance in her voice, as well as a subtle challenge, both of which he continued to ignore.

"Your daughter?" For a brief instant, she thought she detected a note of hurt in the deep timbre of his voice and the fogged gray of his eyes, then realized that it was merely an extension of the shock which had effectively tongue-tied him.

Determined to make her escape before he regained his composure, she lowered her voice and tossed her head in Missy's direction. "I think she's waiting for you." His gaze slowly shifted to the child, back to the mother, then again to the child in an attempt to assimilate what he'd been told. The last hint of mischief wormed its way out as Stephanie murmured sweetly, "And thank you for letting me watch. I am very proud of her." With that, she turned on her heel and made her way off, through the door and on up the hill toward the Grove.

With his class standing right there and Missy waiting expectantly, she knew that he would have been unable to follow her. In fact, she doubted she could have chosen a better time, place, or circumstance to have him learn that she had a child. After all, it had only been a matter of time.

The aura of self-confidence and defiance in which she had been suspended during the momentous confrontation evaporated with each step she took, to be replaced by a return of the upheaval that had plagued her so often since her return to PineWinds. What would happen now? What would he do? What would he say? At best, there would be no change in the status quo, a mere acceptance of the information with which she and Melissa had just floored him. At worst, the revelation could trigger a renewal of the anger, violent anger, of which he had already given her a taste.

But was that the worst that could happen? No. Stephanie knew deep within that the worst was something else, a logical deduction which this new information might inspire. What if he did come to suspect that Melissa was his child? As she thought about it now, that too seemed inevitable—just a matter of time. There were her age, her looks, her ability . . . all coincidence? Close calls? Would he believe that?

Wringing her hands nervously as she paced the floor of her cabin, Stephanie found herself drenched with sweat, perhaps from the warmth of the day and the unusually still air, more likely from her own nerves. On an impulse she changed into her knee-length terrycloth robe, stepped into thongs, gathered together soap, shampoo, and a towel, and headed for the shower house in hopes of refreshing herself, body and mind.

Located behind the middle of the three cabins, the shower house was a totally functional unit, offering two separate stalls, each with its own enclosed dressing room, and a foresection with a deep double sink and—luxury of luxuries for the use of the Grove alone—a washer-dryer combination, recently installed and immensely handy, as Stephanie had discovered. In fact, she had passed more than one period, much to her unexpected pleasure, standing in this very room in deep conversation with Elaine, the female half of Cabin B. Only a year or two older than she, Elaine was both friendly and interesting, a good conversationalist and an equally good listener. And she had proved to be an unsuspecting buffer on more than one potentially uncomfortable occasion.

But Elaine was not on Stephanie's mind at the moment. Indeed, she endeavored to wipe her mind clean of all thought, at least all thought that in any form could cause her distress. Soft and steady in its descent, the warm spray gently coaxed her tension-filled body into a mood of truce, then relaxation, and as shampoo joined the soapy water rushing toward the drain, she began to feel revived and able to think more clearly. Only then did she permit a return to thoughts of Doug, of Melissa, and of her newly complicated predicament. Of the many differing sentiments she had experienced of late, only one remained constant. It was the one thought which had seen her successfully through eight years of building a new life, coping with its new responsibilities. It was the one which had eventually emerged in the aftermath of each of the encounters she'd had with Doug. It was the one which would have to give her direction now, in this latest trial, with whatever aftershocks it might bring. It was the vow to never let herself be hurt as she had once before been, to never let herself be manipulated as she had once before been, to never again love in vain.

Theoretical as she knew this vow to be, she nevertheless felt mentally renewed for having made it. It gave her a base on which to stand, a piece of terra firma to which to retreat when the outside world began to shake and shatter. Realistically, she knew that this vow would see its own shaky moments, that, more than at any time in the past, it would be tried and tested repeatedly this summer, if these early days had been any indication. But she would persevere, she swore, she would!

four

RELUCTANTLY SHE TURNED OFF THE SHOWER and set to work briskly toweling the water from her hair and coaxing her auburn curls into damp ringlets about her head and neck. Leisurely she blotted the rest of her body, savoring the lingering memory of the refreshing pulse a moment longer, then she shrugged into her robe and thongs, wrapped her soap and shampoo in the towel, and stepped out into the fore-section of the room.

As she raised her eyes, she cried aloud, a brief but startled shriek, an involuntary reaction to the sight that confronted her. There he stood, leaning against the front screen door as though he'd been there for quite some time, one hand on his hip, one on the door-knob, his feet planted firmly on the wooden floor. He was still wearing his tennis whites and had obviously, considering the time element as well, just come from the courts. His body was the simplest aspect of his appearance to take in; it was his face that baffled Stephanie. A far cry from the air of bewilderment and disbelief in which she had left him earlier, now his expression bore anger, hurt, frustration, meanness, and, yes, lust—each fighting for its own position of dominance among his rugged features. The picture was frightening, to say the least, and Stephanie sensed, above all, the danger which had quickly obliterated her temporary peace of mind.

In her fright she had dropped the terry bundle with a dull thud onto the floor. Now she clutched at the lapels of her robe, drawing them closer about her, as she kept her eyes glued to his.

"What do you want?" She inhaled unsteadily.

His gaze left no doubt of the answer to her question, his eyes abandoning hers to travel slowly and menacingly over her, missing nothing but what the robe so simply hid. For a moment longer his gaze touched the soft swell of her breasts, rising through the terry cloth cover, before the steel gray rested on her face once more.

"You didn't lose a minute, did you," he stormed suddenly and violently, causing her to shrink from him defensively. Uncomprehending, she sent him a dazed glance; he needed no more invitation than that to rage on. "No wonder you ran out of here so fast. No wonder you never bothered to read my letters! What a blundering fool I was!" he seethed, self-disgust now mixed with the rest as he shook his head in utter disbelief. Instinctively Stephanie sensed where he was headed, and her insides churned in horror.

"What did you do, spend all of your free time on your back after I took care of the dirty work? How many men were there, Stephie? Or was it just one waiting in the sidelines all along?" His bellowing shook her to the core, her knees trembling even as she shook her head from side to side in silent denial of his vile and totally unjustifiable accusations. "You little . . . I should have known. You were much too passionate, much to skillful to have been anything but a technical virgin. And to think that I've felt guilty for so long. . . ." There was a sinister edge to his laugh, which was harsh and throaty and ended as quickly as it had begun.

His eyes flashed in anger now and he took a step forward. "Don't come any closer!" she screamed in warning, but he took another step, then another, until she was backed against the wall and he stood but an arm's length from her. "Stay away from me!" she whispered frantically, realizing even then that he had already cornered her. His eyes settled on her lips, pink and moist and trembling, and she steeled herself for the onslaught of his, but it didn't come.

"What's the matter, Stephie?" he taunted. "You're not afraid, are you? After all, you've been through this before." Slowly and deliberately, he put both hands against the wall on either side of her, imprisoning her as he brought his imposing form that much closer. Stephanie could only stare ahead at the strong brown column of his neck and the ever-steady pulse of the jugular. To further the torment, he lowered his head, bringing his cheek but an inch from hers, as he jeered softly in her ear, "What about your husband, Stephanie? Is there one? Was there one? Where is he now, Melissa's father?"

Stephanie was astonished that she could feel any relief through the maelstrom of emotion and venomous words which had assailed her, yet she did. At least he had assumed that he was not Melissa's father—that was critical! "What's wrong? No answers for me?" His breath was warm against her cheek despite the ice of his tone. Facing the inevitable, she finally spoke.

"I never married Missy's father," she announced

quietly, though refusing to make further excuses for herself or her life-style. "And you're wrong about me, Doug—so very wrong," she whispered. In a gesture of defiance, she dared to look up at him as he lifted his face away to study hers.

Drawing his lips back tightly, he spoke through clenched teeth. "You are a brazen liar, Stephanie! It's all very clear now. I don't want to hear any more!"

Stephanie stiffened in panic. His anger had passed the point of reason, his loathing for her likewise. She pressed back against the wall, which had already begun to grate against her.

"Leave me alone, please, leave me alone," she begged, her jade-spoked eyes wide in fear.

"No way, Steph," he growled. "Damn it, I'm going to help myself to what you so freely hand out." The sound of his words were cut short as his mouth lowered to possess hers, punishing her lips with the full force of his unleashed fury. Angrily he put a hand to her hair, long strong fingers intertwining then pulling cruelly to tilt her head back. Her mouth opened in a cry of pain, only to be smothered further by the lips which reclaimed hers, the tongue which launched a viscious invasion of her mouth's recesses.

Frantically she fought him, pushing against his chest and kicking at his legs, only to find that in one crude movement he had thrust a solid thigh between her own, pinning her helplessly against the wall as the weight of his length overpowered her. With a meager strength she writhed against him, futilely trying to throw him off balance and make her escape. But his body was an immovable warden, guarding its prisoner with a minimum of effort. In evidence of her helplessness he took a thin wrist in each of his hands and pinned them, also, against the wall at shoulder height.

Only then did she cease her resistance, unable to move, breathless and exhausted from her struggles, acutely aware of imminent defeat.

He held her thus while his lips continued their plunder, his kiss degrading her even as she stood, suspended limply before him. When he finally lifted his head, it was to stare down contemptuously at the tears which had gathered at the rim of her lower lids in anticipation of what was to come.

"Tears, Stephanie?" he mocked softly. "Aren't you carrying this a little too far? You know it won't hurt this time." He savored her gasp of outrage and the obvious pain his words had caused before he let her wrists fall. Stephanie was paralyzed, her eyes following his, her breathing short and shallow. In horror she felt his hands touch her shoulders, then trace the lapels of her robe, ever so slowly and tortuously, from neck to waist.

Unknowingly Stephanie moaned aloud, then heard the far-off whimpering of her own final, desperate plea. "No . . . no . . . Doug, no." For, compounding her nightmare in that last movement, as his hands had moved over her, she knew an even greater fear than that which he posed, this one working upward and from deep within—the arousal of stirrings which only he had ever awakened in her.

If Doug was aware of these internal happenings, it didn't alter his intention. "I want to look at you, Stephanie," he stated boldly. "I want to see what changes motherhood has wrought." His words trailed off as his fingers deftly untied the belt that held her privacy intact. Although his body had released her to stand back, a new captor now held her motionless, one whose strength was just beginning to build. At another time perhaps she could have fought it, this sparking flame; now, weakened as she was by Doug's onslaught of hate and hurt and humiliating accusation, she had no chance at all. She had been battered emotionally before the battle, this different and most private one, had even begun.

As she watched his face with growing alarm, his glinting steel eyes left hers to trace a path down her cheek, her neck, and across her throat to the point on her chest where the robe parted. In a deliberately aggressive movement, he thrust a hand under her robe on either side, pushing the protective cloth back off her shoulders, letting his fingers curl electrically around her collarbone as his eyes plundered the wealth of femininity which had been thus served up to him.

Humiliated beyond belief by his demeaning examination, Stephanie's senses came alive, warring among themselves in a skirmish of embarrassment, indignation, and raw desire. Just as she ached to cover her nudity, she craved the touch of those fingers, firm and fiery, upon her.

If she had hoped that he would be gruff and hurtful now, thereby curbing her own unwanted arousal, she was shockingly disappointed. For, as suddenly as he had cast eyes on her nakedness, his touch had changed, softening in the instant and becoming gentle in a way that transported her back, over eight years' time, to a summer night and a bed of pine needles.

Slowly his hands made their way downward from her shoulders, skimming either side of her body to her thighs, as though defining all limits, before moving inward to a more intimate exploration. Stephanie turned her head to the side, her cheek against the wall, closing her eyes in an attempt to erase from her consciousness what was happening. But it was to no avail.

His hands persisted, moving upward now, moving freely, fingers splaying across the scant span of her abdomen, creeping up over her waist, palms crossing her midriff, then pausing beneath the quickened rise and fall of her breasts.

The flame had burst into a searing fire within her, the desire which she had buried so long ago now threatening to engulf her. She cried out as his hands moved up to cup her breasts, then bit her lip in self-punishment as his palms passed seductively over a rosy bud, taut and raised in excitement.

It was a sound she had never heard, strange and hoarse, from the back of his throat, an almost excruciating groan, which caught her attention, drawing her face frontward, her lids up, until she looked into eyes which beheld hers once more. A shudder shook her at the instant of visual contact; it was as though she saw the ghost of that long-ago night in those eyes, that expression. What cruel tricks the mind could play; she was to rue this later! For now, however, rational thought eluded her. As she gazed into that once-beloved and loving face, it lowered, and his lips tasted hers once more, now warmly, sweetly, full of the tenderness and desire which welled within her own.

Mindlessly her body responded, lips parting to receive his, arms winding upward about his sturdy shoulders, reveling in the strength of his neck, the vitality of the thick hair at its nape. His own arms encircled her, crushing her body to his with a delightful harshness that could only heighten her excitement.

It was a kiss of passion, of a long pent-up desire newly released. It was open and giving, wild and heady. His hands caressed her in encouragement as she arched her body toward his, and she knew then that his ardor matched hers. When finally, breathless and trembling, her lips fell away from his, he clasped her to him in a fierce gesture of possession. Then, suddenly, he tensed.

"My God, what am I doing!" he exclaimed in a husky whisper, an echo of his former anger sounding briefly and faintly as a reminder to them both. Abruptly he released her and turned away, his dark head lowering, a tanned hand reaching in exasperation to rub the muscles at the back of his neck. Then he walked to the door and left, without a word or a glance back to where she stood in stunned silence, the bang of the screen door against its frame the final jarring note of the episode.

It could have been a gunshot, the slam of that door, for the traumatic effect it had on Stephanie, illusion exploding before her wide eyes into a myriad fragmentary thrusts of reality, one more excruciating than the next. As the more peripheral fell to the wayside, one by one, two remained to continue the torture—the shock of separation from the warming flame of Doug's sensuous embrace, and the horror that this separation had indeed been a shock.

Senses reeling about her, she staggered forward, clutching her robe convulsively about her, groping for the support of the sink as, slowly, her breathing steadied and her legs became functional. Only then did she hear her own voice, aggrieved and horror struck, reminiscent of the last words he'd spoken. "My God, what have I done!"

What she had done was to respond, yield, even invite the advances of this man whom she had vowed to shun. Worse, and to her growing shame, she had reveled in his caress, indeed had craved more. And, most condemning of all, she had let him know that he still had the power to render her mindless before him. It was an awesome power, if he chose to use it.

By the time she had pulled herself together enough to return to her cabin, a benumbed state had settled over her, a natural defense mechanism, refusing to allow her to contemplate the happening until time had done some healing of its own.

As luck would have it, Doug did not appear at dinner that evening, sparing her one painful reminder of her folly. Neither was he at breakfast the next morning, though by then Stephanie felt she would have been able to endure his presence without breaking out in a cold sweat.

Alone long after the others had finished, she was deep in thought, nursing a final cup of coffee, when a warm hand grasped her shoulder and Sylvie Hampson leaned over.

"May I join you, my dear?" she croaked hesitantly, aware that she had called Stephanie back from the far reaches of contemplation.

Relieved at this pleasant rescue, Stephanie nodded her head eagerly. "Please do, Sylvie! As a matter of fact, I've been wanting to speak to you."

The older woman frowned, her pale lips drawing down amid the host of time-hewn creases. "Oh?"

"No, nothing like that!" Stephanie smiled at the other's sudden seriousness. "Actually, it's good news. I've got contact sheets for you to see. They're beginning to pile up and I'd like to do some enlarging. But you'll have to tell me which frames appeal to you, which you feel would be most appropriate for your book."

"Ah, I see." Visibly she relaxed.

Stephanie continued her progress report. "I'm thrilled with what I've gotten so far. I think you will be too. But you've got to tell me if I am inadvertently missing things which you'd definitely like included."

"Uh-huh. I get the point," the older woman mused thoughtfully. "I'd really like Sonny to see them too. He should be arriving tomorrow or the next day. Can it wait until then?"

"Sure. I have plenty of other stuff to work on anyway," Stephanie assured her. Then she paused, noting the other's reticence, quite out of character for the ebullient director. "What is it? What's wrong, Sylvie?" The woman appeared to be preoccupied, but looked up quickly at Stephanie's concern.

After a moment's hesitation, she ventured forth. "Have you seen Doug?" Her weathered face carried an almost apologetic expression as she awaited an answer.

Stephanie's insides jolted involuntarily. "Ah . . . not since yesterday," she replied quietly, struggling to instill an evenness in her voice to belie her inner thoughts. "Why?" Did Sylvie know something of the goings-on between her and Doug? A sudden coldness gripped her, quivering through her veins spasmodically.

But Sylvie's next words put those particular fears to rest. "He wasn't at dinner last night, nor breakfast this morning. No one seems to have seen him. I'm getting worried." Her face reflected her sentiment. "It's not like Doug to vanish like this."

Stephanie knew that their encounter the previous afternoon must have had something to do with his absence. And, as much as she fought it, she found the worry contagious. Slowly she shook her head. "I haven't seen him, Sylvia," she repeated, a frown furrowing her brow. "I wish I could help you, but . . ."

"How are things going between the two of you?"

Again the jolt to her insides. "Oh, all right, I guess.

We have our ups and downs." She smiled in an embarrassment which the other woman regarded closely.

"He hasn't been the same this summer, Stephie." Sylvie elaborated on her concern. Within her listener, the warring resumed; on the one hand, she did not want to hear a word about Doug, while on the other, she listened with bated breath. "He has been much more tense, preoccupied, brooding. I don't think the others can see it as much as I can." Here was the mother, disturbed by the faltering of a favorite son. Yet, what could Stephanie say? True, their confrontations may have temporarily disquieted him—and rightly they should have. But would the cool, composed Doug Weston have been that bothered by them? She doubted it. And as to what else might be eating at that unfathomable soul of his, she would be the last to know.

Sylvie must have sensed the train of thought. "I just wondered if you might have known anything." she added hesitantly, apologetically.

"I'm sorry, Sylvie. I really don't. We aren't on the best of terms, as you may have guessed. He certainly would never confide in me if he had a problem."

Sylvie gave her a final probing glance before she wrinkled up her nose and whisked her worry off into the air with a wave of her hand. "Acch, he's a big boy. I'm probably worrying about nothing. He'll show up!" She smiled somewhat dubiously as she patted Stephanie's hand. "Thank you anyway, my dear. And I want to see those sheets as soon as my Sonny arrives."

"Sure thing," the photographer promised as she watched her friend take her leave and head out of the dining room. Unbidden, Sylvie's worries sprang back into Stephanie's mind. Where was he? Was he all right? The question stealthily nagged at her as she checked the counselors' bulletin board for her schedule for the day. It hovered in her as she found her way slowly and circuitously—by way of the photo shed to mix a fresh batch of chemicals for the morning's lessons—to the Grove, where she sat down in the warming sun on her steps to jot down some notes on her lesson plan.

F-stops and shutter speeds for bunk seven, she wrote. Could he have been that angry at her? Tripods and close-up filters for bunk ten. Was her presence that disdainful to him? Self-portraits on Azo for the little ones. No, there must have been some other emergency. Burning and dodging for the printers of bunk nine. Where would he have gone overnight? To see his wife? A girlfriend? To her subsequent bafflement her hackles began to rise at the thought of either.

But had he gone overnight? That was the implication, but was it true? Impulsively Stephanie decided to find out. Crossing the Grove, she made her way to Cabin A. She had never been in it, had avoided it like the plague until now. Hesitantly she climbed the steps, her own vague concern—intermixed with guilt feelings galore—urging her onward. At the top, she rapped. No answer. Again she knocked. Still no answer.

Shading her eyes from the bright sun falling against the door, she leaned forward and put her nose to the screen, feeling more like a Peeping Tom than a Sherlock Holmes, yet intent on learning whether he had indeed slept in or not. Against her better judgment, she let her eyes scan the room, identical in structure and furnishings to hers, yet totally different in decoration, and thus, tone, from the masculine brown of the geometrically patterned quilt on the bed to the dignified stacks of books and journals on the shelves to the intimate slant of framed pictures atop the bureau to the casual array of oddly strewn sneakers lying on the floor.

For a brief moment she squinted back at the pictures—photographs of women, it seemed, though she could decipher little else through the diffusion of the screen. And, she reproached herself, her original purpose had been served: Doug's bed was neatly made. Given the fact that he had missed both meals, there was only one conclusion to be drawn. She turned and descended the steps, head down and deep in thought.

His voice, low and harsh, brought her head up with a jerk. "Were you looking for something?"

"N-no. No," she gasped, simultaneously relieved and mortified, blushing under his cold stare. "Ah . . . actually . . . yes. You." Honesty seemed the only way, when one's hand was caught in the cookie jar, she mused. He had obviously seen her at his cabin as he walked down the path. Now he stood opposite her at the bottom of the steps. She couldn't help but notice that he looked drawn and tired, his hair tousled, his clothes wrinkled, his face shadowed in need of a shave.

"You look terrible!" she exclaimed spontaneously, the words having escaped without her permission. In the instant, as she regarded him, the events of yesterday flooded back and she paled in turn.

From his superior height he looked down at her impatiently, his gray eyes flashing their ill humor. "Is that what you wanted to tell me?"

His curtness quickly brought her to her senses. "No. I was . . . Sylvie was worried when she couldn't find you. She asked me if I knew where you were. I just wondered if you'd slept late."

"I didn't," he growled. With both hands on his hips, he was as intimidating as ever. Again Stephanie recalled the last time she had seen him, and her only instinct was to run.

"Sylvie will be pleased you're all right," she mumbled as she moved away toward her own steps.

"What about you, Stephanie? Were you worried?" Through the faint mockery in his tone there was a strange hoarseness such that, with her back to him, she couldn't interpret his intent.

She shrugged with feigned indifference. "I wasn't particularly aware of your absence until Sylvie brought it up this morning," she lied, biting nervously at her lower lip.

Slowly and deliberately Doug walked to where she had stopped. "You never answered my question."

Confused, she spun around. "I just told you—"

"I'm not referring to this morning," he interrupted. There was an odd look in his eyes, an unsureness which was so out of keeping with his character that she attributed it to his tired state. His voice was barely audible when he finally spoke. "That first day I asked you; now I want an answer. Do you really hate me as much as you let on?"

Momentarily taken aback by his bluntness, she lowered her eyes. Then, sighing with resignation, she looked up at him. "I don't hate you, Doug. I never have," she confessed wearily. Then, when she could take the intensity of his stare no longer, she turned and continued on her way, shaken inside but otherwise unscathed. It had been one of the least traumatic of their encounters. Perhaps that was why her mind kept flitting back to those pictures on his bureau.

The next day, amid nonexistent fanfare, Sonny Hampson arrived at PineWinds. As always, the camp seemed to take on a subtle undercurrent of excitement when he was there, almost as though the real business of the summer could not get under way until the Baltimore end had been concluded and he had come north. Shy, quiet, and retiring, he was loved by all. Ofttimes he was seen only at meals, spending the rest of his time at the private cottage at the edge of the grounds, yet his inevitable program additions and the humorous messages passed on by his devoted wife were the hit of any meeting. A surrogate grandfather with a kindly face and a patient way, the campers adored him, particularly looking forward to rainy days when they would be invited, bunk by bunk, to the cottage for a tall tale and a sundae. Even the oldest campers never tired of his understated manner, his wit, and his charm.

Stephanie herself was delighted to see him again. The contact sheets she had prepared were excitedly received by both Hampsons, the only problem being that of choosing which pictures of the many they loved to have printed. In the end they begged Stephanie for most all of them, and she obliged, unconditionally pleased with her photographic success. Despite the inordinate amount of work this undertaking would entail, she relished the idea, especially for its therapeutic value.

There were no further unexpected absences on Doug's part, and Sylvie never again mentioned the first. To Stephanie's relief, aside from that original explosion, there appeared to be no other fallout from Doug's discovery that Stephanie had a child. As for Stephanie, she seemed oblivous to any change in her status. She noted that the two, Doug and Missy, were as close as ever. Although she had mixed feelings about the friendship to begin with, given its existence she felt relieved that Doug had chosen not to hurt the child by taking out on her a grievance he held against her mother. Parting at the end of the summer was natural and inevitable in the camping experience; a midseason rift would have been harder to explain, particularly to one as young and vulnerable as Missy. But as the midpoint of the summer approached, it was her own emotional survival about which Stephanie began to have doubts, as one thing after the other conspired to throw her into the company of Douglas Weston.

"Hey, Steph!" Elaine's voice rang through the screen door as Stephanie was gathering her equipment together. It was a quiet Saturday morning, the last before parents' weekend. Regularly scheduled classes had given way to the gaining momentum of color war competition, leaving her freer to photograph leisurely than during the class-dominated weekdays.

"Come on in, Elaine," she called from the back room, as she rummaged in her spare case for a polarizing filter. "What can I do for you?" she yelled, then grinned as she looked up to find her friend right beside her.

"You can come with us later."

"Where are you going?"

"We thought we'd take a ride down to Ogunquit. First there's the beach. If we can get tickets, it would be fun to go to the Playhouse. If not, we'll just take in a movie. Either way, there are several super restaurants along the way. How about it?" She grinned mischievously. "We all need a break from the institution every so often. Come on, Stephie!"

Stephanie hesitated. Yes, she had the afternoon and

evening off, just like Elaine and Bob did, but she'd toyed with the idea of going away by herself to photograph. "I don't know, Elaine," she began, only to have her hesitation read and dismissed.

"You can bring that thing"—she pointed kiddingly at the camera dangling from Stephanie's shoulder—"if you insist. We'll even stop the car at your slightest call. What do you say?"

Stephanie smiled, pleased at the invitation. "Sounds very tempting." It did. She felt totally at ease with Elaine and her husband, and had to admit that a thorough change of scenery and activity could do her good. Elaine stood expectantly before her as she made her final decision. "I'd love to!"

As the smile broadened on her friend's face, Stephanie noted what an attractive woman she was—tall, slim, and a devout follower of the natural look—long blond hair pulled back into a practical ponytail at the nape of the neck, clothes clean and strictly functional, face sparkling and ever free of makeup. Her spouse was as unpretentious and down-to-earth as she, both in looks and manner. Together they manned the boat house, and, though they had been at PineWinds for several summers and seemed to love working with the girls, Stephanie had suspected more than once that they harbored a secret ambition to sail their own sloop off into the sunset, just the two of them, for one whole summer.

"Great," Elaine exclaimed warmly. "We have a regatta this morning, so we can't be ready to leave until one. How about meeting us at the garage then?"

Stephanie nodded. "Sounds fine. Er . . . what should I wear? I mean, it's kind of a mixed bag you've suggested there."

Her companion grinned in understanding. "I

thought I'd wear a bathing suit under my shorts, then bring something fancier in a separate tote. There's a bathhouse where we can change."

It sounded very simple and a lot of fun. Just for an instant Stephanie had another thought. "Elaine, are you sure you wouldn't prefer to be alone with Bob? I mean, you surely don't get much time to yourselves here."

"Stephie, we'd be disappointed if you didn't come! The more the merrier, for this type of thing. Believe me, if we wanted total privacy, we would go hiking up into the mountains."

Stephanie put up no more resistance. After spending the morning photographing the ongoing sports events, she escaped up into the woods, herself, to do some close-up work with ferns and other low-growing flora by the campfire circle.

Ironically this was one spot which she had avoided all summer, the emotional stirrings it triggered being stronger than she wished. She had even been able to excuse herself from the two campfires that had already been held, though she knew that some photographs of the timeless camp ceremony would be a must for Sylvie's book. It was a simple matter of procrastination. Perhaps her decision to come up here this day was a first step toward breaking through that psychological barrier.

Pleasantly anticipating the afternoon and evening, her thoughts were thus insulated from melancholy reminiscences, as she exposed every last frame of the film she'd carried. Only as she prepared to leave did she turn for a last overall view of the circle; only then did she feel the sadness she had shunned. Hurriedly she returned to camp, depositing her gear and eating lunch before she changed and headed for the garage.

Bob and Elaine's turquoise Rabbit had been pulled out front, and it was toward it that she proceeded. Elaine immediately withdrew her attention from the map she'd been studying and jumped out of the car at her approach, opening the trunk for Stephanie to deposit her canvas tote bag among the others. As they moved back to the side door, Bob appeared at the garage, engaged in conversation with George, the warm-hearted handyman of the camp . . . and Doug Weston. Stephanie swallowed convulsively, a disquieting thought threatening her convivial mood. Surely Elaine would have mentioned it!

At that moment, to her growing distress, Elaine did mention it. Turning toward her with cautious regard, she spoke in a half-whispered explanation. "Oh, Stephie, Bob invited Doug to join us. You don't mind, do you?"

Mind? Did she mind? Yes, she minded! She minded with every inch of her body! She minded more than she'd ever minded before! "No, Elaine, I don't mind." She heard her voice softly contradict her thoughts. What else could she do? Had she known in advance, she would have refused outright. As it was, the four were all here now, and her bag had already been stowed in the trunk. To back out would have been obvious, embarrassing, and insulting. If Doug had hoped to further torment her this way, he would find himself disappointed, she vowed on the spur of the moment. No, he could change his mind, if he wanted to, but she would stick it through and perhaps even enjoy herself despite him, she resolved defiantly. Anyhow, she reasoned, Bob and Elaine would be there all the time.

Stephanie caught the passing look that flickered over Doug's face and then was gone, a kind of stricken horror that must have mirrored her own. A new thought occurred to her. "Elaine," she whispered suspiciously, "did Doug know I would be along?"

This straightforward person was about as incapable of deception as she was of glamor, Stephanie mused, as she watched the measure of apology creep over her friend's simple features. "Bob just told him, I think."

"Looks that way." Stephanie moaned, turning her back on the two men, who had remained at the garage door and out of earshot. At least, she rationalized, the slate was even; neither of them had known in advance of the other's presence, and both would have to now cope with their own dislodged sentiments.

Elaine joined Stephanie, leaning against the car. "What is it with you two?"

"What do you mean?" This was the last awkward discussion she had anticipated having with Elaine on such a potentially glorious day off.

"Relax!" her companion whispered. "It's just that I saw the look that passed between you two a minute ago. And I've seen it before." She took a breath before she barreled on with the bluntness Stephanie had come to expect, and, indeed, respect. "To tell you the truth, Stephie, you'd make a great couple, you and Doug. We've known him for several years now, even gotten together during the winter. He needs someone like you!"

Stephanie felt a chill pass through her at the repetition of the same thought Sylvie Hampson had once expressed. Surely, if Elaine and Bob had seen Doug off-season, they would be aware of his wife. What was it she was suggesting? Why did everyone think that Doug needed her? Everyone, that was, except Doug and herself.

"Are you into matchmaking too?" she cracked helplessly.

"No, silly! Come on, we're all going to have fun!"

Much to Stephanie's surprise, they did. Once the two antagonists accepted the situation—and Doug seemed to have found himself as cornered as she—they retired to the back seat of the VW and managed to conduct themselves with an appropriate amount of civility, even pleasantness. By far the most disturbing part of the ride was Doug's physical nearness, marked at every turn by the brush of his well-muscled thigh against her slim one, both bare below the shorts they wore.

It was several hours' ride to the shore, most of which passed in easy four-way conversation. "Hey, Stephie," Elaine called back over her shoulder from the front seat. "I didn't see your camera. You didn't leave it in that hot trunk, did you?" she asked in mock horror.

"No." Stephanie laughed, brushing a film of perspiration from the side of her nose. Mercifully she had pulled the slew of curls back off her face with large tortoise-shell combs before she'd left, and was now cooler and neater than she might have been and infinitely grateful as she leaned forward to chat with Elaine, knowing only too well that Doug's keen gray orbs would be studying her. "My camera is my work. Even I need a day off sometimes! Besides, the heat and the sand would be anathema."

"When did you start photographing? I don't remember that you used to do it—" It was Doug's deep voice that joined the conversation, only to be interrupted by Bob's tenor. Stephanie had still not quite grown accustomed to that higher pitch; Bob was a stringbean, tall and thin, and each time he spoke she expected a much deeper tone. Now, however, it was not the pitch of his voice which disconcerted her.

"Did you two know each other before?" he asked innocently. Stephanie sat back against her seat, tossing an uncomfortable glance at Doug, while Elaine simultaneously cast a similar one at her husband. Doug was the only one of the group who seemed unbothered, and it was he who parried the inquiry.

"Stephanie was a counselor my first summer here," he explained, before he turned back to her expectantly. It took her a minute to recall what he had originally asked, so thrown had she been by Bob's simple question.

"I . . . I began to take pictures when Missy was a baby. It somehow blossomed from there."

"That Missy is a swell kid, Stephie! What a super athlete!" Again it was Bob, sincere and innocent, again making her squirm in her seat.

This time it was Elaine who came to the rescue. "We all know that, Bozo," she kidded her husband. "But we came here to get away from talk of camp and kids—no offense intended to either you or Missy," she added to Stephanie before she deftly turned the conversation to talk of the tennis tournaments which were taking place in North Conway.

The center of Ogunquit was teeming with summer visitors when the VW passed through on its way to the Playhouse. After successfully securing tickets for the evening performance, the foursome moved on to the beach. Though it was already mid-afternoon, the crowd was large and thoroughly enjoying the brilliant sunshine. Wending their way through the labyrinth of lounge chairs, towels, and sand castles, they finally staked claim to a less congested spot, far from the center of the throng, where the sand was soft, smooth, warm, and inviting. For Stephanie, however, the strongest call was from the ocean, an enticingly cool and refreshing prospect with the heat of the auto ride clinging to her skin. Shedding her shorts, shirt, and sandals, she headed for the water's edge, its initial coldness yielding to pure invigoration as she dived into the waves and swam from the shore. With the surge of the Atlantic numbing in its own way, she felt all worry, tension, responsibility float from her as she swam steadily toward the few scattered wind surfers, whose positions marked her own safe boundary. There was a certain thrill, she mused, to leaving the others behind and joining these few more adventurous souls, here in deeper water.

"Stephanie!" A deep shout not far from her halted her crawl. Treading water, she turned. Doug had just about reached her, his stroke strong and regular. "What in hell do you have in mind?" he growled through the salt water which sprang haphazardly around them.

Puzzled, she squinted. "I'm swimming. Any problem?"

"Not unless you want either to be hit by a surfboard or drawn out by the undertow." The eyes that accused her were suddenly as dark as the murky ocean depths, and she realized only then how far she'd come from shore. Reversing direction and ignoring Doug's glower, she swam toward the shallows once again, her feet sinking into the shifting sand when she finally stood up, waist high in the waves. She had been aware, during the return swim, of the man accompanying her. Now, as she stood panting deeply from the rigor of the swim and its gradually pervading chill, he drew himself to his full height before her, his back to the shore and any onlooking eyes.

"Are you often suicidal, or do you merely like being rescued?" The sun, on its steadfast afternoon descent, was behind him, throwing his form into silhouette, his features into shadow.

Hair dripping down her shoulders, Stephanie shaded her eyes with a glistening arm as she squinted up at him in surprise. He was really angry, though, for the life of her, she couldn't understand why. "Come on, Doug," she chided. "There was no danger. I'm a good swimmer, and I do watch my limits, and, believe me, I was not in any trouble."

Strangely he persisted, the hands on his hips a roadblock of sorts to forbid her passage. "Is that what I should have told Melissa, that her mother was a good swimmer?"

Her lips thinned in frustration. "Really, you're making a mountain out of a molehill."

Water sparkled on his hair, giving him a satanic air as he chastised her. "That was a really dumb thing you did out there, Stephanie. You have a responsibility; don't you think you ought to accept that?"

It took every last bit of willpower for Stephanie not to lash out at him then and there on the matter of responsibility. Clenching her fists in anger, she sidestepped him determinedly and waded the short distance to shore, eyes downcast in contrived concentration on the surf swirling about her legs, her ankles, her feet, then not at all, as she emerged from the water. The absence of an echoing spatter on the wet sand told her that she had not been followed out, and she forced herself into a semblance of calmness, jaw and all, as she approached the blanket on which Elaine and Bob were sunning.

Bob promptly sat up and, taking a paper cup and a

bottle from the insulated bag which they had brought, offered her some wine.

"Mmmm . . . just what I need," she murmured in appreciation, as she plunked herself upon the large beach towel she'd brought. Warming and sweet the wine was, and relaxing it would be, she hoped—anything to revive the good spirits which her self-appointed lifeguard had dampened. Her double-edged thanks did not escape Elaine.

"That bad, eh?" One hazel eye blinked up at her from its restful pose.

Stephanie shrugged noncommittally, already feeling the warming rays that penetrated the moisture on her shoulders. "I sometimes wonder . . ." She heard herself answer quietly, even as her gaze traced the surf line for sign of a dark-haired swimmer. She saw neither that bobbing head nor the look of bewilderment on her friend's face, but rather downed her wine in one thirst-bidden gulp and stretched out facedown on the towel.

Between the strength of the sun warming her back and the power of the wine warming her insides, she was relaxed and content when Elaine announced that she and Bob were going for a swim. Too comfortable to move, she merely raised a hand to wave them off, then fell into a delightfully pleasant state of laziness from which she had no wish to return.

That choice, however, was taken out of her hands and, both literally and figuratively, put into those of another. It was a sudden wormlike cold slithering on her back that shocked her out of her drowsiness. With a start she bolted up, only to be halted midway by Doug's restraining hand on her shoulder.

"My God, what *is* that?" she shrieked in alarm as she

twisted her head around to see what sea creature he had deposited so unceremoniously onto her back.

At her reflexive recoil, he laughed aloud, a deep, rich, beautifully resonant laugh. "A very exotic animal called suntan lotion," he ribbed her, though gently and with none of the impatience with which he had regarded her a few moments earlier.

Buoyed by the wine and struck by the ludicrous nature of her alarm, she joined his laughter, then submitted as his hand pressed her head back down onto the towel and he worked the now soothing lotion into the warm skin of her back. She savored the divine massage, his strong fingers making short work of both the cream and any lingering tension which may have remained in her muscles.

"Mmmm . . . that feels good," she murmured as the delight continued long past the point where the lotion had disappeared.

Suddenly his warm breath fanned her ear with its husky plea. "Truce?"

One lazy lid rose to survey the face that hovered but inches from hers; one auburn brow arched in a moment of skepticism.

"No strings," he assured her. "Just a truce—for today. If not for our own sanity, then for Bob and Elaine's. Yes?" It was the Douglas Weston as she remembered him—steel eyes soft, velvet voice smooth, supplicating smile endearing, his entire person oozing with charm.

Slowly she smiled, bewitched by a brew of wine, sun, and manly appeal. "Why not?" she agreed softly, savoring the peace for a mere moment before a hand came down playfully on her backside. Twisting around with a questioning gaze, she was halted by the amusement skittering about his eyes.

"Now it's my turn," he informed her, the corners of his lips twitching mischievously as he held the tube of suntan lotion out to her.

"I mighta known," she drawled in mock resignation as she sat up and began to paint a surrealistic picture in white on the middle of his back. Whether the wine was now working for or against her, she didn't know. She only knew, as her hands moved in slow circular motions, of the skin beneath her fingertips, firm and smooth, the manly muscles rippling beneath her palms, the gentle contours defining each and every sinew. She only knew that she was as relaxed now, massaging Doug's back, as she had been when he had been the masseur. It was a kind of sweet and heady torture, this physical contact, and she wasn't at all sure whether to be relieved when Elaine ran up to break the spell.

"Brrr! That's really cold!" she exclaimed, wrapping her thin form in a towel as she collapsed onto the blanket. "All quiet on the western front?" she inquired playfully, leaning toward the spot where both Doug and Stephanie had now stretched out.

"Uh-huh." It was a spontaneous response, given in unison, surprising both who had made it with not only its harmonious sound but also its truth. And it was to set a pattern for the day which Stephanie, for one, would look back on as near perfection.

For it was as though all past had been obliterated, the only reality being the present, a kind of heavenly limbo in which no other time had a place. They spent the rest of the afternoon at the beach, snacking on treats that Elaine had thoughtfully packed, lingering long after the rest of the crowd had dispersed. Having decided to eat after the show, they were able to walk a near-deserted stretch of sand, admiring the pink and orange hues of early evening as the dying sun played its swan song on the shore amid the dance of the sand-pipers, scuttling to and fro in rapid harmony with their black-rimmed reflections on the wet sand. It was a most peaceful time of day, one which replaced the long-since quaffed wine as a potent tranquilizer. For Stephanie, the long, bronzed arm resting gently about her shoulders was merely an extension of this natural beauty that touched her.

So precious seemed the attitude of warmth and friendship that enveloped them on the beach that it was with a smattering of reluctance that they changed into the more dressy wear of the evening and proceeded to the Playhouse. But if reluctance it was which caused Stephanie to acknowledge how positively devastating had been Doug's scantily clad form on the beach, it quickly evaporated at the sight of him in his crisp white shirt, navy tie and blazer, and gray slacks—as debonair an image as she could have dreamed. She had never seen him in anything other than purely casual wear, and found herself profoundly aware of his maturity and sophistication, as well as his overwhelming masculinity. As for herself, she was grateful that she'd brought along the fitted linen dress which suited her so well, loosely sashed as it was at the waist, with cap sleeves and a mandarin collar, its smoky orange hue finely complimenting her own healthily tanned complexion. They were, indeed, a handsome couple, she admitted with an abandon of her usual modesty, sparked by the heads that turned their way in admiration as they proceeded down the center aisle to their seats.

The show itself, a revival of one of Stephanie's favorite Rodgers and Hammerstein musicals, *Carousel,* was well sung and skillfully choreographed, doubly compensating for the regretted passing of the memorable afternoon. When the final curtain call had been taken and the house lights had come on, the four headed for a restaurant that had been highly recommended. Stephanie did not flinch when Doug took her hand in his, helping her out of the car, placing a strong hand with a feather touch at her back to guide her. Indeed, she had savored these gestures all day, feeling every bit the woman, protected and cared for. Later, she was to wonder why this stereotypical role-playing had appealed to her on this day. She was to chide herself for nurturing the very vulnerability which she had long ago forsworn. This evening, however, there was no room for practical thought, only for enjoyment.

Unfortunately during dinner, as the four delved into their Chateaubriands, the sharp prong of reality began to poke through the veneer of make-believe, jabbing Stephanie gently with a reminder that, indeed, midnight was approaching and the coach would soon turn back into a pumpkin.

"How is your family, Doug?" Elaine asked, the innocence of her inquiry not lost on Stephanie, whose head swiveled curiously toward him.

He sipped of his Chablis before he answered, looking directly at Elaine as he did so. "They're fine. Mother's doing well, despite her arthritis. She asks for you often."

Elaine grinned. "Please send her our love." Then, sensing the puzzlement in Stephanie's eyes, she explained softly. "Bob and I have thrust ourselves on Doug for our last few winters' vacations," she began, smiling apologetically at Doug before turning again to Stephanie. "You know, skiing-in-Vermont type of thing. His mother is quite a character!"

"You live with your mother?" Stephanie turned now

to Doug, spontaneously posing questions which she might have vetoed on other, less amiable occasions.

Doug shook his head, his gray orbs studying her independently as he answered her. "No. My mother has her own place, a small cottage on the edge of my own grounds."

"Your own grounds? Sounds like you've become a wealthy landowner." She kidded him. "As I recall . . ." Her voice trailed off as she realized that she had nothing to recall. Eight years ago, she had learned nothing about his personal life, despite the intimacy which had capped their relationship. Tonight, on a purely platonic level, she was to learn more. Questioning green eyes lifted to slate ones.

It was as though he had read her mind and understood her unsureness. Quickly, like the impeccably mannered escort he had been this day, he explained, albeit with a touch of reluctance. "Things have changed since then. I don't know about wealthy, but I have been able to buy some land. There's my house, then my mother's cottage."

Elaine's hazel eyes narrowed as she gazed in gentle accusation. "Come on, Doug. Why the modesty? Actually"—she corrected him boldly—"Doug owns a magnificent piece of land in the mountains. His house is exquisite and his mother's is absolutely charming."

Stephanie's eyebrows arched, her head tilted in appreciation. "Very impressive," she quipped softly, unable to totally squelch the tiny thread of curiosity at the rest of the "family" to which Elaine had referred, the other inhabitant of this "exquisite" house. Defensively, she downed her own Chablis, barely catching the look of indecision on Doug's face before the curtain fell on his own gray stage.

Bob, however, was oblivious to the entire shaky

undercurrent. "Tell me, Doug, how did the year end? Much problem with your students?" Again Stephanie's ears perked up; again Doug seemed a shade uncomfortable to be at the center of the conversation, though his gaze held Bob's steadily.

"Not bad. This year's graduating class was a good one; a large number of them were placed in jobs, many others are going on for advanced degrees. No riots, a few demonstrations, a relatively peaceful year overall."

Now Stephanie was thoroughly puzzled. This did not sound like a mere tennis pro talking. What was it Sylvie Hampson had said about a "very demanding position?" Suddenly, she began to feel the germ of an internal conflict nibbling at her. One side had spurned reality for the day in favor of a warm and congenial atmosphere, had wanted to hear everything about the man who was in large part responsible for the creation of that atmosphere. The other side, however, the one which was mother-counselor-photographer, wanted to hear nothing, see nothing, feel nothing. For, she realized with a stark and sober shock, it was the former which could too easily fall in love with Doug Weston, the latter which would not permit it.

It was an entirely private and thoroughly disturbing thought, the possibility of falling in love with the same man who had once hurt her so. Deep in her self-inflicted quagmire, Stephanie was unaware of the frown that had drawn down the corners of her soft lips.

Again, either sensing her distress or reluctant to allow her further insight into his life—she had no way of knowing which from the protective mask which had slid from his gray eyes downward over features suddenly guarded and impersonal—Doug determinedly changed the subject to a more neutral one, launching into a discussion with the experts on the upcoming Newport races.

Stephanie listened with only half-hearted interest, her own face mercifully camouflaging the brooding which had besieged her. Or so she thought.

"Are you all right, Steph?" His warm, low tone startled her as she gave token concentration to the interaction now passing between their married companions. A strong hand had come to rest on her own browned arm, branding her flesh with its searing electricity. As she fought the loud thudding in her chest, her eyes met his in a wordless interchange that was both charged and innocent, intimate and impersonal, questioning and answering. It seemed an eternity that they sat thus, though it could have been no more than a moment. Stephanie felt the force of the conflict pulling unmercifully at her from both ends, its sting bringing tears to her eyes. Quickly she lowered them, nodding as she lifted her coffee cup. "I'm fine," she whispered in contradiction of her own knowledge. With her gaze glued to the sugar bowl, she did not see the momentary softness in his own, the flicker of warmth, compassion, and concern therein, before he turned to rejoin the other conversation.

Overall it was a delightful day, despite those moments of distress and unsureness during dinner. Somehow Stephanie had managed to compose herself and get through the remainder of the evening with no further show of weakness. For, in her own, albeit subjective, judgment, that was exactly what she had displayed—a sure sign of a weakness which, should Doug recognize it and decide to play on it, could lead to her downfall. Indeed, there were trials enough to overcome, temptations enough to resist, without the telltale tears to cloud the issue.

As if to illustrate her tribulation, there was the long drive back to PineWinds. Becalmed by pleasant company, good wine, and pure exhaustion, she dozed off at one point, awakening with a start to find her head resting within the circle of Doug's arm. Instinctively, she jerked away, regarding the eyes which, even in the darkness, held a hint of amusement at her reflexive motion.

"I—I'm sorry," she stammered in embarrassment.

"Don't be," he chided softly, his words held inaudible to the couple in front by the steady chug of the none-too-healthy-sounding engine. "You're tired. Come on," he coaxed, pulling her gently back into the enveloping cocoon. When she tensed involuntarily, he reminded her, "It's just for today. Remember?" She did, though it was not the thought of that declared truce which finally bade her curl against his beckoning form once more. Rather, it was the more primitive force, the need deep within herself for warmth, protection, and comfort. She was unaware of the sigh which slipped unbidden through her moist lips, as she settled herself into the haven and felt its arm close about her, firmly and protectively.

By the time the drive was over, Stephanie was grateful that all four were returning to the Grove, precluding any private and prolonged good night on a secluded doorstep in the glowing moonlight. It had been a day of pleasure, unreal and not to be repeated, a one-time happening which had no place in her normal world. Already she felt a strange emptiness at the thought of the end of this truce which had allowed her such contentment. Yet, it had to be. There was no place for Doug in her life. She had Melissa. She had her career. He had his life . . . and his wife. This day had been an isolated interlude for them both. It was destined to end.

five

STEPHANIE ALLOWED HERSELF LITTLE TIME TO brood on the events of that day as the momentum of camp activity picked up in anticipation of parents' weekend. Not only were there campers' prints to be mounted and displayed along a prominent wall of the main lodge, but she spent every free minute printing negatives which Sylvie had specifically chosen as "musts" for the book.

She saw Doug daily, though he never stopped for more than a brief greeting. If he had felt anything special on that mutual day off, he certainly made no mention of it. Yet, she mused, following one quick run-in on the porch after dinner, there seemed to be a remnant of that same truce in effect, such that they could be friendly and amenable toward one another, with none of the simmering anger and open disdain shown in the past.

For Stephanie, it was a mixed blessing. While she found herself more relaxed without the constant worry of a sudden attack, be it physical or verbal, she felt an equal danger in the subtle charm which emanated from him, a too-frequent reminder of that which could have been long, long ago.

It was on the Sunday of parents' weekend that the past finally caught up with the present, triggering a chain of events whose fallout threatened to permanently alter her own future.

The weekend was to be a vacation of sorts for Stephanie, who, on Sylvie Hampson's direct order, would be a parent, visiting with her daughter, much like the others who came, some from great distances, some from small, to see their own offspring. Although her camera was to be handy at all times to take the token photographs, the first order of business was motherhood; both Stephanie and Melissa looked forward to it.

The sun rose warm and bright on Sunday morning, heralding a day of games, contests, and shows designed to send the parents back home in a contented state of exhaustion. All proceeded well, both for Melissa, whose team won its volleyball game, who placed second in a swimming relay, and easily won her tennis match, and for Stephanie, who watched it all with open pride, a luxury which she did not customarily allow herself.

It was late in the afternoon when the camp cook-out extravaganza took place that the bottom fell out of Stephanie's well-laid life plans. Doug had been in a state of constant occupation during the day, jockeying between his roles as head of the tennis department and head counselor, constantly besieged either by parents or staff bearing a wide array of questions, comments, compliments, and, least pleasantly, complaints. Stephanie had noted his preoccupation and had welcomed it, as it eased the one subtle fragment, the one nagging regret of this parents' weekend. For, much as she fought it, she could not help thinking of Melissa's father, who by rights should be with her now too. Did Melissa mind that she had only a mother? She never had, or so Stephanie thought.

Laden with their fair assortment of burgers, franks, corn-on-the-cob, cole slaw, and drinks, she and Melissa worked their way through the crowds at the food tables to a less congested spot where the two could sit and talk quietly as they ate. There had been precious few times for that during the past four weeks, and Stephanie had looked forward to just these moments with her daughter now. However, someone else had other ideas, she realized, as she watched Doug approach them and put his own plate down beside Melissa. He looked tired, but ruggedly handsome in spite of it.

"How're you doin', Melissa?" he asked gently, pulling one of the child's pigtails as he sat down Indian-style beside her. Melissa, needless to say, was thrilled to see him and, although the private moments Stephanie might have shared with the youngster were now thwarted by his arrival, she felt a sudden quickening of her pulse, a strange wholeness, at his presence.

The time passed all too quickly as they ate, Doug's deft handling of the conversation, such that both Missy and her mother were charmed, astonishing her anew. Melissa seemed entirely relaxed and happy, she noted, the veils which too often shaded her eyes now totally removed, her manner free and open with this man. It was something of a wonder to Stephanie—uncanny, heartwarming, and frightening all at the same time. Particularly when, after they'd finished eating, Melissa threw herself onto Doug's lap and lounged contentedly, her head against his chest, his arms encircling her small body, Stephanie found a sadness joining the other sentiments. What a warm unit they would have made—the perfect family.

Her thought was interrupted by a rather rotund, bald-headed parent, who approached Doug to say good-bye. "Don't get up, Doug"—he waved a hand to keep the other in his obviously comfortable position—"but I just want to thank you once again for everything you've done for our Nancy. Her game has improved dramatically, as has her attitude." He lowered his voice at the last, as he cast a cautious eye at Missy, who was much too intrigued with the ludicrous comparison of her small fingers flush against Doug's large ones to pay him any heed. "My wife and I are very grateful."

"Your daughter is a lovely girl, Mr. Lockwood," Doug replied as he extended a hand up to meet the other's proffered one.

Suddenly, the expression looking down became one of puzzlement, jumping from Missy to Doug and back again. Sensing the train of thought, Stephanie froze.

"I didn't know you had a daughter here yourself," he announced with no small amount of surprise and the tact of an atom bomb. What followed that most innocently delivered comment was encapsuled forever in Stephanie's consciousness.

There passed what seemed to be an eternity of silence before Doug laughed softly. "Oh, no, Melissa is the daughter of our photography instructor, Stephanie Wright." He gestured in her direction, though his eyes shunned hers. Maybe he won't think twice about it, Stephanie prayed silently, her mouth going dry and her breath catching in trepidation. And rightly it should have. For, if he had chosen to overlook the implication of the original statement, there was no way he could ignore the follow-up.

"It's uncanny!" The gentleman laughed heartily at his supposed error. "She looks so much like you!" At that moment Stephanie had to be grateful for small favors; had she still been eating, she surely would have choked! "Well, thanks again, Doug. And Mrs. Wright"—she cringed at the misnomer—"your photos are a huge success! Good-bye." He was gone as abruptly as he had arrived, leaving behind a brutally shattered serenity.

Not daring to look up, Stephanie pulled at the grass beneath her knees. All the while she felt Doug's gaze boring into her, piercing her, devastating her with its newly awakened vision.

"Missy, how about getting me a glass of cider?" Doug asked unevenly, the catch in his voice unnoticed by the child, who scampered away after an affectionate pat to her bottom. Stephanie was barely aware that she had gone, so stricken was she by what had happened.

After a long moment, she heard his voice, deep and low, flecked with an uncertainty that tore at her. "Steph?" She kept her head down, unable to look at him, denying the truth even as she knew he had finally discovered it. Tears welled along her eyelids, then escaped in an ever-slow trickle. What would she do now? What could she say? Things had been going along so well . . . her work, Melissa, yes, even her attempts to exist beside Doug yet without him. Why did it have to happen now? Why in this way—from a complete stranger?

"Where did Doug go, Mommy?" the small voice asked in sudden alarm, Melissa having returned with a carefully cradled cup of cider. Stephanie raised shaky hands to her face, then drew them back across her eyes and cheeks as though she were merely stretching, yet wiping away the tears as she did so. So he'd left . . .

"He—had to—take care of something, sweetie," she calmed her daughter, fighting not to let her own burgeoning despondency become apparent. The situation was out of her control now, but she knew that she would have to speak to Doug later. Melissa must not know yet! She must not even suspect a relationship between Stephanie and Doug!

That the child was totally unaware of her mother's thoughts was evident in the words which next flowed freely. "Doug is so great, isn't he, Mommy? When he was here just now, it was almost like I had a father too!" Her eyes were beaming at the thought, another dagger thrust into Stephanie's gut.

Struggling to recover from this latest jolt, she looked around frantically, brightening as she saw the movement toward the dessert table. "Come on, Missy—they're setting up the sundae makings. Let's get ours." Indeed, a gooey, hot chocolate sundae with marshmallow, nuts, sprinkles, and a cherry was the last thing her stomach could bear at that moment. But the thoughts which monopolized her mind would have to wait until later that evening for their appeasement.

It was an endless few hours before the last of the parents had left camp and Stephanie had seen Missy safely returned to her bunk. Only then was she able to organize the thoughts which had been ricocheting every which way off the corners of her mind since that cataclysmic moment of truth. She knew basically what had to be said; it was merely a matter of finding Doug and saying it. She felt a sudden urgency, which she somehow didn't understand, knowing only that she'd not be able to rest until she'd had her say.

Finding Doug turned out to be the major hurdle. She

began at his cabin in the Grove, but he wasn't there. Neither was he at the main lodge. In fact, no one, of the few faces she'd seen and the few subtle inquiries she'd made, seemed to have had any inkling as to his whereabouts. Had he taken off again as he had done that other time? If so, her own peace of mind would certainly be deferred.

Wrapped in a mantle of desolation, she began to wander in the darkness, following paths which she knew practically by feel, so often had she traversed them of late. The air had cooled dramatically, so typical of Maine nights, and she wrapped her arms about her for warmth as well as psychological comfort. Aimless amblings led her, by chance, to the waterfront, where the gleam of the moonlight low on the horizon caught her eye, tumbling in ripples from one end of the lake to the other.

Then something else caught her eye, a dark, silhouetted form, instantly recognizable as it lounged against one of the two diving boards at the far end of the dock. Ignoring the fear that gripped her, she walked forward and moved onto the dock, her footsteps, quiet as they were, alerting him to her presence much as his had done on another occasion.

Now he turned slowly toward her, as though knowing beyond a doubt that it would be she coming through the darkness. He didn't say a word, merely stood and stared, hands thrust deep into the pockets of his jeans, one ankle crossed over the other as he half sat against the board. She could not see his expression, his face was dark, yet she sensed that there was no anger in his mien. Several feet from him she stopped. All was quiet on this midsummer night, save the gentle slur of the water and the distant chorus of crickets.

"You know," she whispered tremulously.

After an uncertain moment, he nodded, dark hair glistening mysteriously beneath its lunar halo. "I checked the records. Her birth date. You must have delivered early." Stephanie had been prepared for anger, accusation, bitterness. The sadness she now heard took her off guard, wrenching her torturously.

Instinctively, she knew that she had to talk, to explain, to say something to ease that sadness which only magnified her own. Slowly, she walked to the twin diving boards; she would need support, too, if she was going to make it through this new spasm.

"She was two weeks premature," she acknowledged softly, putting both hands down on the board before her, as she kept her back to Doug. A long silence followed her words.

"Go on." His voice was barely audible, its sentiment indefinable, its order startling. What was it he wanted to hear? She hesitated uncertainly. Then, quiet direction came. "Tell me about it. Was it an easy delivery?" Strange that he should want to hear these details, she mused, yet how could she deny him this simple information regarding his own child.

"No, it was long . . . and very difficult," she began slowly. "At one point they even considered doing a C-section. I was in labor for over sixteen hours when she finally arrived, but it was worth every minute," she went on quietly, finding the words tripping over her lips with a momentum of their own. She had never spoken with anyone of this, yet suddenly she felt a driving need to do so.

Once again, the far-off crickets monopolized the night air. Turning, Stephanie dared to look in Doug's direction. Lit by the moon now, having shifted to sit on the side of the board directly opposite her, his pose was one of either deep thought or equally as deep pain, she knew not which. One arm was strapped across his chest, the other bent on it from the elbow, lending his hand as a support for the forehead which was bowed before her.

"How did you manage at the beginning?" he asked without lifting his head, as though a burden weighed too heavily on him to permit that movement.

As she faced him now, it was as if the tables had been turned, giving her the task of comforting him from some pain he had experienced. "My parents helped at first. They loved the baby," she explained, recalling the boundless love of grandparents who were to have such a short time with their only grandchild. Her parents had never questioned her decision not to tell Doug about Melissa, never expressed regret or, worse, embarrassment, about the situation. Now she could only remember the look of joy on their faces when she had brought the baby home from the hospital, when Missy took her first steps, when she began to talk.

"And then?" he prodded further.

"Then . . . they died. Missy was old enough for me to put her into a pre-school program, so I went to work." It all sounded so simple, in hindsight, she mused. How easy it was to forget the lonely nights in that empty house, the hectic mornings, the guilt-filled afternoons—always wondering whether she was doing the right thing for Melissa.

As she studied his moon-gilded features, Stephanie saw Doug slowly shake his head from side to side, then turn his back to her as he straightened his arms and put both hands forward onto the diving board. He seemed to be grappling with a dilemma, one which confounded him. When finally he spoke, it was with a sigh of resignation, as though he had finally accepted what she'd told him.

"I'm sorry, Steph."

Bewilderment overtook her as she sought to understand his reaction. This was not what she had expected, an apology. "Sorry? What are you sorry for?" Lord knew there were plenty of things for him to rue, but did he recognize and admit them?

When he turned to look back at her, there was a fierceness in his manner which spoke of his own inner pain. Taken aback by this depth of feeling, she was further astonished by his words. "I'm sorry you had to go through it alone. I'm sorry I wasn't there to help. I'm sorry I wasn't there to—"

His words were interrupted in the instant that astonishment turned to indignation. "I don't want your sympathy, Doug, or your pity," she snapped, her voice shattering the quiet of the night. "I've managed very nicely on my own all these years. I want nothing from you now—nothing! Do you understand that?" She found herself trembling as she stormed off down the dock. He felt guilty, did he? He felt sorry for her? Damn him, she seethed. That wasn't what she had intended when she had come looking for him. Then she stopped short, realizing that she hadn't yet said what she had indeed come to tell him.

Her checked flight had taken her several yards from where he stood. Now she spoke without turning, her arms stiffened into balled fists at her sides. "I do have one thing to ask you . . ." Her tremulous tone trailed off as she awaited some sign that he heard her. When there was none, she pivoted toward where he was standing, now erect and alert, with a tension she had not seen earlier. He was listening, she knew, so she pursued her point.

"I don't want Missy to know. Not now, not just yet." It was an announcement, rather than a question, and seemed perfectly fitting to her as the sole guardian of the child. As the silence lingered, though, she began to wonder whether he'd heard, understood, or accepted her command. Only then did she rephrase her request. "Please, Doug, don't say anything to her?" Unintentionally, her voice had emerged in a near whisper which underlined the desperation of her plea. To this, he finally responded.

"No, Steph, I won't say anything. Not yet."

Buoyed by instant relief, she turned to leave once more.

"Wait!" His curt order jolted her, its sudden forcefulness sending tremors of fear from one nerve end to the other. Paralyzed, she stood still, unable either to turn toward him or move on. Her pulse quickened as she heard his footsteps, slow and steady, approaching, then passing, then pausing in front. Downcast eyes detected the form looming above her, though she fought the pull of his gaze, now riveting her to the very spot she stood. His voice was confident, velvet-covered steel, when he finally spoke.

"I said not yet. But she will know, Steph. We owe it to her. Some children are not as fortunate; they go through life without parents. No, Melissa is my daughter too, and I'll be damned if I'll have her do without something she can have. She's my daughter too, Steph—don't forget that!"

"Don't forget it?" A bitter laugh accompanied Stephanie's words as the resurrection of her own outrage gave her the strength to look at him. The moonlight was now full in his face, illuminating the line of his jaw, his nose, the slate-hued orbs that challenged her. "Forget it? How can I forget it? He was right, that

Mr. Lockwood. She looks just like you . . . the spitting image. I've seen it every blessed day since that very first, in the delivery room, when they placed her in my hands. I'm only amazed that you didn't see it yourself sooner." Faintly breathless from her tirade, she tried to calm herself in vain; the anger was already aroused. "But, no, you were too intent on ignoring the truth, accusing me of being nothing but a tramp . . . a . . . a . . ." She could go no further. With a choked gasp, she swiveled sideways and put an unsteady hand to her forehead.

After a brief hesitation Doug defended himself, his tone softer, almost apologetic again. "That's unfair, Stephie. We were together for one night. I heard nothing from you after. Times have changed; it would have been very natural for you to—"

"There was no one." She turned back to him, her eyes now glistening with unshed tears. "No one. I've never been with anyone else, Doug!" It was a confession she never dreamed she'd be making to this man, yet it had spilled forth, unbidden, in the heat of the anguish.

Suddenly the entire gist of the discussion had shifted. No longer were they talking of parenthood or Melissa. Now they were talking of themselves, Doug and Stephanie, man and woman. They were talking of an exquisite intimacy, once shared, now remembered. They were talking of desire, need, and fulfillment.

All else fell away into the darkness except the two of them, visually spellbound, on the edge of wordless communication. Stephanie's gaze held his and was held, helplessly, as the interchange commenced, powerful, awesome, inspiring. Within her breast, her heart spoke out in double time, its pulse vibrating dangerously through her body. Her mind's eye saw the hand as it lifted, felt it on her face, first tentatively, then more surely, caressing her cheek, her chin, her jaw, with a near reverence.

She was mesmerized, unable to move, as his thumb traced the contour of her ear, palm and fingers curving softly about her neck. The warmth of his body reached out to her, driving off the chill of the night air. It was as though she had been transported back over time, into the only world which, given the intensity emanating from him and the musky maleness which assailed her senses, really mattered. When his thumb edged forward to circle her cheek, she instinctively turned her lips toward it, savoring its roughness as it feather-touched her skin. A sigh of ecstasy parted her lips as she gave herself up to the heady sensations that had taken control. The attraction was too great, too wonderful to deny.

There was a moment's hesitation when his hands cupped her head on either side and he tilted her face up toward his. She opened her eyes in wonder to behold a sight of gentleness and adoration which only quickened her need. Warm gray eyes studied hers, begging forgiveness, asking permission, wanting to know that she knew it was he.

The moonlight had given him his answer. Reality had fallen far, far away for him too. Stephanie felt the pace of his own heartbeat accelerate in rhythm with hers as he drew her to him, moaning deeply as her body melded into his, hoarsely whispering her name.

Their kiss was new and electrical, charging each with a heady current, driving each toward a pinnacle of desire which seemed limitless. A tremor passed from his body to hers through their embrace, leaving in its wake a weakness which could only be bolstered through renewed touch.

"My God, Stephie," she heard him moan as he tore his lips from hers and imprisoned her fiercely within the bands of his sinewy arms. For her part she was a willing prisoner, reveling in his strength as she buried her face in his neck and inhaled of his intoxicating scent. Rational thought was nonexistent, yet her senses knew that she had missed just this, so painful had been the void he now filled.

As she clung to him, entranced by his manhood, hypnotized in the moonlight, his hands caressed her back, exploring curves and tracing contours, then slipping beneath the edge of her jersey to sear her flesh in a dozen fiery-sweet strokes. She heard herself gasp with delight as his hand moved forward, cupping the soft fullness of a breast, his thumb seeking out its pebble-hard peak, then teasing it into further torment. From deep within her welled the volcano of passion, growing, heating, bubbling, then threatening to erupt in its overwhelming need for his possession, a desire which his manly hardness, bold and heady against her, fed and mirrored.

"Doug?" she begged in a whispered plea, driven only by the awesome need to be one with him again, to be joined with him utterly.

Her feet left the ground as her body was lifted into strong arms and carried from the dock, while her own arms snaked about his neck in immovable coils.

The softness of the sand molded to her as he lay her down, lowering his hard body over her as his lips claimed hers once more, tasting them now in a sensual orgy. Her tongue met his and explored it until, trembling and breathless, she fell back to look at him and drink in his very manliness.

The pleasure was pure and explosive as he drew her jersey over her head to give access to his lips, light and sensuous, covering every inch of her, then lowered her bra to lay bare a host of further delights. Impatient fingers responded by working at the buttons of his shirt, then spread over the breadth of his chest, raking slowly through the finely matted hair which formed its masculine T.

Rolling onto his side, he drew her against him, crushing her breasts deliciously against the roughness of his chest. "Oh, Stephanie," he murmured huskily against her ear. "We've wasted so much time. I want you so much! You know," he went on, drawing back to take in her face, pale and delicate in the dim moonlight, willing his words to carry on the rising thrust of his ardor, "motherhood has made you more beautiful than ever." His eyes fell worshipfully from her face to her breasts, tracing the moonlit outline of the crested curve down over her middle to her waist. Ever so slowly his hand slid beneath the waistband of her shorts to touch her stomach, his fingers splaying over her soft skin as he murmured, "I would have wanted to see you when you were round and heavy, carrying my child." A mere touch of sadness had intruded into the sensual velvet of his tone. It was enough.

In a flash reality was back, stark and shocking, reminding Stephanie of who she was, what she'd done then and almost done now. "Oh, no!" she cried in heartrending anguish, as she bolted up.

"What is it, honey?" He was beside her, sitting as she was, watching as she crossed her hands protectively over her breasts, cowering now from the devastating glow of a moon which moments before had witnessed their passion.

"This is all wrong, Doug," she whispered, hanging her head in misery and shame. "Don't you see?" She looked up at him in pitiful entreaty. "This is merely a repeat—a rerun—It all happened before. I can't let it happen again."

"Why not?" His eyes glittered a challenge inspired by the passionate side of the moon.

"Me. Melissa. You. I should have learned my lesson last time." In actuality her mind was on neither herself, nor her daughter, nor Doug, but rather on another, whose blond-framed features were crystal clear in her memory.

A strong hand, large, warm, and comforting, began a gentle massage of her shoulders, as he voiced his own concerns. "Stephanie, I only wish I could understand you," he began, a touch of exasperation suggested in his voice. "You were as aroused just now as I was. You wanted me to make love to you as much as I did. What is the problem?"

"The problem *is* arousal. Lust, desire, arousal . . . call it what you will; it is a purely physical reflex. But it won't work for me this time. I have my own life. I have my own sanity. I have Melissa. And you . . . you have—"

"What do I have? I've spent eight years wondering," he interrupted impatiently, an unfathomable expression gripping his features. "What do I have? I don't have you. I don't have my daughter. What do you think I have?"

Warning notes cried out within her, threads of confusion which mangled her composure. "You have your work, your home, your wife . . ." At the last her voice had faltered, a mere whisper embodying the dire pain the memory of that one brought.

Doug looked sharply at her, his bafflement evident even through the darkness. "I have no wife. We were divorced long ago."

The words hit her like a wrecker's ball, dashing her well-built arguments to smithereens. Not married? Not married? He was divorced? How could that be? It simply didn't jibe with the image she'd harbored for so long. Yet it would explain both Sylvie's and Elaine's comments that he needed someone. If indeed it was so, then perhaps he was to be forgiven this summer's advances. But what about that other summer? He had been married then. She had seen his wife—as bold and beautiful as could be.

"I don't know. I don't know." She repeated the words in chantlike softness over and over again; she just didn't know! Confusion overrode anger which diluted hurt and thwarted desire. In a daze she fumbled with her clothing, struggling to control fingers that fussed with the clasp of her bra. In an almost automatic gesture of intimacy, Doug's fingers brushed hers aside, then fastened the clasp and drew her shirt back over her head.

Finally, safely dressed once more, she buried her head in arms crossed upon bent knees. "I thought I had gotten over all this," she murmured against her own skin. "In eight years, I've never even been tempted."

"That's it, honey," he began, with all of the eloquence his own work demanded. "Don't you see? We have something very special you and I. And I'm not talking about Melissa—" as she knew he wasn't "—though God only knows how special she is!" He paused to stroke Stephanie's hair lightly, then withdrew his hand as though fearful that his touch would dilute the import of his words. "What happened to us eight years ago was a rarity, Steph. I know. I have not lived the life of a celibate, so I know. When I took you, you were a virgin, yet you opened up to me with a passion that had been hidden within you, just waiting for the right key to unlock the treasure." His voice had taken on a velvety quality, a gentleness that lulled her even as she fought its arousing effect. She knew he was telling her the truth, yet she feared its ramifications.

"And with your own passion," he went on softly, "you stimulated a feeling within me which I hadn't felt before, nor have felt since. It was beautiful. So beautiful." Indeed it had been; in her heart, she knew it. Yet she struggled to reject it. She had her own life, she had Melissa, she had her hard-fought self-sufficiency, she reminded herself once more. And what about trust? She had trusted him once, only to be crudely awakened to the realities of infidelity. And what about love?

Love . . . where was it? At that moment she knew all too dearly where it was, for it welled within her own heart, yearning to be freed from the bonds which held it in check. Yes, she realized in that heart-stopping instant, it was there. Love . . . it was what she had fought all summer, no, for the past eight years. Physical attraction was physical; at least distance could deny it. But love . . . that was a different matter.

As the awesome truth penetrated her battered consciousness, she began to tremble. She loved Doug still, always had, always would. That was the ache which gnawed at her, which drew her to him, begging for release.

A sob caught in her throat as she stumbled to her feet, aware only that she had to get away from him, to think, to breathe, to assimilate all she'd learned on this far-reaching night. But he was on his feet beside her, towering over her as he held her wrist in restraint. His voice was deep and commanding, gentle yet determined when he painted out her future.

"I'll let you go tonight, Stephanie. You're upset and

confused. But mark my words: You will not run away from me this time. You have something I want and until you can see that for yourself, I'll be at your elbow constantly to remind you." He took a deep, labored breath before he repeated his promise, his voice now lowered, though strong and sure. "Yes, Steph, you have something I want and I'll be damned if you'll take it away from me again!"

A wave of disbelief shocked through her at his words. Melissa! My God, he wanted Melissa! From somewhere deep within, a spark of strength motivated her. Unsteadily she faced him, her face grave and deathly in the ashen light.

"You can't have her, Doug. She's mine. I carried her, I gave birth to her, I raised her and I won't let you have her." Her own words fueling her fear, the pitch of her voice drifted to a higher key. "Yours was no more than a momentary biological contribution. She's mine. Only mine!" she cried frantically.

Even in the darkness the puzzlement that creased his brows was evident. "It's not Melissa I want," he whispered incredulously. "It's you."

Now it was Stephanie's turn for disbelief. Gasping aloud, she stared for a moment at the granite hardness of slate-hued determination, then could bear no more. She turned and fled, running on legs which functioned by dint of sheer panic, speeding her directly to the Grove and her own cabin. Once within, she crumbled into a corner, crouching down on the hardwood floor with her knees hugged to her chest and her head buried therein. It was an instinct for protection which sought fulfillment, the even planks on either side of her guarding her from the elements as she fought the awesome predicament that faced her.

Slowly, as her body's quaking ceased, her breathing

evened, and the beads of nervous perspiration dried on her forehead, she began to wade through the sea of confusion that surrounded her.

He wanted her. Not Melissa. Her. Suddenly it hit her, the cleverness of it all. He knew that she would never be separated from her daughter; thus, to have Stephanie would be to have Melissa. Very clever!

So he wanted her. Not loved. Wanted. Was that his game? He had been perfectly clear about his opinion of her as a lover. At least he had not humiliated her along that line, she sniped caustically. And now he wanted her. Wanted her as a lover. Wanted her as the mother of his daughter. *Wanted.*

It was really not much of a surprise to her, the more she wrestled with the quandary. He had wanted her eight years ago and had taken her. She had been naive enough to interpret his tenderness as something deeper, when all along it had been an emotional appreciation of a physical deed well done. A mere act, nothing more.

But what about his earlier words, his note of apology that he had not been with her during Missy's early years? Again there was really no mystery. The man loved children. He was an educator of the young. What would be more natural than for him to want to trace the growth of his own flesh and blood? That he adored children was obvious from his interactions with them at PineWinds. That he had taken to Missy, even before he knew that she was in any way related to Stephanie, was likewise obvious. What was not obvious was what he intended for Missy's future. Would he expect to barge in and assume the duties of a father?

Slowly, as the midnight moments stretched into the wee hours and their passage found Stephanie steady but spent, the force of determination poked its head through the quagmire. Back in Cambridge there was a secure and comfortable life for herself and her daughter; it would still be there, awaiting them, when these eight weeks had ended. She would not let Doug Weston interfere with that life, threatening her peace of mind, tearing her apart emotionally as he had the knack of doing.

For that, she feared, would be precisely the case. She loved him deeply; that sad fact had become abundantly clear to her on the silver sand. But in *his* heart there was no love. If there had been, surely she would have known it. Surely he would have said something among the many words which had been spoken.

And he wasn't even married! What a weird melange of sentiments revolved around *that* small tidbit of information. Perhaps she should be grateful, yet gratitude was the last thing she felt. Perhaps she should be relieved, yet relief was nonexistent. Perhaps she should be happy; what a sadly fleeting quality happiness was! What did she feel then?

Frightened. Unsure. Threatened. Confused. Tempted. Angry. The list went on and on. How much easier it would have been to have dealt with him, had he still been tied to another. Then she could have based her arguments, as she had done over so many years, on the facts of his marriage, his wife, his other commitments, his unforgiveable infidelity. Now that premise had been swept out from beneath her feet. On what, then, did she base her resistance to him?

That she was physically aroused by him she would no longer deny. It was a fact. It was inevitable. It was enduring. Yet there had to be more, much more to life than sexual play and its gratification. There was love for one thing. Of this, he bore none. And there was trust, for another. Of this, she bore none. For never could she forget that betrayal eight years ago. Never could she let herself fall like that again.

Succumbing to exhaustion at the end of that agonized night's journey, she finally undressed and climbed beneath the protective weight of blankets and quilt, intent on seeking an oblivion, temporary as it would prove to be, from her torment.

As she attempted to clear her mind of all conscious thought, one persistent thread remained, stubbornly refusing to be cast aside until it, too, had received due recognition. It carried her back to the afternoon, to the precious moment before all hell broke loose. Once again she felt it, that strange, inexplicably marvelous sense of wholeness which had touched her so ephemerally as the three of them—Doug, Melissa, and herself—had sat together. It was as though only its presence told her of something she had missed in the past, of which she'd never been aware until that very moment, something with which she would have to cope . . . tomorrow.

six

TRUE TO HIS WORD, AND MUCH TO STEPHANIE'S growing consternation, Doug was indeed "at her elbow" as the next days passed. Contrary to those earlier times when he avoided her, now he seemed not only aware of her every move, but present and at the height of charm during many of them. In fact, had she not known of Sylvie Hampson's input into daily schedule planning, she would have suspected that Doug had specifically written himself into her activities, rearranging his own to accommodate them.

Very often she would look up at the start of a class to see him saunter over with determined nonchalance to listen to a lesson, admire some work being done, or merely stand and stare at her, a pleasant expression on his handsome face. From the point of view of the photographer, his presence was unobjectionable; from the point of view of the woman, it was thoroughly disturbing. Ever aware of his closeness, when he appeared over her shoulder, her pulse would quicken alarmingly, her palms become clammy. She knew not whether he was cognizant of this effect on her—but rather suspected that he was. For he seemed to be enjoying himself enormously, judging from his relaxed manner and the all too frequent and devastating grin, broad and white-lined, which lit his features.

Meal-taking and leisure time were even more of a challenge for Stephanie. Again Doug sought out her company; again she was ever aware of him. Unfortunately, during these times, she found herself without the diversions that teaching provided and, thus, more vulnerable to his attentions. In her favor, mercifully, were the other counselors seated at the table, ever present chaperones, ever appreciated for precisely that reason.

For, as if his mere presence weren't enough, Doug went out of his way to initiate physical contacts. Oh, indeed, they were harmless enough in and of themselves—a hand on the shoulder here, a squeeze of the fingers there, a nudging of the knee under the dinner table—each a simple gesture which never failed to electrify her by its sheer simplicity. She found that she could gradually condition herself to expecting to see his face at some point of every hour of the day; but these physical overtures, and the stirrings they invariably caused within her, appeared to resist such conditioning. In fact, far from getting used to the feel of his mischievous fingers, she had only to catch sight of the fiendish glint in his eye, or the suggestive twist of his lip, to feel the rebirth of a quiver deep within her.

He had indeed, in the first day or two, drawn the lines of combat, explicitly declaring his choice of weapon, brilliantly planning his strategy, choosing the line of attack which he knew would hit her at her weakest point.

Even when his direction became apparent, Stephanie had no intention of waving the white flag of surrender. On the contrary, she grew more determined than ever to thwart him, resorting to a few clever countermeasures of her own. When he first began his assault, she had taken the defensive, much as he might have wished, showing him that she was disturbed by the onslaught yet adopting a measure of passive acquiescence. Soon, however, bidden initially by the frustration which had swelled within her, she discovered that to take the offensive, of sorts, was healthier. Thus, she put him to work!

The strategy had its definite advantages, one of which was illustrated dramatically on the day of formal picture-taking, a day which had promised to be, for Stephanie, one of the more rigorous of the summer. There had to be formal pictures of the entire camper population, as a whole, then by individual bunks and specialty groups, plus posed pictures of the camp staff as well.

Off to an early start, she tackled the worst—the all-camper photo—first, directly after breakfast, when everyone would be gathered in one area. Rows of benches had been set up on the front lawn of the main lodge, and she set to the task of arranging the girls in long lines in order of height. True to form, Doug was at her shoulder, looking, suggesting, just being there. It was enough to distract her from the more urgent work of the moment. Suddenly inspiration hit her.

"Doug," she suggested over her shoulder, where her sixth sense told her he would be, "why don't you take the taller half of the group. Start, say, with Judy, over there"—she pointed to a medium-sized camper—"and put them in order all the way to the tallest. Maybe they'll hear you more above their chatter than they are hearing me!" Whether he was pleased at her acknowledgment of his usefulness, or merely pleased to be put to use, she cared not. It worked, both removing him from her elbow and getting the work done in half the time.

Subsequently, she set him to work carrying her equipment, lining up individual bunk shots, and then sent him back to the photo shed to return some film which had already been exposed—and which could have easily remained in her pocket, but which was just as well in her cooler darkroom. And, thus, his idle fingers were kept sufficiently busy and diverted from other, more dangerous enterprises.

From that point on, she managed to give him a chore or two whenever he appeared. Certainly aware of her tactic, he never objected to it. And there was some inherent satisfaction for Stephanie to have an assistant, even as potentially distracting a one as Doug. If nothing else, it gave her a reason for not fighting his presence; as long as she could tell herself that he was making himself useful, the annoyance wasn't quite as bad. There was, unfortunately, one sad side effect to the turn the war had taken.

Cheryl, the redheaded ceramics instructor, broached the topic one morning as they sat finishing their coffee after Doug had been called away from the table for some important discussion with Sylvie Hampson.

"Doug seems to be pretty hung up on you, Stephanie," she commented innocently as the two watched his tall, handsome frame disappear into the lounge.

A hair too quickly, Stephanie protested, "Aw, don't be silly, Cheryl!"

But the other was dead serious. "No, really! Are you two going out or something?"

Or something? "Not on your life." The jade spokes

flashed indignantly at the thought of someone suspecting it. Yet, it seemed that more than one person had. Several days after the first incident, she was approached by her old friend, Babs, head of the waterfront department.

"Say, Stephie." The buxom woman had suddenly changed subjects at midstream of a totally different conversational bent. "You and Doug are the talk of the camp!"

"Me . . . and Doug?" she feigned ignorance, becoming more uneasy with each such reference.

"He's been very attentive, hasn't he?" the other kidded her. Stephanie shrugged, knowing all the while how very attentive he'd been of late. Indeed, had circumstances been different, she would have been in seventh heaven with the same attentiveness that now rankled her. It was not long after, moreover, that the topic was raised once more.

"Tell me, Stephie," Elaine asked one early evening when the two women were in the shower house, "are things going as well between you and Doug as they look?"

Stephanie glanced at her friend in a dismay that was quickly supplanted by acute frustration. "There isn't anything going on between us," she snapped peevishly, then softened her gaze in immediate apology.

Hazel eyes grinned in amusement, undaunted by the harsh response. " 'Methinks the lady doth protest too much.' And that's not the way it looks, Stephie . . ."

Blushing under her tan, Stephanie was curious. "Exactly what do you see?"

"Hmm." The other tapped her lip with a forefinger in mock contemplation. "He seems to be with you an awful lot. Is he helping you with your classes or something?" Or something. "Then there were those pictures the other day—the arm-around-the-shoulder type of thing."

"Come on, Elaine. You know Doug does that to all the girls," she protested, becoming increasingly angry with him, even in his absence, for having put her in this embarrassing situation.

The blond ponytail swung from one shoulder to the other as Elaine shook her head vigorously. "Uh-uh. Not this summer. It seems he's reformed. Haven't you noticed the difference yourself?"

Mildly disturbed, though infinitely more perplexed by the comment, Stephanie feigned indifference. "I really haven't noticed a thing. But believe me, there's nothing at all between us!" she concluded with a forceful declaration, in turn met by an equally forceful look of skepticism on her friend's face, which Stephanie promptly ignored. She didn't forget it, however, and the next day she raised the issue accusingly with the overeager suitor himself.

It was late at night. Stephanie had spent the evening hours in total leisure, curled comfortably in a chair before the fireplace in the main lodge, a book opened, though unheeded, in her lap. The evening had grown chilly; the fire offered a warming glow, which, although most of the other counselors had long since departed, she was reluctant to relinquish for the cold walk back to the Grove. As it was common knowledge that Doug was at his weekly meeting with Sylvie and Sonny, going over the next week's schedules, Stephanie felt relatively safe from his attentions that evening. Unfortunately she lingered a bit too long; there was, indeed, a price to be paid for her self-indulgence.

With a robust slam, the outer door of the Lodge opened and closed, footsteps announcing a late arrival rather than the more customary departures at that hour. Reflexively she turned to identify the newcomer—though the sound of solid footsteps left little doubt, in this predominantly female-populated environ, to whom they belonged—her eyes following his as he skirted the room and disappeared beyond her, through the open arch of the dining room and thence into the adjoining kitchen. Suddenly aware that there was no one else left in the room, Stephanie told herself to be grateful that he hadn't stopped, though, in truth, there was a strange feeling of disappointment, which she promptly rationalized as the loss of an ideal chance to blast him for the unacceptable attention he'd been drawing to them as a twosome. Gripped by an odd uncertainty, she gazed at the flames for a few moments longer, then closed the book and sat forward to rise from her sheltered perch.

"Don't leave yet." The deeply smooth voice halted her, its command as seductive in itself as had been so many of his directives of late. Raising her head at his approach, she could not have moved had she wanted to, mesmerized as she was by the smoky gray sensuousness of his eyes. In an instant he was before her, a steaming cup in either hand, one of which he offered her. "Hot chocolate. It's very cool out; you'll need it to get you back to your cabin." His invitation was scrawled between the lines, his entire carriage and subsequent stance elaborating on it. He was, indeed, the image of self-assurance, standing tall and straight, yet casual and at ease.

Every rational instinct cried out for her to refuse his invitation, to excuse herself and quickly make her escape. Some other more powerful instinct, however, forbade it. "Thank you," she heard herself say as she reached to accept the mug, and in so doing sent the last remnants of reason cowering in defeat. "I didn't know you were so handy in the kitchen," some further voice spoke out from within her, its tone teasing in its own shy way.

One dark eyebrow arched at her unexpected good humor. "There's a lot you don't know about me. How else do you expect a bachelor to eat?"

He had taken a chair beside her, his long frame easing to its graceful curve. Now, as he propped his feet up leisurely on the raised brick of the hearth, he sipped his handiwork and gazed thoughtfully at the fire. "Actually," he began, "I do have someone to do the cleaning. You women are always better at that," he cracked, baiting her with a challenging glance her way, then continuing before she could argue, "but I do my own cooking. I rather enjoy puttering around."

"Funny, you don't strike me as the type," she retorted with her own bit of sexism surfacing despite his efforts to gloss over his own, "though I do agree with you about cleaning."

The dark head cocked, puzzled. "Is that so?"

"Uh-huh. You're right; women are better at that. The few men's places I've seen have been absolute pigsties, and when I once hired a cleaning service, two men to come in and clean, as a treat for myself, I actually had to clean up after them!" Her eyes danced above the steaming mug as she regarded him, noting with satisfaction that her putdown had been well taken, a satisfaction subtly enhanced in his next question.

"What men's places have you seen?"

There was a sudden flicker in his eye which bespoke of something which she could not understand. Nonetheless, she savored the slight upper hand she seemed to have been temporarily given. "Oh, friends, colleagues, that sort of thing."

The flicker hardened suddenly into a more defined

piece of flint, his voice similarly lowered. "I thought you said—"

"I never said that I had become a hermit," she interrupted in frustration, correctly perceiving his implication. Tilting her chin a bit higher, she glared at him. "Although you may not know it, it is possible to have friends of the opposite sex without resorting to bedroom antics. Not that it's any of your business in the first place!"

Doug's voice evened and his gaze relaxed once more. "Your jaw is clenching again, Steph. Did I hit a raw nerve?" The satanic smile that shaped his lips hit a very different nerve, though only his words alerted her to her own momentary tension. Taking a deep breath, she remained still, drinking the cocoa as she struggled to regain her earlier composure. In its breach, that tiny voice of reason once more urged her to retire from the fray; in its recovery, she looked him in the eye and defied his accusation.

"No raw nerves, other than the ones you cause. If I didn't know better, I'd suspect you of jealousy." She turned the tables with this indictment of her own which seemed, in turn, to shake him before he grinned wickedly at her. Quickly, she parried this potentially devastating twitch of the lips and barged on to give attention to one truly raw nerve that had been gnawing at her. "Which brings me to an even more important matter." She eyed him in annoyance. "People are beginning to talk."

This he found, much to Stephanie's chagrin, to be enormously amusing, an unsuppressed smile overspreading his strong features. "Really?" The voice was a smooth drawl, neither in the least surprised nor disturbed. As though to underscore his unconcern, he slid further down in his seat, stretching himself out lazily as he turned his gaze smugly toward the fire.

It would have been impossible for her not to sense his indifference on this particular matter. But then, why should he be concerned? Hadn't he created the situation? "Well, you may not care what rumors fly," she snapped, careful to keep her voice from carrying to the rooms upstairs, "but I certainly do."

"And you feel the rumors are false?"

"They are."

"Is that so . . ." It was neither a question nor an exclamation that he had made, but rather an extension of the pensive gaze he cast to the flames.

Suddenly impatient, Stephanie sat forward in her seat. "Doug, I know you think this whole thing is very funny, but I don't agree with you. And neither will Melissa, when she sets her heart on rumors and then finds it broken!"

Now she had his undivided attention. A thick swath of dark hair fell across his forehead as he turned to face her, his gaze piercing her with its determination. "It won't be."

"How can you be so sure? She's a very perceptive child. If she doesn't hear it from someone else, she's apt to see it herself, with all of your carryings on. And, if you think I have any intention of selling myself to you, you're sadly mistaken!" Unconsciously, in her frustration, her voice had begun to rise along with the color in her cheeks.

Before she could repair to the depth of her chair, Doug sat forward himself and took one of her hands into his. "Shh, love. They'll think we're having a spat," he teased softly through the maddeningly mischievous smirk on his face. How beautifully his bright white teeth contrasted with the dark tan of his cheeks, she mused helplessly, then remonstrated herself in the instant, frowning and dragging her gaze away from his.

"You're exasperating," she snorted, pulling her hand from his and shrinking back into the furthest corner of the chair. Mercifully he made no comment, but rather shifted toward the fireplace, and, taking the nearby poker, stirred the coals of the fast-shattering logs to coax a final, fast flame from the wood.

Determined to resolve the issue in some form or another, Stephanie persisted. "Please, Doug, will you cool it?"

For a moment he crouched in concentration before the fire, the silhouette of his handsome features—forehead, nose, lips, chin—a striking portrait of devastating masculinity before the red glow. The only sound in the room was the occasional crackling from the hearth's core, a ticking of the seconds of eternity.

Slowly he turned his head toward her, a fiery gleam, the devil incarnate, in his eyes. "That depends . . . on how nice you can be to me."

Stephanie's jaw dropped open. Madness, absolute madness! He would stop pursuing her if she came to him on her own! What kind of sadist was he? Or did he take her for a fool? What could she say to him? To outwardly decry his proposal would only serve to invite further trouble, yet to say nothing would imply a tacit agreement. Fortunately he saved her the decision.

"Come on." He took her hand and drew her out of her chair, scooping her empty mug up beside his and leading her toward the kitchen. "It's late. Let's go to bed." Had his voice been louder at the end, intended specifically for any listening ears, or had it merely been her imagination?

Immediately she stiffened. "You've got to be crazy."

"No, honey. Not crazy. Very sane. And very human." His eyes slid seductively over her, touching each curve in turn. "But," he sighed wistfully, "alas, very, very tired. I'll walk you to your cabin, then bid you a reluctant good night. Can you object to anything as harmless?"

His lead had taken her through the kitchen to its rear door, the empty cups having been deposited in the sink along the way. No—she had recovered slowly from his visual caress—there was nothing wrong with their walking back to the Grove together . . . if he could be trusted. But could he?

The question was put to a grave test when they emerged from the building into the cool of the night. Without benefit of either sweater or jacket, Stephanie wrapped her arms about herself and shivered reflexively, missing the warmth of the fire. In the next instant a strong arm drew her toward a different source of luxury, this one alive, warm, and moving in perfect harmony with her gait. Reason never had a chance; the heat which his body offered her was too lovely to resist. As though sensing the possibility that she might have drawn away, he crooned down against her hair, much as he might have to a skittish filly, "Atta girl." Barely audible, yet soothing, it entranced her with its low murmur, hypnotized her with its nearness. At that moment Stephanie knew indeed that she would have to trust him not to take advantage of her, since she doubted she could trust herself not to succumb, should he try.

They walked in silence—and total comfort, she was to realize much later, when reason began to function once more. With the steps of her cabin lying just beyond, they stopped, he to turn her toward him, she to be turned. A strange feeling of contentment had pervaded her being during that all too short walk, a feeling she was reluctant to relinquish. His hands took a gentle hold of her shoulders, thumbs resting tenderly against the sensitive cord of her neck. She looked up at him, mindful only of how handsome he was, how charming he could be, how badly she ached to feel those firm lips against her own.

"Sweet dreams, Steph," he whispered huskily, as those lips touched her forehead; then he turned and walked off toward his own cabin, his form etched in silver, animated yet growing smaller, until she heard his footsteps, faint but discernible, on the rise of steps, then the soft bang of the screen door behind him as he, too, became a poignant memory.

Sad to say, just as the warmth of the fire had quickly evaporated, thus did the warmth of the spell he had cast over her. With her own door now shut behind her, it seemed that there was not a drop of heat within. What had she done? She cried. He had charmed her and she had been charmed. He had cajoled her and she had been cajoled. Indeed, in theory, he had seduced her and she had willingly submitted, loving every minute of it! What had possessed her? those rational instincts urged. Was it need? Desire? Love? Yes, she admitted readily; it was all of these things. And it was something more. That feeling of wholeness which had stuck so in her mind, which plagued her consciousness relentlessly—tonight it had manifest itself in a sense of contentment. A magnificently beautiful, eminently divine sense of contentment such as she'd never known before.

But how could it be? How could such a feeling of contentment exist in the presence of this rogue, who had done so much to shatter her peace of mind, past and present? Small consolation it was that he had proven himself trustworthy for this evening alone. She wondered cryptically how long it would last.

Evidently Sylvie Hampson had do doubts whatsoever regarding his trustworthiness. Indeed, the next day she and Sonny left for several days back home in Baltimore, entrusting the directorship of the camp to none other than Doug. But if Stephanie had suspected that he would be too busy to bother with her, she was sorely mistaken. He seemed to be as adept at juggling the additional administrative duties as he was at juggling her all too vulnerable sensibilities.

"You don't seem at all fazed by the added responsibility, now that Sylvie and Sonny are gone." She confronted him at dinner that evening as he deliberately escorted her to the seat of honor on his right at the director's table.

"I'm well accustomed to administrative duties. These are minimal by comparison," he replied with a shrug of dismissal. Stephanie, however, was in no mood to be dismissed. All summer she had wondered, ofttimes against her own better judgment, about the "very responsible position" he supposedly held during the winter months. Now, emboldened by his own insistence that she sit with him and the resultant rise of a defensive indignation within her at this decidedly open claim on her affections, she yielded to the persistent curiosity.

"What do you do?" Casually she tossed him the question.

"For Sylvie?" Casually he tossed it back, the twinkle in his eye betraying his purposeful avoidance of the issue.

"You know very well I'm not talking about for Sylvie," she scolded, impatience conveyed in the set of her jaw. "What do you do all winter?" There. It was out. Very blunt and straightforward. Would he evade a direct answer, as he had always done her more indirect inquiries in the past?

"You really want to know?" Still, the twinkle in the eye.

"Yes."

"Why?"

"Why not?" She could play his game too, she congratulated herself.

"It's my life." His dark head tilted, one eyebrow lifted, and his gray orbs bore into her as though he had just stated an irrefutable fact. For a minute she sensed a specter of the unfathomable anger that had possessed him at the start of the summer; then it was gone. Fortunately, with the reassuring presence of the rest of the camp eating busily and talking noisily about them, her wits remained finely honed.

"No, no, my man," she taunted, taking pride in the almost imperceptible note of surprise which her own confident manner had been able to stir in this undauntable lord. "It was your life," she corrected, enjoying herself too much to pay full heed to the far-reaching ramifications of her words. "But, as you seem to be so intent on convincing me, things may have changed. It's a two-way street, Doug. Perhaps I'll begin to make demands on you as the father of my child. Perhaps you do owe me something. So"—she took a breath as she repeated her original question—"I'd like to know what you do all winter."

If she had hoped to set him back with her threat, she had underestimated his self-confidence. Again he answered her question with a question, and that infernal glint of humor which now played about the faint laugh lines at the corners of his eyes. "Do you want to know as the mother of my child or as my lover?"

"I am not your lover!" she snapped back testily.

His voice was husky as he leaned slightly closer to her, his eyes exploring the soft curve of her lips as he spoke. "Not yet. But you didn't answer my question."

"As Melissa's mother, of course," she retorted, angry more at her own loss of composure than at his insinuation.

With an almost arrogant movement back in his chair, he gave her the answer she'd been seeking. "During the winter, I am the president of Northern Vermont College. It's a small school, fairly experimental in educational concept. It's north of Montpelier, nestled into the mountains in a magnificent region of the state." He paused, smiling smugly at her. "What else do you want to know?" The victory was sweet as he watched Stephanie grapple wordlessly with the information he had just sprung on her. President of a college? Certainly a very responsible position. But president?

"How long have you been at the college?" she asked through her amazement, not quite able to verbalize his title.

Naturally he saw right through her. "I've been at N.V.C. since before I met you," he informed her with a smirk, "as president for the last four years."

Stephanie looked down at her plate, totally unaware of its contents. Well, she mused wryly, he certainly was a step above the tennis pro. It explained many things.

"What? No comment?" The deep drawl brought her attention back to the source of her wonder. No, she realized, she had no comment. But should she let him revel in his coup? Mustering her wits about her, she faced his penetrating gaze once more, forcing a sly smile of her own.

"Well, I am pleased to hear that you are gainfully employed. It does make Missy's future seem very secure." There was no victory in her words. Immediately, she hated herself for having spoken in such a snide and mercenary manner, thoughts which had no basis in reality. Even though Doug might well be able to offer the child things which Stephanie herself could never be able to handle financially, she knew that she would neither ask for nor accept his assistance. After all, she had come this far without him.

There was, for Stephanie, that strange void that was evident only in comparison to the fullness she felt within when she was with him. Yes, to her growing chagrin, she had to confess that she enjoyed his company—albeit forced as it was upon her—even the moments of battle which sparked so many of their encounters. It had almost become a challenge—the sparring for oneupmanship. Deep within she was beginning to suspect that her chances for winning the long-range war were slight, a nagging thread of worry, faint and distant, yet very, very real it was! But in the meanwhile, the everyday chores which consumed her time and attention conspired to keep that possibility in a distant limbo.

Over the course of the next few days Stephanie actually found herself enjoying the meals they ate together, the congenial conversational turns, the little bits here and there that she learned about Doug. He seemed to have temporarily shelved the idea of physical seduction, and, other than the constant sensuality of his gaze, the electricity in his hand as it brushed her shoulder, the mesmerizing sight of a muscle flexing as he moved an arm or a leg—all of these causing reactions within her—there was no further threat.

On the day that Sylvie and Sonny were due back, Stephanie had closeted herself in her darkroom, determined to catch up on her backlog of developing and printing. Only here did she feel safe from Doug's company, protected by one of the few locks at PineWinds, a simple device on the door to prevent any unexpected intrusion at a critical point when prints might be accidentally exposed by unwanted light and thereby ruined.

In truth, however, it was merely his physical presence that could be kept out of the room, for, increasingly, Stephanie found herself printing negatives of her daughter . . . and Doug. They were indeed magnificent, if not from the photographic standpoint then from the meeting of minds they captured, the heartfelt rapport between father and daughter. Most had been taken with a telephoto lens from a safe enough distance to preclude her detection by the subjects. Many she had blown up further, selecting a small part of the frame, perhaps only the faces or heads and shoulders, perhaps including the entire bodies. All had been executed to perfection, with an added something most photographers sought but rarely attained.

On this particular day she had made several such prints before moving on to the more urgent camp pictures. With safelights illuminating the way, she had just taken a piece of printing paper from beneath the enlarger and was about to submerge it in developer solution when she heard the outer door of the photo shed open and close.

"Stephanie?" Doug's deep, sensuous drawl was immediately recognizable.

"I'm in here, Doug," she called out, "but you can't come in!"

"Why not?" He was at the door of the darkroom area now, his voice sliding smoothly through the light-tight partition.

"Because I'm working! You'll ruin the print I've just exposed."

He was not to be deterred. "I'd like to watch." The door handle jiggled as he tested it. "Open up, Steph!" he ordered calmly.

Slipping the paper under the rippling surface of the chemical solution, she firmly repeated her refusal. "Uh-uh. You'll have to wait. I can't let the light in!"

"How long?" Was that impatience, she wondered with a pert grin.

"Oh, a couple of minutes or so," she drew him on, as she nonchalantly rocked the tray of solution, one eye on the timer and the other on the gradually forming image. Silence followed her declaration, during which she pictured him lounging expectantly against her door. Leisurely, she transferred the print to the stop bath, then the fixer.

"I'm waiting." His sing-song tone sounded through the smooth pine, a kind of good-humored impatience slight consolation for the fact that her time was quickly expiring. She said nothing, merely continued to agitate the print, turning it over and again periodically to assure even saturation of the solution. "Stephanie . . ." Now there did seem to be a warning, telling her that she could put him off no longer.

"Almost . . . almost," she yelled out one last time, then lifted the print by the tongs and dropped it into water, before switching on the overhead light and, finally, opening the door. With her hands on her slim hips and a look of exaggerated disgust on her face, she regarded the smile Doug now showed her. "Must you be so impatient?" she snapped, even as she felt any reluctance at seeing him evaporate under the power of his smile.

"Only when I want something very badly," he replied arrogantly. "And right now, I want to watch you work." The door slammed emphatically behind him, stressing the finality of his thought. The brief glance he cast her way, with its devastating gleam of the eye, reminded her that she was as caged as she'd felt on other occasions, when cornered by this towering man. Most disconcerting, though. This time she was neither frightened nor sorry that he was here.

In a motion of pure self-defense against these emotional stirrings which threatened to sidetrack her more rational instincts, she quickly returned to the enlarger head to remove the negative she'd just printed and replace it with another.

"Very nice," she heard Doug murmur from where he stood beside the basin of completed prints. Only then, in a moment of futile panic, did she remember the prints she had finished earlier, prints which would be right beneath the ones at which he was looking. Impulsively she switched off the overhead light, her only hope to divert his interest and thus prevent him from seeing these more personal pictures.

"Sorry," she murmured, "but I need relative darkness again." Without further explanation, she switched on the enlarger and began to focus the negative at the proper level of enlargement.

Suddenly the voice was deeper and closer, no farther than several inches from her ear as he leaned over to watch from behind. "No need to apologize; I like the darkness," he crooned, deliberately seductive, his breath warm against her ear as was his body so close by hers.

"Doug . . ." She protested his nearness as the battle

began within her once more. How could she concentrate with him practically cementing himself to her? How could she hold her hand steady enough to function with her nerve ends beginning to quiver?

"What is it, Stephie?" Again the deliberate drawl, touched this time with mocking innocence, curled her insides. Oh, he knew precisely what he was doing. Inhaling deeply, she searched for some makeshift argument to get him to leave. Finding none, she heard herself blurt out the truth.

"I can't concentrate with you at my shoulder," she cried out in frustration, shocked by how quickly she'd reached that point.

"Then don't concentrate," he urged softly, as he turned her around and kissed her, ever so tenderly, on her moist lips. For an instant she indulged herself, tasting his manly tang, relishing in the hardness of his lips as they gently moved over hers. Then she drew herself back.

"No, Doug. I have to get this work done," she protested, as much for her own benefit as for his.

"Can't it wait for just a minute?" he murmured against her cheek as he nibbled at her earlobe.

"Just a minute? Is that really your intention? Just a minute?" she challenged him, as she struggled to escape the erotic muskiness of his being.

"Just a minute," he assured her, standing back and eyeing her keenly.

Crossing her arms staunchly across her chest, she sighed in exasperation, knowing that her only hope was, indeed, to get him out of her domain. "All right. You'd better hurry. Your minute is ticking off."

Before she had even been able to detect the smile of victory that appeared in the yellow glow of the safelight, he took her arms, unwrapped them from each other, and put them around his own waist, drawing her, as he did so, firmly against the taut line of his body, imprisoning her in his own arms as he bent his head to kiss her again, to her dismay, without the slightest hint of hurry but rather in one long, sensuously electrifying, drugging kiss, from which he released her—when his time was up—reluctantly.

"There," he teased, his gray eyes probing hers. "Was that so bad?" So bad? she asked herself. My God, it was breathtaking, so warm and giving had it been! Yet, she couldn't tell him that, though surely he would have suspected from the subtle softening of her own lips beneath his that she was far from immune to his embrace. No, she couldn't admit that, or he might take it as a willingness to surrender totally, and that she would not do!

Parrying his question, rhetorical as it was, she forced a frown. "Okay. Your minute is up. Now, will you leave, please?" She pointed emphatically toward the door with one slightly wavering finger.

"I never said I'd leave." He corrected her smugly. "But I will stand back while you work since I seem to distract you so easily!" Stephanie glared at him, searching for an appropriately snide rejoinder, when he went on. "Could it be, my sweet, that you are vulnerable to the cravings of the flesh, just as I am?"

It was a gasp of outrage that erupted involuntarily, coinciding precisely with the moment of acknowledgment that he was correct and the moment of dismay that he should know it so surely. "Ooh, you're impossible," she growled, as she switched on the room light and faced him. "You can explain to Sylvie why these prints aren't completed." Turning on her heel, she stormed out of the darkroom, then the studio, emerging into the bright sunlight in a state of muddled infuriation.

Damn it, she swore. Leave it to Doug to ruin her good intentions, not only relating to the unfinished work but also to her badly needed composure. Why was she so very vulnerable to him? Unfortunately, the answer to that question was no mystery at all. Love did all kinds of foolish things to a person; all too vividly she had learned that lesson. And now she was about to fall into the same trap, if she weren't very careful!

The more she thought of it as she strode angrily toward her cabin, the more she realized it was her own fault, this latest encounter. She had softened to him noticeably; he must have sensed that. She had enjoyed his company of late; he must have sensed that. What more natural a conclusion was there for him to reach than that she might welcome more? It was so difficult, she fumed, so difficult to remain indifferent to him, so difficult for her not to . . . love him. But it wouldn't do, she clenched her fists determinedly; it just wouldn't do!

Anxious to expend some of the nervous energy that had been building in her, she changed into her bathing suit and headed, not for the waterfront, but for a narrow path by the water which led, after about a ten-minute walk, to the cove, a thoroughly private, delightfully small and intimate stretch of sand. She dropped her things and promptly plunged into the cool water, warming rapidly against her skin as she swam vigorously out toward the middle of the lake. This was swimming at its best, she gloried. No chlorine, no threatening waves. Instantly she conjured up a picture of the ocean, of a similar strenuous swim, of Doug's sudden appearance from the shore.

She shifted direction, half expecting to see his dark form pursuing her as she headed back toward the sand. But the way was clear, quiet, peaceful—all the things she wanted. It was only a faint twang that plucked at her heartstrings at that summary appraisal, but she determinedly ignored it in favor of the warming, healing sun that awaited her on the shore.

The exercise had indeed been invigorating, and a good deal of her tension dispersed when she finally stretched out on her back on her towel, letting the gently rhythmic lapping of the foam-edged water lull her into a brief sleep, warmed as she was by the sun's rays, protected as she was from the rest of the world by the tall wild grasses that surrounded the cove.

It could have been no longer than a few minutes that she slept, judging from the position of the sun, relatively constant in its midafternoon perch. But, as she slowly opened her eyes, she was immediately aware that something else had changed, and intuition told her exactly what that was.

"How long have you been watching me?" she asked, turning her head and lifting an arm to shade her eyes as she regarded Doug. Any annoyance at his intrusion into her private shelter was immediately swept away by his appearance. He, too, wore a swimsuit, slim fitting and none too roomy for even his lean hips. Above and below spread his long, bronzed frame, manly, roughly haired in all the right spots, similarly muscled. Oh, she had seen him thus clothed, or unclothed, as was more accurately the case, but for some reason, perhaps coming right from the sweet bliss of sleep, his devastatingly handsome physique affected her even more than usual.

"Not long—maybe five or ten minutes," he answered, forcing her to recall her original question.

"You must be very tired. Are we working you too hard?" He cast a winning smile her way as he teased; struggling to maintain an even keel, she closed her eyes to both the sun and his alarmingly endearing expression.

"I'm not complaining," she murmured dismissingly, hoping that he'd take the hint and let her lie in peace. But he had no intention of doing so.

"I saw the pictures you printed." He startled her with the change of subject. "They were remarkable."

Stephanie looked at him askance, recalling the bunk pictures she had been in the midst of printing when he had so rudely interrupted her. Skepticism intermixed with modesty in her reply. "There's nothing particularly remarkable about pictures like those; they happen to be very straightforward group shots, simply posed, all smiles."

"Those aren't the pictures I'm talking about, Steph." He caught her up short. "I saw the prints you made of Melissa and myself. You captured something very special." His eyes had taken on an almost distant expression, one which she had never seen and could not quite pinpoint.

However, she knew very well what her own feelings were regarding the photos and the depth of feeling that had gone into both the taking and the printing of them. To her dismay, a flash of heat brought a rush of color to her cheeks, and she looked away again in a desperate attempt to camouflage her much too explicit feelings.

"Where do I stand, Stephanie?" His words brought her head around with a jerk, their directness cutting through her. Blankly she regarded him, fully understanding his meaning—they seemed to flow along the same wave length, the two of them—yet totally incapable of answering him.

"You may not realize it," he went on softly, "but there is an awful lot of you in those prints." In response to her gently furrowing brow, he proceed. "Your love for Melissa must be very, very strong."

"It is," she replied without hesitation, shading her eyes as she squinted up at his back-lit features. From where she lay, the sun glinted off the natural sheen of his dark brown hair, giving it a healthy, vibrant, please-touch-me feeling that beckoned to her with a cruel temptation. Struggling to keep her attention on the conversation at hand, she elaborated. "Melissa is my whole life."

"What about your work? Don't you love that?"

"Yes. In its own way. And what about you? Do you? Do you enjoy your work?" It was a dual inspiration which spurred her into the discussion, desirous not only of learning more about him but also of diverting the attention from her own life. For a short while, he humored her.

"Sure, I enjoy it. I wouldn't do it if I didn't."

"What do you like best about it?" She studied his face, noting the straight lines of his nose and jaw, faintly moistened under the heat of the sun.

He thought for a moment before answering, his slate gaze skimming the surface of the lake. "Teaching," he concluded. "That's always been my favorite part."

"You teach? I thought that presidents were too busy with administrative work to bother with such mundane issues." Her eyes flickered, first in surprise at the revelation, then in humor at her tongue-in-cheek accusation.

In turn he smiled understandingly. "Not all of us.

Fortunately N.V.C. is small enough to permit me the time for other luxuries, such as the very mundane business of teaching." He mocked her gently. "It's the interaction with the students that I've always found most meaningful."

"What do you teach?" she asked shyly, enthralled by the newly revised image of him.

Suddenly, as though realizing that it was his own private life that was now under the microscope, he studied her suspiciously. "Psychology. But you're the expert at that; you've very nicely managed to shift the focus of our discussion, haven't you?"

Flecks of guilt tinged the color on her cheeks as she smiled innocently. "It's just that you don't talk much about yourself. It's always me doing the talking. Well, I'm curious too!" Instantly she regretted the frankness of her argument.

"What cause could you have for so much curiosity?" he taunted, pleasuring in the crimson stain which now darkened her features. For her part, there was the agonizing anticipation of the ultimate exposure, the heartstopping fear that he would pinpoint the source of her curiosity. Yet, for some unfathomable reason, he spared her that final humiliation. Instead he merely furthered her milder embarrassment. "Your face is much like your photos, Steph."

"W-what do you mean?" she stammered, realizing that the steady flow of his deep voice had already begun to do its spellbinding number on her.

"Just as your jaw is sure to clench when you are tense, or tired, or annoyed—as you were back in your darkroom with me before—your cheeks are sure to flush when I begin to hit too close to home." He paused, subtly assessing the effect of his observations. Stephanie merely looked at him, unable to tear her green gaze from his bold gray one. "Am I hitting too close to home, Steph?" he asked in a husky whisper which sent spirals of excitement twisting through her.

Well under his trance, she was unable to refute his words, unable, indeed, to speak at all. "Am I?" he repeated, so softly that his words were a mere humming caress of her whirling senses. It was only the weakest remnant of a fleeting resistance which bade her shake her head, slowly and with an utter lack of conviction that must have been evident immediately to Doug.

Allowing no hint of protest, his lips replaced the soothing beauty of his voice, warming her, teasing her, coaxing a response from her which she could no more deny than she could her love for this outrageously perplexing man. It was a soul-reaching kiss, dredging riches from the depths of her which she would have surely withheld, had she been of sound mind. But the mind had no role in this particular exploration, as she yielded to the irresistible call of passion.

"God, you're beautiful," he whispered hoarsely into her ear as he leaned over her, his strongly sinewed arms straddling her body as she lay on the golden sand. When his head lowered again, her lips parted to meet his, driven open by the wildfire which burst, as though from the explosive flares about the sun above, to course through her veins. Moving instinctively, her hands crept up his chest, then over his shoulders, shyly exploring the rippling muscles that lay just below the hard surface of his deeply browned skin.

What heaven was this? she asked herself, floating in the passion-induced delirium which he had inspired. Two people, alone, making love . . . *Making love? Oh, my God, what I am doing,* she screamed within. Even as he stretched a tanned leg over one of hers and she felt his manly hardness against her, she stiffened. Stop. He has to stop. It can't happen again. "No, Doug, please don't," she pleaded from the far-away reaches of sanity, a weak voice which aptly illustrated her own most critical position.

To her surprise, Doug didn't fight her. Rather, he made a strangely painful sound as he pulled himself up off her and sat up, several feet away and facing the water. His breathing was as labored as hers, small satisfaction that he had been as aroused; she watched timidly as he fought to even it. Only then did he look at her, his eyes devoid of the anger she had expected.

"You know my intentions, honey," he crooned, both his tone and the endearment crinkling her token resistance and touching her much against her will. "But I'll never force you. When the time is right, we'll both know it. And, believe me, that time will come!" There was a momentary flicker of hardness before his gray eyes softened once more. It was all Stephanie could do to hold her hands in check, to keep them from reaching out to him to draw him back to her. Mercifully, at that moment, he bounded up and away from her.

"Where are you going?" she asked in alarm, only much later to be alarmed that she had asked.

"I need a cold swim," he called bluntly over his shoulder, his meaning obvious as he kept his back to her and waded into the water, soon to be swallowed up in the gray-blue depths. When his head finally emerged, he was a good twenty feet from shore and steadily moving out, his powerful crawl propelled by the thrust of his own thwarted energy. Given the need for a cold shower herself, Stephanie headed for one, gathering her things together and setting off for the privacy of her cabin, as far from Doug as possible.

As her legs took her quickly through the willowy

grass, her mind took up a chant, mournful and poignant. He knows! He sees! He understands! Was she, in fact, discovered? Did he, in fact, recognize her love? Had he, in fact, understood? Would he, in fact, wait? Wait? For what? Did he really expect her to come around to his way of thinking? Did he really expect her to become his mistress, knowing that he held no further feeling for her than that of the mother of his child? Did she really expect that she'd be able to resist?

It was a chant comprised of questions, one following the other, one echoing the other, one supplanting the other in the maelstrom of emotion that seized her. It all boiled down to that final question: Would she, in the end, be able to resist that which he so deliberately offered?

seven

THE MOMENT OF DECISION WAS TO COME MUCH sooner than either of them had expected. Right on schedule, Sylvie and Sonny returned from Baltimore, and the final three weeks of the camp season were off and running, crammed to the hilt with parties, competitions, shows, special events—all to build to the climactic final banquet, held on the last night—the undisputed highlight of the summer season.

With the return of the directors, Doug eased up on Stephanie somewhat, though perhaps the growing momentum of the summer had finally begun to gain on him too.

Stephanie spent practically every evening in her darkroom, busily printing the scores of pictures which each of the campers would carry home as a cherished momento of the summer. Remembering very clearly how much she had treasured the photos from her own camp years, she stubbornly stuck to the work, intent on finishing up ahead of time and thereby being able to relax and enjoy those last few days of the season. In truth, she was pushing herself too hard.

"You look exhausted," Doug commented one evening at dinner, after he'd spent much of the meal in studied silence. "Are you feeling all right?"

Touched by his concern, though ever-cautious not to look too deeply into his pointed observations, she shrugged. "I'm feeling fine, just a little tired. There are so many pictures to be printed. I'm afraid I may have tackled a little too much this time." She picked at her food, then finally put her fork down. "I was planning to do some work tonight. Is there anything else more urgent on the schedule board?"

Doug shook his head, dark gray eyes not leaving her face for a minute. "Nothing at all. But don't you think you'd be better off to get some rest?"

A deep sigh accompanied her gently shaking head. "I really can't, not until I've done at least part of this work."

"The work will wait. You're way ahead of schedule. Come on. Ease up!"

He was right, yet she hated to lose her lead. And, she mused, what an odd experience it was to feel that someone was concerned. But then, why shouldn't he be, she scolded herself. After all, she was the mother of his child!

"So you'll leave it for tonight?" he persisted.

Auburn curls bobbed back and forth once again. "No. I'd really like to do a little. But I think I will quit early. After a while one gets bleary-eyed, anyway."

Doug eyed her skeptically. "You hide behind that camera, don't you? You escape into that darkroom of yours as though it can take the place of—"

"Excuse me, Doug. I've got a lot to do," she broke into his gradually spilling thoughts, refusing to hear more of the accusations which she knew had much more truth to them than she'd care to admit. Pushing that truth into the hidden recesses of her mind, she hastened toward the photo shed, promptly picking up where she had left off earlier that afternoon. Mercifully, the escape worked once again, if not for as long as she might have hoped.

About two hours later Doug was at the door, knocking impatiently. "Come on, Steph. That's enough for tonight," he yelled through the locked door. "Open up or I'll break in your damned door!" Had she not known better, she would have suspected he'd been drinking; yet, she did know better. No, he was merely determined, for whatever reason, that she get some rest, and she was too tired to fight him.

He actually helped her put everything away, store leftover solution, discard what was no longer usable, wash out trays, wipe down counters, and lay out wet prints on drying screens for the night.

"They really do look good!" he complimented her, as he paused to examine some of the prints. "You must be pleased. Have you ever done anything like this before?"

"Well, I've never done it at a camp," she replied, wiping her hands on a towel as she scanned the room a final time to make sure everything had been properly disposed of, "but I have done similar things for schools."

"Do you always do the work yourself? Don't you ever use a lab?" he asked, showing a return of the concern which both touched and puzzled her, as he shut off the overhead light and ushered her to the door.

"When it involves color I do. Black and white is different though. I love the darkroom work, and the results are always better if I do it myself. Labs have a way of making things muddy." The door closed behind them and they headed up the pine path toward the bunk row, walking in peaceful silence for a bit before Doug spoke.

"How about spending the day with me tomorrow?"

"The day?"

"Sure. You have a full day, just as I do." *I wonder just how that happened,* she thought suspiciously. "We can take off and do something really different. The forecast is good and I was hoping to cross over into New Hampshire and drive up Mt. Washington. There are plenty of other things to do in the same area. The Kancamagus Highway is beautiful; the Flume is right on the way. Have you ever seen it? Or the Old Man of the Mountain?"

Momentarily carried away by the memory, distant but clear, of the spots he'd mentioned, she responded with pleasure, "I haven't seen them for years! You're right—that whole area is beautiful!"

"Great! We can leave right after breakfast!" he concluded confidently.

"Whoa!" she dented his premature satisfaction. "I haven't said I'd go. I really should stay here, at least for part of the day, and make up for the work you just dragged me from." It was a feeble excuse, she knew, but she wasn't quite sure if she could parry his advances, or, even more simply, his alluring masculinity, for an entire day.

As though sensing her train of thought, his voice lowered in a seductive mockery. "Just think of the wealth of subject matter for your camera around and through the White Mountains."

In spite of herself, a smile broke through her lips. "You certainly know how to twist a girl's arm, don't you?" In the darkness she could not see his expression, though his voice betrayed a definite grin.

"Ten o'clock?"

"I don't know." She hesitated. "I was actually going to spend the afternoon retracing Route 302. Missy and I saw some terrific scenery the day we drove up; I've been meaning to go back and photograph it all summer. This may be my last chance."

As they passed by the bunk row, all quiet now with its campers long asleep, Doug mapped things out in his mind. "I tell you what," he finally suggested softly. "You come with me in the morning and we'll return via 302 later in the day. Hmm?" Once again she was cornered. There was now only one logical reason why she should not go, and that one his next words summarily disposed of. "What if I promise not to molest you?" Again there was the unseen smile, now joined by a similarly unseen twinkle, mischievous and telling.

"Is that a promise?" she asked as she eyed the dark form beside her.

"Promise."

Without further hesitation, and ignoring the faint cries of caution from within, she agreed. "It's a date then." Only after she'd accepted his too tempting proposal did she stop to wonder whether he would indeed stick to his promise, whether indeed she wanted him to. But at least it had been made, and that would be enough to satisfy the more rational elements of her own constitution for the time being.

Things did not work out quite the way either of them had expected. Stephanie was finishing her breakfast the next morning when Doug joined her, promptly digging with relish into his own scrambled eggs and bacon, as she watched in amusement.

"Are you sure you have enough there?" she mocked softly, estimating at least four eggs in the mass heaped on his plate. "Cholesterol is not the best thing for you, you know," she added.

A dark eyebrow arched high into his forehead. "Are you concerned with my health now?" He teased right back.

"Oh, no," she assured him calmly, and smiled as she ribbed him. "But you're getting to that age . . ."

In retaliation he leaned toward her and spoke deeply by her ear. "Then I guess I'll just have to help myself to a little more. I'll need a lot of energy for the demanding day ahead of me." His eyes studied her long enough to catch the passing dismay.

"You promised, Doug," she warned.

"My, my," he chided. "You seem to have a one-track mind, my sweet. I was talking of all the sight-seeing we'll be doing." It was a playful kick she delivered under the table, but any further response he might have made was forgotten as the camp secretary approached them.

"Stephanie, you have a phone call in the downstairs office. It's an Alex Gardiner."

"Alex? Now what would he be wanting?" She spoke half to herself as she got up to follow the secretary. Brow furrowed in puzzlement, she excused herself and left, unaware of the suddenly sober expression on Doug's face.

Five minutes later, when she still hadn't returned, he made his own way into the office after her. She was standing with her back to him, staring at the receiver she had just cradled.

"Who is Alex Gardiner?" he boomed, causing her to jump. Then he caught his own breath when she turned and faced him. Her cheeks were ashen, her eyes wide in horror. When she spoke, it was in a weak and tremulous whisper.

"He's . . . he's a neighbor . . . a good friend."

"What did he want?" Had she been in a normal state of mind, she would have rebelled against the possessiveness of his tone. As it was, she barely heard it.

"I asked him to keep an eye on the house while we were away . . ." She looked out the window, her mind's eye far away.

"And?"

Suddenly she looked back at him, an agonized helplessness in her eyes. "The house had been broken into—ransacked—"

Instantly his voice softened, as did the expression on his face, all thought of jealousy vanishing. "When?"

"Last night."

"Much loss?"

She lifted a shaky hand to the taut muscles of her neck. "I don't know. He didn't know. He's not that familiar with my family's things. But he said that there was an absolute mess there." A shiver passed involuntarily through her, and she shook her head in disbelief. "I've lived all my life in that house. Somehow I never expected anything like this. You know, it happens to other people, not to you. I don't really know what to do first—"

"You go get ready and we'll leave right away." It was a firm voice taking over control. "We can be there by noontime. There will be the police to see, insurance people to talk with, cleaning up to do."

She raised rounded eyes to his. "I can't drag you down there to that mess on your day off. I'll just drive down myself—"

"You'll do no such thing," he interrupted, his slate gray eyes seconding his determination. "You'll need some help. Besides, I want to get a look at this Alex fellow." The corners of his mouth curved up in an attempt at lightness. Again she was too numbed to object to the implication.

In truth her major sentiment was relief that there would be someone with her to face whatever was there—as well as whatever was not. "Are you sure?"

His answer was the strong arm that draped over her shoulders, drawing her with him to the door. "Come on. Let's get ready to go." His voice was so steady, his touch so reassuring, that Stephanie never seriously considered the alternative. And, when they did arrive in Cambridge just before noon, she was doubly grateful for that.

She was unusually quiet during the ride down, her mind skipping from room to room in her family's house, picturing each as it had been before, wondering in each case what she might find. As she directed Doug through the local streets, she grew even more worried.

"Just relax, honey." He comforted her, squeezing her cool hand for just a moment. "Everything will be all right. It's always worse in anticipation." A feeble smile was the only reward he would get this time, though, as her imagination continued to work overtime.

"Alex found the door open this morning. He said he locked up when he left though," she explained as she fumbled with her key at the lock. Finally Doug brushed aside her trembling fingers and opened the lock himself. Unfortunately her imagination had not been terribly inaccurate. As Doug quickly moved to open some windows and relieve the stifling air, she gazed around her in horror. The place had indeed been ransacked—furniture overturned, books thrown from shelves, clothes emptied from drawers, beds pulled apart.

There was a note from Alex by the phone, telling her that he'd already alerted the police and that she should call them when she arrived. Doug had already done so.

Meanwhile, becoming more and more ill as she walked from room to room, exclaiming aloud at each new bit of destruction, Stephanie began, under Doug's guidance, to list everything that was missing. All of the usual things had been taken—television, stereo, radios, photographic equipment which had been in her pantry-darkroom, bicycles.

"My mother's good sterling," she shrieked as she ran into the dining room to the armoire in which that treasure had been stored. Gone—every last piece. "Oh, God," she moaned softly as she dropped into a nearby chair. Doug was at her side in an instant and it was to him that she turned defeated green eyes. "The set was a wedding gift from my father to her. She adored it, polished it every week, used it whenever she had the slightest excuse . . ." Her voice trailed off in a misery eased only by the warm fingers on her shoulder.

Compounding her grief, similar fates had befallen her father's coin collection, her mother's jewelry and several priceless etchings that had been in the family for years. Each torturous discovery brought a new wave of agony, the sorrow of memories and momentos now besmirched, tainted, and, in the last cases, gone.

The police came and went, declaring that they would do everything possible to track down the culprits, though claiming that these cases were nearly impossible to crack. The insurance company was duly contacted and informed, requesting detailed lists of what had been taken—further prolonging the ordeal for Stephanie, whose stomach had already cramped over on itself, stricken as it was by each new realization of another long-cherished item gone. Alex stopped in briefly at midafternoon, to talk with them both, and express his regrets; then he returned to work.

By late afternoon Stephanie was fading steadily, exhausted to begin with by the schedule she'd set for herself during the past days at camp, crushed emotionally by the reality of the havoc surrounding her, overwhelmed by the hours of work which lay ahead, cleaning and putting things back in order. Closed up as it had been all summer, the house was still hot and stuffy, the now opened windows introducing nothing but humidity. She was unaware, as she worked, of the perspiration dampening her hair and her clothes, of the darkness beneath her eyes now contrasting sharply with the pallor of her cheeks. Doug, however, was ever mindful of her state.

"Let's go get something to eat, Steph," he suggested, righting the last of the furniture which had been overturned. "You need a break from this"—he cast his own wary eye about the wreck of the living room—"and we could both use some nourishment, not to mention a little air-conditioning." A sturdy forearm lifted to wipe the line of sweat from his own brow.

"But I have to get this all cleaned up," she objected, "or we'll never get back tonight."

"I've already called Sylvie and told her not to expect us back until tomorrow." Stephanie looked up in surprise. "She agrees with me that you should get everything in order here before we return. And," he went on quickly, his gray gaze steadying her even as it studied her unsteadiness, "she will explain to Melissa if your absence is noticed—covering up appropriately, of course. There's no need for the child to know about this"—his eye once more scanned the room—"at this point."

Even if she had had the strength, Stephanie couldn't argue with his reasoning. It would take a while to straighten up, but it was better to get it all done now than have to think of coming home to it at a later point, or, worse, having Missy see it.

They ate at a small Greek restaurant just on the outskirts of Harvard Square, an old favorite of hers, its consistently good food a needed reminder to her that some things, indeed, did remain the same. As Doug had promised, she did feel better, somehow more able to put the entire ordeal into perspective. After all, she told herself, these were only things. . . .

The gloom set in once more, however, when they returned and began the arduous task of putting things back where they belonged. Doug took the downstairs, dealing primarily with the hundreds of scattered volumes which had been part of the family's diverse library. Stephanie took the upstairs—the clothing and more personal items. Unfortunately she progressed much more slowly, trying to cope, as she folded jerseys, sweaters, nightwear, and underclothes, with the idea that some unknown person had been through these most personal things. Finally, in a fit of disgust, she crammed her arms with piles of the most personal of the items, charged downstairs, and threw the lot into the washing machine.

"Everything feels so—filthy!" she explained, when she confronted Doug's questioning gaze in the living room. "It's like . . . like rape!"

His long frame uncoiled as he stood and walked to the door where Stephanie was standing. His voice was quiet and calm, urging her inside. "Come and sit down while I finish these last few things. Then we'll tackle the upstairs together." He was so understanding, so considerate as he gently eased her into a chair, that she willingly complied. What would she ever have done without him today, she asked herself, and a forboding feeling of emptiness coursed through her as she watched him work. Within a few minutes' time, he stood, brushed his hands off on his jeans, and beckoned for her to come. Obediently she climbed the steps, by his side all the way, his arm lightly at her waist. She was only marginally aware of the climb, so intent was she on drinking in the comfort which his very nearness delivered.

At the top of the stairs he hesitated, debating something in his own mind before moving past her to the doorway of Melissa's room. "Let's start here," he stated quietly, as he entered and surveyed the room. In this instance it was Stephanie who did most of the work, poignantly inspired by the random exploratory wanderings of a father about his daughter's room. Periodically she would offer some anecdote referring to a particular stuffed animal, doll, or vacation momento resting on the white dresser; occasionally he would ask a question, wondering about this photograph or that, examining in detail the shelves as each book in the child's growing collection was replaced from the haphazard heap on the floor. It was a touching scene, one which she knew she would remember always. Never before had she seen Doug's face looking so utterly vulnerable.

"You never had any other children?" she asked impulsively, puzzled by the look of near-wonderment on his face. For a minute it was as though she had spoken a foreign language, the look he cast her was so uncomprehending. "When you were married . . ." she explained softly, timidly.

Slowly he shook his head. "No. That was one of our great differences. I wanted children; she didn't." Suddenly the pieces fit together, enabling Stephanie to understand how much Melissa meant to him. It was a distinct feeling of guilt that engulfed her for the moment, guilt at having, for seven years, deprived this man of the child he'd always wanted. Once again she found herself wondering what the future held. And it was no longer a far-off date, the future. There were little less than three weeks left of camp; what would Doug want of Melissa at its conclusion?

Lost in her own quandary once more, a quandary far removed from the immediate mess of the ransacked house, she closed the last of the drawers on Melissa's clothes, stood, and wandered off into the hall, leaving Doug behind to his own private sentimental journey.

What was she going to do? She loved Doug, she loved Melissa. Also she knew that Doug loved his daughter, an infinitely greater complication than those she'd already considered. But Doug didn't love her, and she couldn't trust him. Oh, how she wanted to trust him! He had been so wonderful today—she would have been lost without him. But his dealings with women were another matter entirely.

Aimless wandering brought Stephanie to the door of her own room, whose contents were relatively organized and repaired, save the load of clothes now in the dryer. There it was—the bed—her big brass bed—in which she'd lain and dreamed of Doug so many times. Now he was here, back in her life, in this very house which was hers. What was she going to do?

It was—being here in this familiar room with this man, the only one she would ever love, so near—the last straw. Dark as an ominous thundercloud overhead, the psychological burdens of the day, indeed those of the entire summer, gathered into one potent mass within her, crashing suddenly in a blur of tears which could be withheld no longer. Weighted down by the crushing emotional turmoil, her weak legs gave way and she slowly slid down the oak frame of the door, reduced to a knotted heap on the floor. Desperate for comfort, she hugged her stomach, pressing back against the doorframe as silent sobs racked her, tears streaming down her cheeks unchecked in the wake of her whirling emotions.

Control. She had thought she had everything in control. But she'd lost it all! There was Melissa and their self-sufficient life-style, now threatened by a father's concern. There was the house, ever her haven, now plundered and violated. There was . . . there was . . . Doug, whom she loved with all her heart. Oh, how painfully she loved him! How much she wanted him! How much she needed him!

All the illusions she'd painted of a life of contentment, just her daughter and herself, had been shaken, then erased during this summer of discovery. How empty life seemed, how meaningless the future promised to be without Doug to make things whole! But he didn't love her. He desired her, and perhaps he respected her work and her accomplishments as a mother, but he didn't love her. And, in the absence of love, she would never be able to hold him when the physical desire was sated and he no longer craved her offerings.

Could she take the chance? Could she knowingly introduce her daughter to the delights of a life which was destined only for eventual pain and separation? Could she expose Melissa—and herself—to a repeat of the agony which she had suffered eight years ago?

Cheeks wet with multiple rivulets, she raised her tear-filled eyes to the bed in which she'd slept, alone, for so many years, in which she'd lain, heavy and swollen in those last months of pregnancy carrying Doug's ever-growing child within her womb, in which she'd dreamed of his holding her, kissing her, carrying her with him to heights which had been reached but once before. In a futile effort to erase the image, she buried her face against her knees, which she brought up to clutch defensively, her disheveled tresses falling on either side, the rebirth of quiet sobs shaking her.

Suddenly from amid the turbulence came a steadying force, a hand, strong yet gentle, curving around her neck in a tender massage. "Don't do this to yourself, honey," the velvet-edged voice crooned by her ear, the hand relaxing as she raised her face to his. He was squatting before her, his features close and understanding, his hand now steadying her shoulder.

Driven by some incomprehensible need to explain something—anything—to him as well as to herself, she heard the broken whisper which was her own voice, striving to express her thoughts. "I feel so . . . h-helpless, Doug," she began, the tears cascading in fresh torrents, "s-so weak, so c-confused." But that was all; there were no more words, no more thoughts to be shared as her fluid green eyes pleaded for the comfort she needed.

Doug's large hands framed her face, tilting it to his as his lips commenced a slow and thorough clean-up of the tears which had streaked her cheeks, tears which his mere touch now succeeded in stemming.

His tongue tasted the salt from her eyes, her cheeks, her jaw, kissing away her distress even as it threatened to ignite a new current of torment, sweet torment, within her.

He paused, looking down at her with eyes of the softest gray flannel. "Let me help you, Steph. Please let me." *Please*—he had never used that word to her before, though it wouldn't have made any difference had he said nothing at all. It was his body which spoke the volumes, offering her a kind of help which she was too weak to refuse.

In an instinct for survival, she threw her arms about his neck, clinging to him as to a lifeline thrown to rescue her from stormy seas. "Do help me," she cried in unsteady breath, his arms encircling in response to her plea, crushing her against him as he absorbed the pain which had so devastated her.

She heard his murmur, soft and low, whispered yet thunderous to her consciousness. "I will, honey. Trust me." In that instant, she did trust him. She had to trust him. She needed him more than she'd ever needed anyone. She loved him, though she couldn't tell him that. But she could show him, and she would, she vowed, as very slowly the trickle of strength seeped from his throbbing pulse to hers, coursing through her bloodstream with electrifying speed. All else fell away, save the present. Yes, she would trust him. She loved him too much not to!

How long he held her there, crouched as they both were on the threshold of her bedroom, it mattered not to either. In his embrace she felt the aching of the day past, the many days past, begin to fade into oblivion. It was as though he sensed her need for the transition, as though he needed it too. There was no rush, never any rush, when the two of them were together.

When her breathing eventually forsook the irregular spasmodic legacy of weeping, he took her breath away with a long, leisurely kiss that devoured any lingering shreds of memory, even as it sealed his pledge. Drawing his lips from hers, he cast his own pleading glance into her hazy eyes. "Trust me?" It was as though he had read her mind and somehow knew that this, indeed, was her biggest fear. Yet reality had already receded; she nodded silently in answer to his plea.

His hands slid beneath her and he lifted her into his arms, her own tightening around his neck as he carried her the short distance to the big brass bed. When he laid her down, it was as though she were a china doll, for the near timidity he showed. Then he kissed her again, his lips gently coaxing her into a response which had merely been held in abeyance, waiting for expression.

Moving of their own volition, her arms traced the path of his, from wrist to shoulder, as his steady fingers unfastened, one after the other, the buttons of her blouse, pushing aside the cotton fabric at last and sinking down to let his lips roam exploratively over her creamy smooth skin. She clutched at the firmness of his shoulders as he eased her up a bit, only enough to slide the blouse off her arms and release the catch of her bra, discarding it along with the blouse onto the floor.

Her eyes never left his as they caressed her in the soft light of the lamp on the bedstand. The rosy peaks of her breasts thrust upward beneath his very gaze. When his hands joined in the erotically sweet torture, she moaned in ecstasy, awed by the delight surging through her.

But it wasn't enough to be touched, without touching

as well. For so much of love was giving, and she wanted, more than anything, to pleasure him too. Her hands skimmed his rough cheeks on their way down to the buttons of his shirt, releasing each, then allowing him to remove the covering completely. It was even greater delight, this touching of his body, this raking of her hands across his tufted chest and over the smoother skin of his shoulders to cascade langorously down his arms and then bridge the gap to his rib cage. His own moan of pleasure was heady music, making her even more aware of the tightening knot within her, begging for release.

Suddenly and simultaneously their patience seemed to exhaust itself, overcome by an urgency which eight long years had conspired to build. They were in each others' arms, clinging, gasping for breath, struggling to get closer than the remaining clothes would permit. Without a word, he released her to unbuckle his belt and remove his pants. In mirrored movements, she followed, lying back finally on the smooth sheets of the bed and reaching her arms out toward him. It was an invitation which he had long awaited, and he accepted it readily, lowering his warm, lean body next to hers and tracing her unfettered curves from shoulder to thigh and back, exciting them both beyond belief. If the tension within her, the coiled knot of desire tormented her, his state was no different.

With a frenzied movement, he took her, smothering her cry with his kiss much as he had done on another occasion. But rather than the streak of pain which had prompted the last, this one was the outcry of ecstasy, a sense of fulfillment born by the act of total possession. Arching toward him, she timed her body to his thrusts, feeling herself soar upward, higher and higher, to the apex on which he stood, sharing the explosive passion of the summit, before plummeting together slowly back to earth.

A long arm molded her to his side in firm embrace as her breathing steadied and she lay, quivering yet satisfied, against him. Their bodies were bathed in a mingled wetness, silky beneath fingers that reassuringly stroked, as spent fragments of desire refused to be dispersed.

When he came to her again, it was with a luxuriant slowness, so very different from the frantic coupling which they'd demanded earlier. This time each held back, savoring the touching, the kissing, the exploring, heightening the peak of desire which catapulted them, finally, through miles and miles of ecstasy-driven oblivion, to a state of mutual elation.

Bodies intertwined, they lay, at last, on the verge of a drugged sleep amid the warm night air. There was a brief moment of loss when Doug turned away from her to switch off the light and thrust them into shadowed darkness, a moment of separation which foreboded the future, but which was quickly forgotten upon his return. Once again Stephanie melted against him, reveling in the closeness, the sense of wholeness and fulfillment which she craved.

Her impulse was to thank him—to thank him for being there to help her through the ordeal, to thank him for the ultimate joy she had just experienced, to thank him for the blissful lethargy she now felt, to thank him for all the good things—and to tell him of her love. "Doug, I—" she began in a whisper, only to be silenced by a gentle finger at her lips.

"Shh. No words tonight. Tomorrow. We'll talk then." An involuntary shudder ran through her as she recalled the similar phrase he had spoken years ago.

Then the arm about her tightened, drawing her head against his chest and repelling those fears, as the steady beating of his heart beneath her ear lulled her into a deep, dreamless sleep.

eight

THE WARM CITY AIR HUNG HEAVY ABOUT THEM during the night, the faint whir of a passing car or the distant whine of an emergency siren the only sounds to compete with the slow and steady breathing of the lovers, spent and satisfied, now asleep. But once, Stephanie ventured from the delightful abyss of exhaustion to surface to a momentary disorientation, instantly remedied by the strong arm that curved about her slender waist, drawing her back against the contours of his firm, male body.

When the pale blue light of dawn filtered through the open window, she stirred, turning instinctively to regard the figure beside her. Never before had she spent the night with a man, never before had she felt so complete as a woman. For the first time, she noticed the length of his thick, brown lashes, lying richly around the curve of his resting lids. Anew she admired each feature, at ease as she had never seen them. She suppressed the impulse to trace each outline, to skim each contour, to sample each texture, reluctant to disturb his own deep sleep.

Quietly she slid off the bed and walked to the window, gazing out at the rising skyline, clothed as she was from the outside world only by the gown of bounteous greenery, the lush summer growth of the maples outside the window. The morning was pure and still and peaceful. As its calmness pervaded her soul, so a clarity of the evening past came to her . . . and a vision of the future.

She could not live without Doug. Whether he loved her or not, she knew that she needed and wanted him. The heights they had shared the night before, to which she had risen from the very depths of pain and confusion, had been incomparably beautiful. They had, indeed, shared once more that very special ecstasy which had existed before. She could neither deny its existence nor her own need for it. In those hours of exquisite lovemaking, her decision had been made for her. She could not bear the thought of returning to a life devoid of this man. And, whether he wanted her as mistress, lover, wife, or mother of his child, she knew she had no choice but to agree.

Still as an alabaster statue before the window, she heard the rustle of movement on the sheet, then an echoing whisper. "Steph?" he called to her. Slowly she turned to see the outstretched arm of the man she loved, beckoning her back to him. Yes, her decision had been made. With no uncertainty she covered the short distance between them until his arms once more encircled her, holding her a willing prisoner against the sinewed strength of him.

"I won't let this night end," he vowed huskily against her forehead, then began to kiss and caress her until she felt the familiar warming tingle creeping from her loins to envelop her in a cocoon of exhilaration. In the moments of play, he taught her with mastered ease how to fondle and tease, how to touch and knead and thereby heighten her own near explosive yearnings and his. Long moments later, when the molten flame of passion had been fanned and quenched once more, she drifted off amid the wonderment of a delight which ever-deepened itself and its delirious fulfillment.

Golden shafts of sunlight poured through the window when her red-tinged lashes finally fluttered, then raised to present the new day to love-dazed eyes. The silence about, most noticeably the absence of the regular breathing by her ear, told her of Doug's earlier awakening. Tucking her curls behind her ears, she saw that he had not only arisen but that he had dressed as well, the clothes discarded during the evening's passion now gone. Walking into the adjoining bathroom, she smiled, eyeing the moisture on the shower door and the towel neatly draped over the rack. He certainly had a way of making himself at home, she acknowledged admiringly, as she made to follow his example.

Turning, she happened to catch sight of herself in the mirror, the remnants of steam on its edges framing an image of radiance which she barely recognized. Her cheeks had a pink flush amid the tan, her lips a sensuous fullness, her eyes a dewdropped opalescence. Shyly, her gaze fell lower, to the rounded swell of breasts alive and electrified hours before under Doug's expert caress, their rosy points thrusting upward in remembrance. Blushing, she quickly reached for a clean towel, threw it over the shower door, then stepped inside.

Twenty minutes later, when she descended the stairs, she heard Doug at work in her darkroom, doing his best to replace the things which had been dislocated. He looked fresh, hair still glistening from his recent shower, unbelievably handsome even in yesterday's wrinkled clothes, with yesterday's growth of beard lightly stubbling his face.

It was that endearing smile that greeted her as he looked up. "Good morning, sleepyhead!"

"Hi!" Her voice surprised her, soft and shy. "You should have woken me!"

His attention returned to the technical books he was stacking. "You needed the sleep. I only hope I'm putting things in the right place."

Stephanie's green-tinted gaze touched the shelves of the darkroom, jolting her in reminder of their main business. "It's better than I'd be able to do. I still feel sick when I look around." Hesitantly she looked toward the kitchen. "I'm afraid I can't offer you much food, since the refrigerator's empty, but," she brightened, "I can scrounge up some instant coffee."

When she returned to him, Doug's face had taken on a preoccupied expression and now, as he looked up, it was as though he had been wrenched from some distant quandary. Too quickly, he smiled. "That'll be fine. We can get something to eat when we've finished up here."

Puzzled by his abrupt change of mood, Stephanie pondered its cause as she boiled water and then added it to the coffee crystals she had measured into each of two mugs, finally handing one to Doug, who had come to lean against the kitchen sink to watch her.

"We have to talk, Steph," he burst right out, gesturing for her to sit at the small round table in a corner of the room. Silently she complied, her eyes never leaving his, curiously studying the hardness of the gray slate.

"Why did you run away?" His question, like a bolt

out of the blue, seized her confidence in a choking hold. The look of bewilderment which gripped her fine features prompted him to elaborate. "Eight years ago. On that last day. Why did you leave without waiting for me?"

Like broken scenes under a flashing strobe, Stephanie's mind flickered back to that torturous day and the many others that had succeeded it. As much as she wanted to tell him the whole truth, she found herself unable, for some strange reason, to verbalize the one thing that still terrified her, she realized, in spite of her newly made decision. Refusing to meet his penetrating gaze, she stared down at the reflection of her own face in her coffee cup. "I was confused, unsure of things." Her voice echoed those sentiments, causing him to confront her further.

"And now? Are you still confused?"

She faltered but a moment longer, knowing that, although there were still many things that concerned her about a future with him, on the issue of being with him she had no doubts. "No."

"I want you, Steph. I told you that once before." Not a muscle in his body moved, so intent was he on what he said. "But I want an answer now. Are you going to run away again?" Now she did meet his line of vision, shocked to see its calculating attention to her every breath. Why she felt like a recalcitrant child being scolded, she could not say. Neither could she muster any anger to defend herself against his mildly accusatory tone.

"No," she replied softly but firmly. Facing him as she was, something seemed suddenly wrong. He was too dispassionate, too businesslike for the kind of proposal he seemed poised to make. She began to perceive of herself as the kept woman, the mistress, rather than the lover she had been last night. It was a fine distinction, but one which made a world of difference to her. What had changed since last night, or, more correctly, since this morning, when they had made love so breathlessly in the pale dawn light? Where was the softness in his eyes, the openness of that gray slate that had welcomed her then? Had it only been her imagination? No. Suddenly she realized that she had repeated the same error she had made on that night in the woods by the campfire. Then, as last night, she had interpreted his feelings as something more than in fact they were. He wanted her, he desired her, he craved her—but that was all!

Only when her heart grew noticeably heavier did Stephanie realize what she had hoped. It had been, and would always be her greatest hope that he should love her. That was her own dearest desire. Yet, even as she knew what he was offering her—and its limitations—she knew that she would hold to her decision. "No, I won't run away this time," she repeated solemnly.

Dark brown eyebrows jutted down over his eyes, a look of skepticism marring his usual fluidity. "What? No fighting?"

"No." Firm and calm. She had come to terms with herself.

"Why not?" It was a challenge, carried on the reed of a velvet-toned piper.

"I'm tired of fighting it, Doug," she answered simply, resting both elbows on the table as though to illustrate that emotional fatigue of which she spoke. "And, besides," she added, a measure of self-protection thrown in, "I have Melissa to consider."

Contrary to all of her expectations, he frowned at the mention of the child, stirring anew her own perplexities concerning the man. His pitch was cold-edged steel when he finally spoke. "I see."

Did he? she asked herself. If so, what did he see? And why did she feel guilty? With puzzled eyes she watched him put his empty coffee cup into the sink, then walk to the window where, hands jammed into the rear pockets of his jeans, he stood and stared. Taken off the hook of those piercing gray eyes, Stephanie felt a resurgence of the emotion which would always bind her to him. In a gesture of frustration, she jumped up and strode to the sink, rinsing both cups before propping them upsidedown on the drainboard. So confused was she by his manner that his next words floored her.

"I want you to marry me."

In all truth, it had entered her mind, along the twisting road of her emotional wanderings, that he might want, for Melissa's sake, this very course of action. It was something which, eight years earlier, she might have rejoiced to hear. Now, however, it was a proposition being made for all the wrong reasons. It was as a business proposition, a prospective merger between two entities. Yes, she wanted it for her own, totally nonbusinesslike reasons. Yes, she would accept, even knowing of his limited feelings toward her. She would enter into this marriage with open eyes and a clear head.

"Yes. I will marry you." As he turned his head toward her, their gazes locked, bound together momentarily by something unfathomable to each. Then, it snapped, bringing reality back with a force. If she had expected him to glory in his victory, she was in inexplicable error.

"Then it's settled," he murmured nearly inaudibly, as he approached her. Placing a light hand on either shoulder, he feather-touched her cheek with his warm lips, much as an older brother might have done, then moved away toward the door. "Let's finish with the upstairs. Everything down here seems pretty much in order. We ought to be on the road by early afternoon." And he was gone, his footsteps reverberating through the worn runners leading up the oak steps to the second floor, in infinitely calmer tempo than Stephanie's racing pulse.

Then, it was settled. They would be married. As she mulled the idea over in her mind, she moved in a trance, retrieving her clean clothing from the dryer, folding each piece neatly, then following her fiancé (how strangely inappropriate the term sounded to her ears) upstairs. But she loved him! Of that she had no doubt. She knew that she loved him! Why, then, did she have that gnawing in the pit of her stomach?

The last bits of straightening were completed within the hour, the windows closed and locked up once again, the front door bolted as they headed out for something to eat, then retraced yesterday's route back to PineWinds. It was a quiet ride, much as the one down had been, though so much had passed in the interim that it seemed an infinitely more awkward silence now.

For her part, Stephanie had no regrets about their fiery passion-sharing the evening before. It had been a fiery, passionate, and—yes—sharing experience. She had no remorse whatsoever for having given of herself to the man she loved, or for having welcomed the ecstasies he offered. A nagging worry at the back of her mind was the distinct possibility that another seed could have been planted in that euphoric lovemaking adventure, that indeed she could be pregnant again. It had happened before; perhaps their union would once more bear fruit. Much to her own amazement, this thought held neither worry nor fear. After all, she had seen how Doug loved Melissa; surely he would love another child as well. And they were to be married; what more could she ask?

Aye, that was, indeed, the rub! There was more she could ask—his love. For suddenly it became clear. Only with his love would come the total commitment that would finally convince her of his devotion and his fidelity to her and her alone. When and if that day ever came when he swore his love for her, then would she know the full meaning of joy.

As they drove now over the highway, there was intermittent conversation, always of an impersonal nature and increasingly spaced from the one previous. By the time they slowed onto the narrower country road, silence hung as a thorny barrier between them. The few furtive glances she sent his way returned the image of a man at war within himself, eyes dark and brooding, nostrils tensed, jaw clenching involuntarily. The look was such an antithesis of that of a man having made a supposedly pleasing decision that Stephanie could not help but question him.

"Is anything wrong?" She broke the stillness, her seat-belted form as stiffly posed as his.

It was as though he'd forgotten her presence, for the startled look he gave her. Quickly regaining his composure, he spoke in the same coolly indifferent tone that had chilled her so at the start of the summer. "Of course not. Should there be?" As the recipient of a sadly forced smile, Stephanie would have rather gone without it.

Shaking her head in outward denial and inward confusion, she turned her face to the window, watching the passing scenery without seeing anything.

What was eating at him? she wondered. He was so different—so totally different from the warmer, more friendly and attentive person he had been since that pivotal day when he had learned the truth about Melissa. Perhaps he was just tired. Perhaps he was worrying about the work he'd neglected back at camp. Perhaps he had some other, entirely independent problem on his mind. Or, she cringed, perhaps he was already having second thoughts. Perhaps she had not pleased him as a lover after all. Perhaps he would have rather she'd refused his proposal. Perhaps . . . perhaps . . . perhaps. Sensing the build-up of a deep-seated tension, she gathered the power of resolve within her to exorcise these haunting possibilities, forcing them out of mind and, thus, out of her present reality.

The exorcism failed miserably. During the next two weeks each of the disturbing what-ifs returned again and again, with burgeoning fury, as Doug's mood went from bad to worse, spreading not only within the sphere of their private interaction but extending as well into his work. When Sylvie approached her, finally, to ask subtly whether there was something bothering him, Stephanie could merely blush and stammer feebly, adding an I-don't-know to the list of complaints eroding her own self-confidence.

They saw each other less frequently. Indeed, it was as though, despite their marriage agreement, they had returned to that earlier summer pattern of laissez-faire. For Stephanie, considering the love which gnawed at her from the inside out, it was sheer hell, the only saving grace being his evident decision not to announce their marriage plans publicly. Of that humiliation, considering the sourness of his disposition, she was mercifully spared. For, when they were together, they were more estranged than affianced, their conversation formal and stilted. Nor was there any warmth of a physical nature, though the rapid approach of the end of the camp season left them little opportunity for such.

Stephanie was swamped with work, doing little or no photographing, now, but rather moving doggedly toward the completion of the girls' pictures. It was little consolation, as she found herself wilting noticeably under the pressure, that Doug suffered similarly. She had of necessity noted the drawn look gripping his features, the tension pervading his mood, the exhaustion which seemed to have completely overtaken him.

As if things hadn't been bad enough before, they took a turn for the worse on the night of Melissa's play, at the start of the final week of camp. Although the child's role was a small one, she had nonetheless been ecstatic at her inclusion as a member of the cast, and, as always, her excitement was contagious, particularly where her mother was concerned. As it was to be the evening's entertainment, Stephanie had gone directly from dinner to the photo shed to finish up some work before the curtain was due to rise. Leaving ample time, she headed up the pine path to the hall where the performance was to be held. It was at a point not far from her destination that she was confronted by Doug, barreling double-stride down the path toward her.

"Where the hell have you been?" he thundered angrily, pulling up but inches from her, hands struck boldly on his hips, his dark features menacing in the fast-waning daylight. This was the last thing she had expected, only anticipating eagerly Melissa's thespian debut.

Her voice held that very note of surprise when she answered. "I've been touching up several prints in my darkroom. What's the matter?"

"Aren't you aware that your daughter is going to be in this play and that you should be there, or is your work too important for that?"

"That's unfair, Doug!" she protested, refusing to be cowed by his fierce visage. "I have plenty of time to get there. For Pete's sake, the play doesn't begin for another ten minutes, and Missy specifically told me there was nothing I could do for her backstage."

"And how am I to know where you are? Did it ever occur to you that as Melissa's parents we should be going to the play together?"

"No, it didn't occur to me, to tell you the truth," she snapped back with growing frustration. "Maybe I've gotten in such a habit of being a single parent that I can't think of things like that. Maybe," she spat out before she could restrain herself, "I thought you wouldn't *want* to go to the play with me. I seem to have become a sudden thorn in your side." Her gasp was one of dismay that she had blurted out this last, most honest sentiment. Yet, it had been there, on the sidelines of her thoughts, for too many days now.

So preoccupied had she been with what she said, that Stephanie did not catch the note of hurt that had tinted her last words. Doug, however, had. Softening noticeably, he took her elbow gently. "Let's go. Missy will be heartbroken if you miss it." There was no further word, no apology, no explanation, neither affirmation nor rejection of the premise she had put forth. And, in light of the event which was to start momentarily, she did not pursue the matter. She did, however, note the warmth, the pride on Doug's face when his daughter recited her part, a warmth which vanished immediately when he caught Stephanie looking his way. If she had had doubts before, he now made it obvious. She was, indeed, a thorn in his side. And, reluctantly, she began to have second thoughts about the decision that had been made on a warm, loving, memorable night seemingly an eon away.

With each passing day the camp season edged closer and closer to its final climax, the banquet. Excitement was rampant among the campers, all of whom seemed ecstatic with the book of photographs they'd received, all of whom were intent on having every camper and counselor autograph it. Not only was Stephanie thrilled at her success in completing the job with several days to spare, she was relieved as well to have the greatest pressure of her work eased. There was no immediate rush for Sylvie's prints, and it had already been agreed that she would finish them up at home within several weeks of the camp's close.

For the first time, Stephanie did have time to relax, yet this was somehow the most formidable assignment of the summer. Just as the tempo of camp had approached a near-fever pitch, so her relationship with Doug seemed to be doing—though in a negative, rather than positive, respect. Following Melissa's play, he had been brusque and standoffish. He appeared to have caught none of the excitement which had seized the rest of the camp, or, if he had, he shared none with her.

Each day her torment increased, until she sensed that they were headed for a confrontation which would determine things one way or the other. Mercifully she had no inkling beforehand of the situation which was to ignite the explosion.

It was on the final morning of camp, when the work

of packing trunks and duffel bags occupied the rest of the camp, that she decided to grab at her last opportunity to drive through some of the nearby towns to do the personal photographing which had so tempted her earlier. With her own packing completed, she took her camera and several extra rolls of film, and set out quietly. She knew that this was the only way she would be able to escape Doug's angry presence, which followed her everywhere at camp, if only in her imagination, and which had already reduced her to a jingling mass of raw nerves.

The diversion worked well. Several hours later, when she pulled up in the parking lot behind the garage, she felt both pleased with the frames she'd exposed and refreshed from the out-of-camp sojourn. Hauling her gear behind her out of the car, her head snapped up at the sound of her name, called with some urgency in his thick Maine twang by George, the mechanic.

"Sylvie's lookin' fo-aya," he yelled from the rear door of the garage. "Says it is impo-a-tant."

Waving in appreciation of the message, Stephanie set off at a brisk pace for the main lodge, wondering absently what the matter of immediate concern could be.

"Stephie, thank goodness you're back!" the white-haired woman exclaimed when Stephanie bounded up the stairs of the balcony. "There's been an accident. Melissa tripped over an open trunk and hurt her foot. Doug suspects it may be broken." Stephanie's face went ashen, her heart stopped beating in fear for her child's condition, yet the first words out of her mouth surprised her.

"Doug?"

Sylvie explained, as her warm hand extended in a

comforting gesture to Stephanie's suddenly cold one. "He's taken her to the hospital to have it X-rayed." Whether it was the director's total acceptance of Doug's role, or the sympathetic expression which graced her weathered features, Stephanie realized that, how ever she had discovered it, Sylvie was now fully aware of the father-daughter relationship. "They've gone down to Portland."

"All the way to Portland? But that's nearly an hour away!"

"Doug knows a doctor, an excellent orthopedic man, who will be waiting to meet them. Actually"—she checked her watch quickly—"they should be arriving there in just a few minutes. Doug was quite concerned." Whether the last was a word of comfort or warning, Stephanie did not linger to discover. Armed with the name of the hospital, its address, directions for reaching it, and the name of this eminent orthopedist, she departed at once.

Driving steadily southward, she was acutely aware of the worry that tensed her every limb. Yet, the worry was not as bad as it might have been in the past; for she knew that the child was in as capable and loving hands as hers would have been. It was a new experience, she realized, to share the burden of parenthood.

The emergency room was quiet at this lazy summer's noontime. Stephanie had no sooner sought to make inquiries at the information desk, when a firm hand took her elbow from behind. "She's being X-rayed now. You might as well have a seat and wait. They'll tell us when she gets back."

Whirling around, her own gaze of concern met a dark and impenetrable mask. "Doug! How is she?"

"I don't know. That's why they're taking X-rays," he replied coolly.

"W-what do they think?"

"Broken foot."

She winced in sympathetic pain. "Was she very uncomfortable?"

Doug's tone softened subtly, perhaps from the thought of his brave little daughter, perhaps from the obvious worry on her mother's face, perhaps from a combination of both.

"She's a good little sport." A meager smile shadowed his lips, telling of his own anxiety. "Yes, it hurt her quite a bit. But she was more frightened than anything."

Stephanie sat in the chair he'd offered and now gazed at the floor, recalling the many bruised knees, splinters, cuts, and scratches her daughter had suffered as a matter of growing up. Never before, though, had it been anything as serious as this.

"How did it happen?" she asked timidly, raising her jade eyes toward Doug, who had leaned back in his chair and with one hand was massaging his forehead in a gesture of fatigue. Without looking at her, he answered.

"It was a simple accident. Trunks were open all over the floor. She was trying to jump over one to get to hers and she fell."

"Why didn't you wait for me to get back?" The words were out before she had even realized that the thought had been racing about the back of her mind during the entire ride down.

Finally finding an outlet for his own frustration, Doug lashed out at her in a deep growl. "We didn't know where the hell you were! Or, for that matter, when you were planning to return. Do you always just pick up and take off like that?"

She was as taken aback by his anger as by her own

urgent need to explain. "I—I just went to take some pictures. I couldn't have been gone for more than two hours," she told him timidly.

"That was two hours too long," he barked, his gray eyes hard, cold, and boring into her. "It would have been easier had you been five hundred miles away and we could have at least gotten you on the telephone. This kind of injury should be taken care of quickly. If the bone has to be set, it is best done as soon as possible."

Stung by his putdown and increasingly worried about her daughter, Stephanie shot out of her chair and moved to the other side of the waiting room. As much as she resented his intrusion in the issue of her personal behavior, she sensed that he was right. She should have left some word of her whereabouts. Why hadn't she?

"Doug?" It was a strange male voice she heard as she turned to see the object of the call quickly cross the room to its source, a middle-aged man, bespectacled, with thinning blond hair, and dressed in the white coat that immediately identified him. In response to Doug's movement, Stephanie joined the two, who, after proper introductions were made, led her to her daughter, sitting forlornly atop a white table in the casting room. The child brightened at the sight of the adults, particularly her mother, who immediately hugged her, albeit gingerly and with due caution.

"How does it feel, sweetie?"

"Oh, okay, I guess. It kind of hurts though." Melissa turned beseeching gray circles toward her. "I'm not going to have to miss the banquet tonight, am I?" What should have been a triumphant note on the unqualified success of the summer for the child now became a tremulous plea. Simultaneously mother and daughter turned to the orthopedist. His answer was not long in coming.

"I think she may be able to go . . . under certain conditions. Melissa, you have two little bones which are broken—a simple break—right about here"—he pointed to a spot just below her toes on the small bare foot—"so I'm going to put a cast on. If you're not too uncomfortable and you be sure to prop the foot up high on something, there's no reason why you can't go. It may take you a little while to learn to maneuver with crutches, but I think Doug, here, can help you a little with that."

Thus, while Stephanie and Doug looked on with a mutual helplessness, a thick plaster cast was applied, from knee to toe, warm, white, and weighty, on the youngster's slim leg.

"I'd like to take one last picture of it now, just to assure that the bone is well aligned," the doctor informed them as he wheeled Melissa off, and the waiting resumed. Grounded by heavy silence, a current of tension staticked through the air.

"Look, Stephanie." Doug finally broke the stillness, his face a closed mask of steel confronting her. "I know you're not terribly pleased that I'm here, or, for that matter, that I exerted my own authority to have Melissa treated by my friend, but I have only done what I believe to be best for my child."

"She's mine too, Doug, or are the last seven years suddenly worth nothing?" Again she was shocked at the vengeful pitch of her own words, puzzled as much by it as by Doug's entire manner toward her. Had he tired of her so quickly after but one night of pleasure? Or did he simply despise her so very much?

Thunderous sparks grated against gray flint. "You'd better make up your mind, Steph. You can't have it both ways. Either you trust my instincts and accept me as the rightful father of your child or you stay the hell away!" Her gasp of disbelief was met by a fast-receding expanse of back, as Doug returned to the less explosive atmosphere of the waiting room.

What did he want? her senses screamed. Was he saying that he didn't want to marry her? Was he saying that he would live without Melissa after all? Or—and her stomach lurched at the sudden thought—was he telling her to leave Melissa with him and desert them both. Was that at the crux of his earlier accusation?

She was given little time to ponder these heart-rending possibilities when her daughter was wheeled back to her, fitted to crutches—pathetically small—instructed on their use in the presence of both adults, and finally settled on the passenger's seat of Stephanie's car, her foot propped appropriately high on the seat beside her. Doug followed them in his car, instructing Stephanie to wait until he arrived at camp before attempting to remove the child from the car.

As much by way of escape as anything else, Stephanie poured all of her attention into her concern for Melissa, who seemed to be but minimally disturbed by the accident, now that she knew she would not have to miss the grand finale of the summer. Doug trailed them all the way, his presence and eversteady pace behind her giving Stephanie a headache. When he pulled up behind them in the parking lot, he immediately got out of his car, took Melissa in his strong arms, carrying her, as though she weighed little more than a bird, up to the main lodge.

"Don't you think she should try using the crutches?" Stephanie cast him a skeptical glance as she tried to keep pace with his long stride, noting the eagerness with which Melissa clung to his neck—like mother, like daughter, she mused wryly—and the firmness with which he held her.

"On a gravel road?" he snorted back disdainfully. "She'll have plenty of time to learn. Let's prop her up in the lounge now and she'll be able to watch the preparations." He was right, she saw in hindsight, marveling at how little Melissa questioned his having taken over the reins. Suddenly a fearsome thought seized her.

At the first opportunity out of the child's earshot, she cornered him. "Did you say anything to Melissa about us?" she asked, suspicion eroding her bare semblance of composure. "She seems totally acclimated to your presence in all this."

The square jaw grew even more rigid. "*She* happens to trust me," he seethed, accusation coating his words, before he stalked off angrily away from her. His words, his tone, his accusation, his manner all conspired to multiply her torment as the afternoon progressed. Convinced that Missy was well attended, waited on eagerly as she was by several of her bunkmates and a counselor, not to mention all those others passing through the lounge who stopped invariably to greet the child, Stephanie completed Melissa's packing, which the unfortunate accident had interrupted.

What would she and Melissa be doing in a week's time? Where would they be in a month's time? What, indeed, did the future hold? Could she marry Doug? It had seemed so possible back in Cambridge; but things had changed since then. Or, rather than changing, had they merely become more prominent, all the drawbacks of their relationship? They had barely exchanged a warm word since. What basis was that for marriage?

Haunted by these seemingly insurmountable uncertainties, she stopped in at the photo shed for a final time, double checking to make sure that everything had been well-packed for storage, wondering when and by whom this equipment would be used next. In further attempt to fill the hours before the touted banquet, she wandered about the waterfront, the boathouse, and the Arts Center, chatting with friends she found at each.

But inevitably her quandary reasserted itself as soon as she was alone. What was she to do? As she reviewed the day's happenings, she realized that she had, indeed, come to depend on Doug, that even had she been around at the time of Melissa's fall she would have immediately sent for him. She did trust him, she knew, as she had known for quite some time now, as the father of her child. But as her husband? That was another matter. Had he not once already demonstrated to her his flair for infidelity? In that case, she had been the instrument in the deed. In another case, in what role would she find herself?

How she managed to sit through the banquet, Stephanie would never know. The only face she saw was Doug's, right up there beside the director's. The only speech she heard was Doug's, dealing with good sportsmanship and emphasizing how much he'd seen of it this summer. The only satisfaction she received was the glow on his dark features when the campers gave their own tribute to him, well-deserved and heartfelt by campers and counselors alike.

It was a bittersweet finale for a bittersweet camp season. At its end, Stephanie accompanied Doug as he carried Melissa to her bunk, and only when the child had been tucked safely into bed, did she leave. It was with undisguised surprise that she found Doug waiting for her on a nearby tree stump, rising to meet her as she carefully descended the dark steps.

"Is she all right?"

"Uh-huh."

"Does Beth know to keep checking to make sure the pillows are under her leg?"

"Yes."

"Are you going to the staff party?" His voice was cool and even, much as it had been toward her—angry moments excluded—since the episode in Cambridge.

Stephanie put her head down. Loving him as she did, the obvious scorn he felt for her was more than she could bear. Blindly she began the short trek to the Grove. "No. I'm really not in a particularly festive mood." She hadn't given much thought to the party, so embroiled had she been in her own dilemma. And, given the bleakness of her present outlook, she would have never made it at the celebration.

"Good." The added element which entered his tone chilled her.

Puzzled, she stopped and faced him. "Why do you say that?"

"Because I'm tired and would like a good night's sleep."

"And what does that have to do with me? You don't need me to put you to bed." An odd thought flickered in the back of her mind; disturbed, she resumed her pace, with Doug falling into a matching one.

"Tonight I do." The tone was deep, throaty, and hard as rock.

Nervously she stepped up the pace. "What are you saying, Doug?" she asked, eyes now straight ahead on the cabin, her sanctuary, which had finally come into view.

"You know damn well what I'm saying! And don't act the outraged virgin—because you're not."

"You must be crazy," she muttered under her breath, pain tearing into her heart at his implication. At some point his hand had encircled the flesh of her upper arm and now tightened as he directed her toward his cabin, rather than hers. His retort was no less acid.

"That's the most profound thing you've said to me in a long time. I am crazy, but, so help me, there's nothing that can change matters." Still puzzled, confused, and growing steadily more frightened, she tried to pull away.

"Let me go, Doug. I have no intention—"

"I don't give a damn what intentions you may or may not have. Right now, I only know what I want," he growled angrily. "I've been wanting it since that last time, only I've curbed my appetite, as they say. But I'm too hungry to deny myself any longer." They had reached the stairs to his cabin, and he all but dragged her forcibly up and through the door.

A sick, nauseous feeling seized her stomach, and she grabbed at it convulsively. "Don't do it, Doug. It's . . . disgusting!" She meant exactly that, though it had been a purely emotional reflex speaking.

He had not bothered to light the lamp, and in the darkness he towered above her as a menacing form. "Disgusting? Is that what you think now? That didn't seem to be your reaction last time, if I recall correctly," he taunted before bellowing, "And just why is it so disgusting?" The force of his mien quaked through her.

She wasn't ready for this, she told herself, as she began to back away. There was only confusion, hurt, anger, and, yes, love, to render the others even more devastating. "Just forget it," she whispered haltingly.

"No. I can't forget it. Not before. Not now. What is so disgusting?" His hands clamped down on her shoulders to effectively prevent her flight.

Stephanie fought the churnings within her, certain that she would faint if he didn't release her. "Not now. I don't feel well. Please, just let me go. We can talk tomorrow."

"That's what we were going to do last time," he screamed, "but you turned and ran before we had a chance. Why should I trust you this time?"

She shook her head in disbelief. How did she suddenly become the villain? "Oh, God," she begged in a mere whisper, her dazed eyes imploring her captor to free her, "don't do this to me!"

"I'll do whatever I want with you," he snarled harshly, shaking her violently in proof of his point. Whether the darkness was within or without, Stephanie no longer knew. She was amazed that she even heard his next words, so muddled were her very senses. "Now, tell me what's so disgusting about my wanting to make love to the woman I—the woman I'm going to marry?"

Her only defense was anger. Where it originated, she knew not. Neither did she know from where it derived its strength. It shocked her as much as it did him, her final infuriated outburst. "It's disgusting when it's only physical! It's disgusting when it's filled with anger! It's disgusting when there is no love—"

nine

THERE. SHE HAD FINALLY SAID THE WORD. CERtainly not in the context in which she would have liked. But she fully believed in what she had said. As physically attracted as she was to Doug, his absolute loathing of her poisoned any joy she might have felt at the union. What had happened to make him hate her so, particularly in these last two weeks? It was an unfathomable issue for her, and one with which her distraught being could simply not cope!

All of a sudden, she realized that she was free, that the hands which had held her prisoner had dropped from her shoulders. It seemed that her words had jolted him as well. Now he stood, hands dangling limply at his sides, staring blankly at her. What a travesty it was, this scene of pain and suffering! What a travesty of a love which could have and should have been so very beautiful!

Whirling around with a spurt born of sheer panic, Stephanie ran to the door, finding herself moments later sprawled in tears on her own bed. Time lost all meaning as uncontrollable sobs racked her tension-filled body, finally subsiding and giving way to an utter desolation she had not known since she had cried herself to sleep in her home in Cambridge, following the cataclysmic awakening on that morning eight years ago. Now, however, sleep eluded her, as she tossed and turned on the wings of anguish, wondering what she had done, what she had not done to render such a potentially loving, charming, caring man an unfeeling monster. And worse, what was she going to do now?

Of only one thing she was certain: She could never marry Doug. Never, knowing how strong his feelings of hatred were toward her. Never, knowing how steadfast, despite all, was her love for him. Never, knowing how positively masochistic would be the outcome of such a merger.

As the night wore painfully on, the ache in her heart grew until the nausea returned with a vengeance. By dawn, she had lost the contents of her stomach, grateful only that she had been able to eat so little at the banquet the evening before. Exhaustion mercifully granted her an hour or two of sleep, albeit fitful, but by seven thirty she was up and whipping around her cabin, packing the last of her things with an energy produced from raw nerves. The irony of her action, unfortunately, did not escape her; hadn't she unpacked these same things in a very similar state of nervous combustion but eight weeks before, on that very first day of camp? How long ago that seemed now. So very, very long ago!

Peeking out her screen door to see that Doug was nowhere about—also, much as she had done that first day, she recalled with a shudder—she hastened to Missy's cabin. To her chagrin, Doug had beaten her there and now sat, waiting, on the front steps.

"They're just getting dressed," he explained, greeting her jade orbs with a look of exhaustion. Groomed immaculately as always, the fatigue etched around his eyes and mouth suggested that he had gotten as little sleep as she. Without a word she made to pass him and go in to assist her daughter. Long, strong fingers seized her wrist as she passed, firmly yet gently, and totally devoid of the anger which had characterized his touch last night. "Look, Stephanie. We have to talk this out. I've got to spend most of the morning getting the right groups on the right buses. How about if we meet this afternoon? No fighting. No touching. Just talking." It had to be done. She knew it as did he. Not trusting her voice, she merely nodded before disappearing into the cabin.

It was a truly agonizing morning. Stephanie stayed with Melissa throughout, their own plans calling for them to leave for Cambridge later in the afternoon, stopping for dinner along the way. There were tearful partings from many friends, fond farewells to others. For Stephanie every minute brought her closer to one other farewell, the one she would of necessity be bidding to Doug later. Oh, yes, she knew that he would expect to see his daughter from time to time, but those details would be worked out later. Tonight she would be returning to Cambridge, to the life which she had so carefully designed for herself.

Lunch was a quiet affair, with only a handful of campers remaining, and those staff members still present in a state of numbed anticlimax. Doug ate with Stephanie and Melissa, chatting with his daughter as his intense stare probed Stephanie's very soul. What he saw, if indeed his eyes of steel were able to penetrate the layers of pent-up anxiety which slowly and torturously consumed her, she had no way of knowing, as she fought to keep her own eyes on the chicken sandwich which had been barely sampled, then rejected on her plate. When they had eaten as much as any of them would or could, Doug scooped Melissa up into his arms, grabbing her crutches in the process, glancing at his watch likewise.

"Missy and I are going for a walk. We'll be back soon. I still have packing to do." His deeply intoned words had been aimed at no one at all, yet Stephanie honed in on them. What did they mean? she asked herself. Was she to wait here at the main lodge for him? But this was no place for the type of discussion theirs was destined to be.

In an effort to waste time—for, had she her way, she and Melissa would be loading their own car already—she wandered around the grounds, trying to recall all the good things that she had experienced this summer. Yet, it was hopeless; her frustration only mounted as she found that the only memories that held any meaning for her were those that involved Doug—sitting with him on the soft grass, sunning with him on the warm sand, swimming with him in the cool, invigorating water. There was so much that had been good. What had happened?

Slowly, she headed back toward the Grove. He would be packing now. Undoubtedly he would have found a suitable diversion for Melissa such that they could be alone. And what better opportunity was there, she asked herself, a tightness growing steadily in her throat at the thought, for her to tell him her final decision?

The imprint of fresh tire tracks on the dirt road leading to the Grove brought her head up from its downcast pose. As her eyes fell on the red Volvo station wagon backed up to Cabin A, a corner of her stomach cramped in involuntary reminder of a similar scene eight years ago. Then the car had been blue, and an older model. Perhaps he had borrowed this car to carry all of his gear in one trip, she reasoned. Taking a deep breath and mustering every ounce of courage which her strangely shaky body held, she mounted the steps and boldly entered the cabin.

Eight years evaporated in that heart-stopping instant as Stephanie found herself face-to-face with a blond-haired woman she had seen only once before in her life. The figure was as slim and elegantly clad as it had been then, though time had matured the face, and the hair was now much shorter in a stylish bob that whirled silkily as the woman's head came up to meet Stephanie's paralyzed gaze. Trembling hands gripping the doorknob for support as Stephanie stood, staring incredulously, at the spectral image.

"Stephanie?" The voice was soft and tentative, the face holding none of the arrogance which memory had imagined. Yet Stephanie knew the face. How could she ever forget it? What was this woman doing here? He was divorced, supposedly. "You are Stephanie, aren't you?" the woman prodded gently, dropping the clothes she held into the open suitcase as she sidestepped the bed and approached the mute arrival. As Stephanie's brow furrowed in bewilderment, the other's mirrored it. "I—I'm sorry," the blond-haired woman finally stammered, "I must have made a mistake. Were you looking for Doug?"

The mention of his name sent the blood flowing through her veins once more. "Yes. Er . . . I *am* Stephanie," she murmured belatedly. "And you are Diana."

Surprise totally altered the contours of the other's face. "That's right," she bubbled, with a genuinely warm grin. "You have a very good memory!" *How could I ever, ever forget,* Stephanie shrieked inwardly! Yet, incomprehensibly, the other seemed thoroughly pleased to see her. "Doug has told me a lot about you. He's usually so very secretive about things, but I guess this time he had to share his news with someone." What was going on? This couldn't be, could it, Stephanie cried! Mercifully, Diana appeared satisfied to carry the conversation on her own shoulders, as she chattered on enthusiastically. "I'm so glad he found you again this summer. You know, he was really distraught when he lost you the last time!"

The look of disbelief on Stephanie's face finally drew the other up short. "Is something wrong?" Diana asked. "You look deathly pale. Are you feeling all right?"

Suddenly aware of her rudeness, Stephanie managed to speak. "I'm sorry," she began hesitantly. "It's just, well, I didn't expect to find you here . . ."

Diana quickly picked up the ball, smiling warmly as though relieved to understand the dilemma. "Didn't Doug tell you we'd be here?"

"We?" Was there more, she winced?

"Sure. Joel and Mother are with Doug, I believe." Her eyes took on a conspiratorial sparkle. "They're hatching some special scheme with Melissa right now!"

Melissa? Joel? Mother? What in the devil was this all about? Here she had trounced into Doug's cabin to tell him that she wanted no more part of him and she seemed to have fallen into some bizarre family gathering. It was, ironically, Diana who came to the rescue.

"Doug didn't tell you anything, did he?" Her tone was deep, in an accusatory way. Slowly she shook her head. "You know, I love him dearly, but I'm afraid that brother of mine has a lot to learn!"

Stephanie scrunched up her nose and frowned. "Brother?" It was a whisper, barely audible, more mouthed than spoken.

"He really didn't tell you anything about us, did he?" Diana said apologetically, now totally serious. The dumbstruck expression which greeted her gaze was ample response. Swearing under her breath, she grabbed Stephanie's hand, pulled her farther into the cabin and sat down next to her on the edge of the bed, carelessly pushing aside suitcases to make room.

"I'm sorry! You must be totally confused! Let me explain. I'm Doug's sister. I always come to help him pack at the end of the summer. Mind you, not that he really needs my help." She smiled a warmly affectionate glow. "But I guess I like to indulge him after not seeing him all season! He calls every week or so, but we still miss him terribly. He is, after all, the only brother I have!"

Stephanie listened in a benumbed state. Brother? "And who is Joel?" she heard herself ask.

"My husband. We've been married for three years now." The friendly eyes studied Stephanie's still-ashen visage. "Are you sure you're feeling okay, Stephanie?"

Stephanie, bewildered, focused on the floor during this last explanation, and now lifted her eyes to meet the concern of Melissa's aunt. "I had no idea," she murmured, still groping blindly with the concepts. His sister? This stunning blonde was his sister? "It just didn't occur to me that you were brother and sister." A choked breath cut into her as she realized the awesome proportion of her error. Her voice was a bare whisper, faint and tortured. "I've made such a mistake, Diana, such a terrible mistake!" As though to hide from herself, she covered her face with her hands, shaking her auburn-tinted head back and forth, muttering over and over the same words, ". . . a terrible mistake . . ."

In a futile attempt at comfort, Diana put a gentle arm around Stephanie's shoulder. "It can't be all that bad."

"Oh, it is. It is!" Beseeching eyes lifted toward those which were now filled with puzzlement. "Thank you, Diana. You've cleared up something for me, but I have to be alone for a while," Stephanie gasped falteringly as she stood and, finding the door handle through rapidly misting eyes, ran out.

It was a flight motivated by pure anguish, sheer misery, utter heartache. Tears fogging her vision, she ran blindly through the woods, unaware of the encroaching growth which threatened, within several more years, to obliterate the path entirely. It was an inexplicable instinct that propelled her on, drawing her to the very spot which she had assiduously avoided all summer. Struggling over the occasional fallen log, she flew along the path with the perseverance of a homing pigeon, her mind a random conglomeration of kaleidoscopic memories as her feet kept her moving ever onward, deeper into the woods.

It was just the same, she saw when she arrived, breathless and heart torn, at the clearing, as intimate a campfire as one could ask, as private a spot as one might wish, and, for Stephanie, as emotionally charged a haven as she would ever find. It was here, eight years ago, that she had committed herself to Douglas Weston, in what she now realized was to be an everlasting pledge of a love which refused to die.

Knees collapsing beneath her, she sank down onto the cushion of pine needles. A terrible mistake—she had made a most terrible mistake. And she had lived with it, unwittingly, for eight long years. Like an idiot she had jumped to the conclusion that Diana Weston had been Doug's wife, that he had been married but had neglected to tell her, that he had been blatantly unfaithful to his wife and thereby shown himself to be unworthy of her own trust. And, all along, there had been no marriage, no wife, no infidelity. What would have happened had she known the truth then? What would their lives have been like? She had felt so sure, on that beautiful night in this beautiful spot eight years ago, that Doug had loved her.

But it was too late! Tears streamed down her cheeks at that frank realization. No wonder he had been so angry with her! No wonder he had felt himself the injured party! No wonder he hated her so! Yes, he hated her, and he had every reason to do so. A hollow feeling filled her, plunging her into a bleak pit of emptiness. It had been a terrible, terrible mistake, and she was going to have to live with its consequences for the rest of her life!

"Stephanie? Stephanie?" Her head flew up in alarm, tapered fingertips reflexively brushing away the moistness from her cheeks. "Stephanie?" It was unmistakably Doug's voice coming nearer with each call. How could she face him having learned what she had about herself and her own unforgivable ignorance. She searched frantically about for a route of escape but saw none. Sitting crosslegged on the pine needles, she pulled her knees up to her and buried her face in their makeshift shelter.

"Stephanie!" He emerged into the clearing, the crunching underfoot halting suddenly as he regarded her huddled form. "Here you are, thank God! What in the hell did you run off like that for?" he bellowed angrily. "You did it to me once before, and you were planning to do it again, weren't you?" Her breath came in short, uneven gasps as he thundered above her, yet she had no defense at all. "What's this about a terrible mistake? Diana said you kept repeating it. What in the hell do you mean by that?" He paused for a breath amid his tirade, but still she remained silent. "Stephanie," he growled in warning, "I asked you a question. What is this terrible mistake you've made?"

As tears welled again, her shoulders shook under quiet sobs, each new spasm cutting deeper and deeper into her. Words choked in her throat. She had no idea where to begin, what to say, how to apologize.

Suddenly his voice was no more than inches from her and noticeably softer. It could have been her imagination, that feather-stroke along the back of her head. "Please don't cry, Steph. It hurts me too much." There was a pain in his voice as he crouched down before her. "Once and for all we have to talk this all out. We have all the time in the world now. Melissa is with her grandmother, and my brother-in-law is entertaining them both while Diana finishes the packing." He took a deep breath, infused with several uneven gasps of his own. "You and I have to reach some understanding, one way or the other."

Stephanie found his steady, pacifying tone to be effective and contagious, her own sobs abating, the flow of tears stopping. "Now," he began quietly, "what's this about a terrible mistake?"

The silence seemed eternal before she could gain the courage to lift her face to his. Pale and tear-streaked as it was, the sorrow which she felt was written over it, capitalized in the misery-laden eyes, the trembling lips, the hollows beneath her cheekbones, the despair that pervaded all.

"I've been a fool. I thought—" she paused, unsure that she had the strength to reveal the depth of her blunder to this man whom she worshiped.

"Go on," he prompted gently. "You thought . . ."

"I thought—" She stopped again, unable to face him in this moment of her humiliation. Shifting away from his gaze, she stood and moved several feet away, leaving her back to him, her face protected from his penetrating examination. "I thought that Diana was your wife," she finally blurted out softly, cringing anew at the magnitude of her error. Standing as she was with her back to Doug, she could not see that he had risen also and now stood, arms crossed over his broad chest, a puzzled light in his gray eyes.

"What's so terrible about that?" He surprised her with his response, her head rising in disbelief as she sought the threads of reason in the intertwining evergreen boughs before her eyes. "She straightened you out, didn't she? Then there's no harm done." How could he brush it off so easily, unless . . . unless he'd not fully comprehended the extent of her folly.

Suddenly anxious only to enlighten him and thereby secure her freedom, she turned and faced him, head on, her green eyes sparkling clearly through the few lingering tears. "No, Doug. You don't understand," she began, slowly mustering strength as the words began to flow. "Eight years ago, when I went to see you that last morning, she was there, in your cabin, packing your things." The frown which gradually appeared, drawing the corners of his firm mouth down somberly at the corners, was sign enough that he had, himself, returned in thought to that day. "When she introduced herself as Diana Weston, I stupidly assumed that she was your wife. I don't know why," she went on quickly, thinking aloud now, "but I jumped to that conclusion and ran. I thought you had used me to be unfaithful to her. I thought you'd intended to tell me about her that morning. I thought . . . I don't know what I thought." She hesitated, looking defensively down at her own sandaled foot, now poking self-consciously amid the pine needles. What use was it? she asked herself. He was right. It was about time they had it all out; she could not live a deception any longer.

"I loved you, Doug! You have no idea how much!" she murmured breathily, eyes still glued to the dark forest floor. "And when I thought you were married, I knew it was hopeless. What had been so beautiful to me was suddenly marred. I was hurt and confused and heartbroken. That's why I never read your letters. I couldn't bear the thought of loving you the way I did and not being able to have you." Her trembling hand sought her forehead in a gesture of incredulousness, at what had happened then as well as what was happening now. "No wonder you hate me. I can't blame you for that. . . ." Her voice trailed off, as a pair of tasseled brown loafers entered the range of view by her feet.

"How could I ever hate you, Steph?" His voice was low and sweet and soulful. "I've never wanted any other woman as I've wanted you . . . to be with, to talk with, to share with, to do with—all of those things which our lovemaking, magnificent as it was, could only complement." While Stephanie was still groping with the meaning of his words and their tone of truth and sincerity, a firm hand cupped her chin and drew her face up to meet his. What she saw in those open, gray eyes was echoed in his next words. "Stephanie Wright, I love you. I love you as I have for the last eight years."

Her ears could not believe what they heard, her mind could not assimilate it, yet her eyes saw it and her heart felt it. In the instant of discovery, she was in his embrace, her arms clinging to his strong neck as she cried uncontrollably, tears falling against the warmth of his throat.

"Shh, honey. Don't cry. It hurts me to see you cry," he murmured against her hair, his breath a warm whisper to her ears.

"Just t-tell me that y-you love me again," she sobbed, her knuckles white from the fierceness of her hold.

"I love you, my sweet. I love you. I'll tell you again and again, every night and every day, as long as we're together." His vow was sealed with a kiss, punctuated by the last of her sobs, lingering a moment longer before slipping into oblivion.

"Oh, Doug," she finally murmured through the delirium of happiness which had unconditionally conquered all of those other emotions in the psychological battle. "I never thought I'd hear you say those words. I was sure you despised me!"

A deep chuckle greeted her. "Oh, I tried. Don't think I didn't! I was as hurt and confused as you on that day you disappeared. I thought we had really created something special." Another chuckle followed, this one lighter and more mischievous, as he hugged her even closer to his long, muscular frame. "I guess we did just that—we have living proof." His eyes darkened in a moment of sorrow. "I only wish I'd known. Then we might have cleared all this up so much sooner!"

"I'm sorry," she whispered, releasing one hand to stroke the frown lines from beneath the swathe of dark hair on his forehead. "I'm so very sorry. We've all missed so much!"

"Don't I know it," he agreed huskily, as his lips claimed hers briefly before he held his dark head back once more to study her. "I didn't know what to do when I saw you here this summer. It was as though you'd deliberately come back to torture me. I tried to ignore you, to hate you, to annoy you myself, but I only succeeded in loving you more! When I learned that you had a child, you can't imagine my jealousy, the hurt that it wasn't by me." He smiled warmly. "Then, when I discovered that she was, I knew that I could never be without the two of you again. I tried to convince myself that my feelings toward you were solely as the mother of my child, but it didn't work. When we spent that day together in Ogunquit, I saw that I would adore you all the same, had you never had a child. It was just you and I then, just you and I in Cambridge, and I loved you to distraction."

"But you became so cool to me after that," she interrupted, "so indifferent, even angry."

The gleam of love was brilliant as he looked down at her upturned features. "I was shattered to think that you had agreed to marry me only because of Melissa. You said—"

"I know. I was hurt and worried," she broke in again, determined as never before to tell him everything. "I knew I had to marry you. I loved you too much not to. But I was defensive, and I didn't want you to know how I felt. In my own warped mind," she remonstrated herself wryly, "I had been badly hurt once. I swore it would never happen again. You can imagine how I felt when I saw history repeating itself!"

"Oh, God, how I love you." Doug's deep growl was enchanting music to her ears.

"And I, you," she whispered, opening her lips for a kiss which was to ignite a series of fireworks at her every nerve end. Snaking her hands through the thick brown hair above the nape of his neck, she held his head closer against her, reluctant to let the kiss end.

When at last they surfaced for a gasping breath, he gazed lovingly at her starry features.

"I want you to know something, Stephanie," he began soberly, the urgency of his expression conveying his need for her to know. "I think you are absolutely beautiful. When I make love to you, I feel complete. You excite me and satisfy me in unimaginable ways. Yet"—he stroked the side of her cheek with a long finger—"if there were no such thing as physical attraction and lovemaking, I would still adore you. Your beauty is inside—your personality, your determination, your resourcefulness, your warmth. I will always love you."

It was this verbal caress that put Stephanie on an emotional high she had never known existed. And she knew that there was only one acceptable way of sealing their vow of love; her insides quivered at its thought, the knot in her belly cried out for release. Only a total oneness would satisfy her now.

"Let's make love, Doug," she whispered by his ear, the flush inspired by her forwardness only adding to her glow.

"Mmm, I thought you'd never ask," he growled thickly against her lips in the instant before he covered them in a drugging kiss, an opiate to drive away all hurts of the past, leaving only bliss and ecstasy ahead.

It was a long time before either spoke again, other than the whispered words of love and desire which heightened their passion-winged flight. The late afternoon sun filtered its deep yellow gleam through the dense pine fronds, throwing a myriad of shadowed patterns on the naked skin which was a tangle of arms and legs, fronts and backs, shoulder, hips, and torsos.

Stephanie exhaled a long sigh of utter contentment.

"I love you, Douglas," she repeated, never tiring of the words.

A long brown forefinger traced the line of skin from the hollow of her throat to the cleavage between her love-swelled breasts, circling them in gloried possession as she gasped ecstatically. "If you say that once more, we'll never get back to camp."

"I'm not sure I want to. This place, this little clearing is so very special, even though there was no campfire this time."

Impulsively she drew her fingers from the top of his muscled shoulders down to his rib cage. In retaliation, he kissed her, hard and demanding, leaving no doubt as to the effect of her wayward touch. It was the low croon at her ear which thrilled her most.

"We don't need one. The fire's right in here," he touched her low on the abdomen, then took her hand to guide it to the matching spot on his own manly body. "It's been burning here, all this time, all these years. The ember—that sweet ember which has refused to die—it just keeps glowing and glowing, sometimes bursting into flame, other times fading to a faint red memory, but ever alive. I love you, Stephanie."

Mischievously she growled back in echo of his own words, "If you say that once more, we'll never get back to camp."

It was a gasp of reluctant disengagement that slipped from his lips as he lithely bounded up from their pine bed, pulling her up with him and pressing her nude body to his one last time. "I'll never let you go, Steph. You know that, don't you?"

She smiled, a soft and loving curve gracing her lips. "I'll never forgive you if you do!" She raised her face and kissed him once, sweetly, on the tip of his chin, before suffering to be released from the masculine contours which fit her own exquisitely.

"Until tonight, my love," he exclaimed, as he playfully bent his head to nip at a pebbled peak, before it was once more hidden by clothing.

"What do we do from here, Doug," she asked, pulling on her own shorts as she watched the jeans which he donned, slowly removing the long, tanned, sinewed legs which she so admired from view. The zip of his pants, loud and final, echoed through the woods before he answered, searching now for the wide leather belt which had fallen beneath her cotton shirt.

"Now, we go back to check on the family and to finish packing," he suggested, as, the belt uncovered, he threaded it through its loops. "Then, we send Melissa home with Mother. They'll both love it—they hit it off right away, kindred spirits, almost." He paused, gazing intently at Stephanie's face. "I know the joy your parents must have felt, Steph. You spoke of it earlier this summer. I saw it today on my mother's face."

Stephanie stiffened. "Does your mother know that Melissa is yours?"

"Correction, my sweet. *Ours.*" He put his hands comfortingly on her shoulders. "I didn't tell her. But she saw it immediately; Melissa looks exactly as I did at that age."

"Did she . . . mind?"

"Mind?" he roared good-naturedly. "It was the dearest thing I could have ever given her. She was thrilled, although I explained the situation, so she won't spill the beans before we see fit to tell Missy. Diana and Joel know nothing other than that I intend to marry you." He paused, measuring his words in light of the slight discomfiture which flitted over Stephanie's features. "Will it bother you to leave Melissa with my family? Do you trust me enough to trust them?"

Mesmerized by the warm gray orbs as she was, Stephanie knew that she would never again have cause to question him. Putting a hand on either side of his face, she drew his head down until their lips met. "I trust you with my life, my love, my everything."

"If you don't button your damned blouse, you may change your mind," he rasped, his hands having already crept in the open sides to caress the smooth skin of her back. With her body drawn as it was in intimate closeness to his, she felt his own state of arousal and immediately stepped back to button the blouse.

Moments later, as they walked hand in hand down the verdant path, Doug spoke his thoughts aloud. "There is a justice of the peace near the college who'll marry us. I want you mine, legally and every other way, before the weekend."

Questioning eyes locked into his. "Why the weekend?"

There was a twinkle of mischief in the gaze that he returned. "Because the only airline reservations available, should we decide to take them, are for Saturday night."

"Reservations?"

"Our honeymoon," he explained, savoring the element of surprise to its fullest. "A week in Paris."

Stephanie's eyes widened in amazement. "Paris? Oh, my God, I'd love to photograph Paris!"

With mock anger, Doug turned to imprison her in the iron band of his arms. "To hell with photography. You may not see the light of day for a week," he threatened playfully, as he kissed her hard.

She, too, was in a playful mood, though she spoke

in all earnestness. "For that matter, Doug, why don't we just go to some quiet little Vermont inn. I'd rather be with you for a week, alone and quiet, without the distractions a city like Paris would offer. We can go there another time. I want to get to know you, to *really* get to know you, and to have you get to know me. Would you mind?"

It was a long moment before he answered, the wealth of tenderness in his gaze multiplying by the second. "You're a remarkable woman, Stephanie Wright! And you're on. A week in an inn—alone!" He hugged her boldly before she found herself abruptly released. "I can't believe how you manage to muddle my mind so! I nearly forgot. I've only been waiting eight years to give this to you." Digging into the rear pocket of his jeans, he drew out a small, tissue-wrapped object and carefully peeled back the translucent white layers to reveal a brilliantly sparkling pear-shaped diamond, exquisite in quality, set on a thin band of gold.

Stephanie gasped aloud as she looked from the ring to her lover and back. "It's magnificent," she whispered, afraid as yet to touch it.

"Will you marry me, my dearest, dearest love?" The voice was deep and resonant, a breathtaking melody to her ears. The jewel was forgotten as she looked at his face, framed as it was, halo-fashion, by the sheen of sunlit hair.

"Yes, I will marry you, my dearest, dearest love," she promised, adding a soft and gentle kiss of adoration into the bargain.

She was startled when he reached for her finger, tearing her gaze back down from his face to the hand which now bore the sign of their betrothal. "Thank you. It's so beautiful."

"As is its wearer," he told her softly. "I bought this eight years ago. Actually I had gone to pick it up when you so unceremoniously popped in on my sister." Stephanie raised her eyes in renewed apology for her blunder, only to find a gentle understanding in his. "I've held it for you ever since, even long after I thought you were gone forever. I had my sister bring it up with her today."

Her arms crept over his shoulders. "Will you ever forgive me, Doug? I was so wrong not to trust you."

Long, strong hands stroked the curls about her face. "There's nothing to forgive, honey. It was as much my fault as yours. I should have told you how I felt before I'd presumed to take your virginity. I should have told you more about myself and my family and that first marriage which lasted for all of two years, so many years ago. I was wrong . . . and I'm sorry for that!"

Giddy with love, Stephanie pinched him playfully in the ribs. "Just make sure it doesn't happen again," she growled in mock fury.

"It won't," he pledged, as he kissed the tip of her nose. "Now, let's get going. I want to get this family thing over, so I can have you all to myself again."

Suddenly Stephanie stopped short in her tracks. "Oh, Doug, I must look a mess. Crying and all . . . my hair . . . these wrinkled things."

"Shh. You look absolutely radiant." In the love-drenched reflection of his eyes, she believed him. "In fact," he went on, "if I didn't know better, I'd wonder if you weren't pregnant." He regarded her suspiciously, as the thought popped into her mind for the first time since that morning after.

"Do you know better?" she teased, as she mentally calculated her dates.

He gasped excitedly. "Are you? We do have a pretty good record for one-night stands, you know."

"With your virility, there's a good chance. And I was violently sick last night," she retorted playfully. "But, I don't think so. Only time will tell for sure."

"Would you be happy, Steph?" he asked hesitantly.

A broad smile spread over her features. "You bet! I'd love to have more of your babies. But . . ." she paused apologetically, "I'd really like you to myself for a while. I mean, we already have Melissa."

Doug put a protective arm around her as they resumed their homeward journey. "This time around, we'll go through it all together, though you have to understand that we'll have a few certain people knocking down our doors to babysit. And I happen to know that there is a small prep school not far from N.V.C. which has no photography program to speak of . . ."

Stephanie giggled happily. "You have it all planned, don't you?"

"I'm proud of you, Steph. What you've done, what you've become, what you've made of your life alone. I just wonder if you'll ever really need me." There was a thread of doubt in his tone which underscored his words and touched her profoundly.

"I've always needed you, Doug, only I never realized it. There was a void, a big blank that I managed to cram full with my work and Melissa, so that I could pretend it wasn't there. But then I'd wake up sometimes in the middle of the night, frightened and lonely and missing you. I'll always need you, Doug. I could never love anyone else!"

"That's my girl!" he crooned huskily, hugging her to him, side to side, hip to hip, a strong arm about her shoulder, secure in the knowledge that she was, finally and forever, his.